*Alison's*

# Automotive Repair Manual

**Also by Brad Barkley**

*Money, Love*
*Circle View*

# Alison's

# Automotive Repair Manual

*a novel*

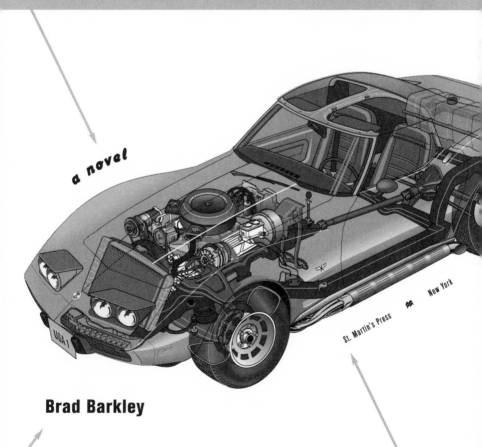

St. Martin's Press ❧ New York

**Brad Barkley**

www.stmartins.com

Illustrations by Precision Graphics
Design by Susan Walsh

Library of Congress Cataloging-in-Publication Data

Barkley, Brad.
    Alison's automotive repair manual : a novel / Brad Barkley.—1st ed.
        p. cm.
    ISBN 0-312-29138-8
    1. Widows—Fiction. 2. Automobiles—Conservation and restoration—
Fiction. 3. Corvette automobile—Fiction. 4. West Virginia—Fiction.
5. Grief—Fiction. I. Title.

PS3552.A67137 A78 2003
813'.54—dc21

                                                                2002035886

First Edition: March 2003

10  9  8  7  6  5  4  3  2  1

*For my children, Lucas and Alex*

# Acknowledgments

Deepest thanks to my agent, Peter Steinberg, for help and encouragement above and beyond the call. Also to my amazing editor at St. Martin's Press, Alicia Brooks—I could not have invented a better editor. I am grateful to others at St. Martin's for their generous support and faith in the book, particularly George Witte, editor in chief; John Cunningham, associate publisher; Matthew Shear, vice president and publisher; and Kevin Sweeney, production editor. Thanks also to jacket designers Steve Snider and Sarah Delson for both their talent and perseverance. I'm grateful to my friend Susan Perabo and the mysterious Anthony Tuck for casting their eyes upon early drafts, to Tina Lombardi for the crash course in dams, and to Frostburg State University and the Maryland State Arts Council for financial help. Thanks to all my friends in Maryland and West Virginia who lent me their stories and names, to friends scattered everywhere or gathered on a Thursday night, to my parents, and, finally, to Mary, for far too many reasons to list here.

A car can massage organs which no masseur can reach. It is the one remedy for the disorders of the great sympathetic nervous system.

—JEAN COCTEAU

# *Alison's*

## Automotive Repair Manual

# 1

The garage was no more than a decaying shack, covered in torn asphalt shingles, tilting at the end of a long gravel driveway. Alison Durst squinted against the late-afternoon sun, waiting for her brother-in-law to open the garage door. Bill tried several keys, shook his head at each one, until finally the rusted lock clicked open. Alison and her sister, Sarah, helped him pull as the door slid upward, angled and creaking, dropping fragments of broken window glass. They ducked under a low-beamed ceiling hung with cracked garden hoses, a sled dangling from a nail, and strands of Christmas bulbs, into a stilled grayness, slats of light flecked with dust motes. In one corner leaned a bent snow shovel and a badminton net scrolled around its aluminum poles, and in the other a tangle of tomato stakes and twine, a wooden cutout of a reindeer, the edges worn and feathery. And at the center of all the clutter sat a junked Corvette, covered in dust, the tires mushy, silver paint peeling in strips.

"Well, you asked, so now you've seen the famous car," Sarah said, rubbing dirt off her hands. She snapped on a lightbulb hanging from an extension cord, half an old coffee can for a lamp shade. The jarring light draped everything with shadow. The floor was nothing more than packed dirt, the air full of wet smells, the car's interior a dull maroon, stringy with cobwebs.

"Famous like what, the Hindenburg? The Titanic?" Alison said. It was about the saddest car she'd ever seen; it looked fossilized. "How much did you pay for it? Or did they pay you?"

"My nephew defaulted on the loan," Bill said. "We'd cosigned. Fifteen hundred later, boom, there you are." He gestured at the Corvette. Earlier that afternoon, Bill and Sarah had argued over how much money to send that same nephew for his eighteenth birthday, which was how the subject of the car came up in the first place.

Until then, Alison had never heard of it, never bothered to even peek in the garage. Sarah had wanted to send a card that read, "You Now Owe Us Only $1,400. Happy Birthday!"

"Deadbeat nephew," Sarah said, frowning at the car. "You forgot deadbeat."

"Now, now," Alison said. "Some of our best relatives are deadbeats." This came out wrong; too quickly, she thought of Marty and turned away, pretending to inspect the paint.

"We sank most of our money into eight-track tapes," Sarah said. "Want to see those, too?"

Alison looked at her sister and smirked. Sarah gave her back an identical smirk, her own dimples, like Alison's, lengthened by age into creases edging her mouth. Their father had pegged them "the twins," though Sarah was two years older. Even now, halfway through their thirties, they both still had the same graying corkscrew hair, the same slight hips and breasts, arms so long, they would hold them awkwardly, crossing and uncrossing them, jamming their hands in their pockets.

"How does it drive?" Alison asked.

Bill shrugged. "We never actually drove it. Tow truck backed it in, and that was that."

Alison walked around the car, stepping over a weed eater, a tangle of tire chains. "And you've had this how long?" she asked.

"A long time, too long," Sarah said. "I keep telling Bill, let's just scrap the thing."

"Well, I can't believe you never told Marty about it," Alison said. "You didn't need to scrap it." Marty would have insisted on saving the car, the way he'd saved console stereos and televisions, his VW van, the Pong video game from the bowling alley. He had rescued obsolete things the way other people rescue dogs from the pound. Things were more pitiful than people, he'd told her once, because when they got old and wore out, they didn't have guilty relatives around to pretend otherwise. The pack rat's apologist, she'd called him.

Sarah said something else about the car, but Alison only half-heard her. She was lost in thought, absently trying to list the sixty-six British monarchs, the same list she used to let her students memorize for extra credit—*Ethelwulf, Ethelbald, Alfred the Great.* She did this unconsciously, a habit she'd acquired in grad school and carried over into her teaching, her version, she thought of it, of biting fingernails or tapping pencils. It annoyed her, had annoyed Marty when they'd sit on the couch to watch a ball game, and he'd glance over and catch her squinting at the ceiling, her lips barely moving. But for these past months she'd indulged the habit, rather than hiding it away. Better this obsessive cataloging of the past than growing silent and brooding over some Jeep commercial on TV or a rack of flannel shirts at Sears. It was distraction, a noisy game. Without it, she would catch herself thinking of Marty in the present tense, as if he were only off somewhere in the woods riding dirt-bike trails or in the basement drinking coffee with Lem Kerns. Or worse, she would think of the morning of the day he died, those hours beginning their ugly echo inside her, and so she would close her eyes and start listing the monarchs, the Bill of Rights, the names of the Popes, the divisions of the Magna Carta, muttering like the old ladies in church bent over their rosaries. But she could never keep it all in her mind, couldn't recall if the third concern of the Magna Carta dealt with royal forests or towns and trades, or who succeeded Edward the Elder. The past, like the present, seemed a shifty, deceitful thing.

"Did you hear me?" Sarah said.

Alison looked at her sister.

"Ali, I'm trying to tell you," Sarah said. "We got the car *after* Marty's accident. A few weeks after."

"Well," Alison said, "when you said 'a long time,' I just thought . . ."

"It *has* been a long time," Sarah said, too quickly. Bill busied himself untangling the tire chains. "Two years now," Sarah added.

Alison looked away, her eyes adjusting to the dim light of the garage. "Thanks for the update," she said. In the dust blanketing the hood of the car, she scrawled WASH ME with the tip of her finger. She could cry right then if she nudged herself over into it, or she could nudge herself the other way and smash the windshield of the car, throw things at people she loved. Heat tightened around her chest, her eyes warming. She breathed the smell of fertilizer and rust, of wet dirt, gasoline, old leather.

Sarah sighed. "Okay, listen. Six months ago, we'd've probably lied about having any car, knowing it'd make you think of Marty. Wouldn't we, Bill?"

Bill smiled and shrugged, his face pink, hair neatly parted, as if he were about to have his school picture taken. He looked at Sarah and said, "That's exactly right." Good old Bill. Always so agreeable, so embarrassed by all of this. Alison felt grateful then that he'd gone along with her moving in, dragging the mess of her life behind her.

"So, that's probably a good sign, don't you think?" Sarah said. Alison shrugged, then nodded. How did she know if it was good or not? Maybe she should've looked it up in one of those god-awful books that friends had pressed on her in the weeks after the accident. *A Path Through Grief* was one title she remembered. *Embrace the Silence, The Passages of Living.* Like the names of the soap operas her mother used to watch at the Laundromat while she folded bath towels. The only help any of those books provided had been in giving her someone to resent for a few distracting weeks. She would open the back flaps, look at those smiling book-jacket faces, read the overview with its blueprint for grief. As if all those experts had gotten together to scout the emptiness of her first months after, to chart the topography of her loss. She read enough to figure out that they didn't know much beyond how to sell books to vulnerable people. The first night she arrived at Sarah's, she'd walked out in the dark and flung the stack of them as far as she could, one by one, into the lake.

"You know what?" Sarah said. Awkward, her words clumsy. "This two-year mark coming up, I think that will be your time, when you're, you know, back on your feet?"

The two of them stood watching her. Sarah had said the same thing at the six-month mark, the one-year mark, and again at eighteen months, and the statement had slowly bent itself into a question, just as she knew Sarah's concern had bent into impatience.

And who could blame her? Two years *was* a long time. But Alison wasn't some *widow*, running around in a black dress and veil, not anymore. Somehow, though, her mourning had evolved into a kind of indolence, an inertia of stunted feeling.

Alison looked at them standing in the door of the garage, and behind them their A-frame house angled against the evening sky. It had always looked out of place, that house, without some mountains around it, a ski slope or two. But this was Wiley Ford, in West Virginia, and instead of mountains there were only ancient, low hills, ground down like the teeth of some fitful, sleeping child. The house glowed above its lawn, above the lake which belonged not to it but to the town. Soon the house would be filled with the usual crowd, the old people, dancing and dancing, flooding the living room with vibration and movement.

"So, Bill, what year is this car?" Alison said, sidestepping Sarah's question. She opened the door and leaned into the maroon interior. Dust and oil smells, mildew, rot.

"A '76," Bill said. He scratched the back of his neck and frowned a little. "Kind of an off year for Vettes. Ain't even worth all that much."

"Are we about done with the tour?" Sarah said.

"Actually, the body doesn't look that bad," Alison said. "I mean, no rust."

"Fiberglass," Bill told her. "Doesn't rust. But look under." He tossed her a tiny flashlight he kept clipped to his shirt pocket (he repaired telephone lines for Bell Atlantic). As she crouched to look under the car, she lost her balance and pitched forward onto her knees, her clogs falling off her feet. The Ocean City shark's tooth she wore on a cheap silver chain slipped out of her T-shirt and dragged in the dirt. For all these months upon months she'd felt gawky, cramped. That was the best way she knew to think of her grief, her guilt—like trying to change clothes in a tiny elevator, everything clumsy, the ground moving beneath her. She clicked on the flashlight. What little she could see beneath the car looked like the landscape of Mars, inverted. Rot and corrosion, thick layers of hardened mud. She tapped underneath with her knuckles, and a shower of rust covered the back of her hand.

"That can't be good," Alison said.

"None of the glass is broken," Bill said. "That's a plus, I guess."

"Bill always finds something nice to say," Sarah said. Alison smiled at the dirt floor, letting the flashlight sweep under the car, all those parts and cables and tubes she knew did *something,* could be named, fixed, replaced. Somehow about this appealed to her, the order of it, maybe. Parts working. Synchronization. The logic of gears. Just then, Bill bounced the front bumper to test the shocks, and, along with the rust, four tiny gray balls fell from under the car and landed in the dirt. She inched closer, shone the light on them, trying to see what they were—lumps of mud, maybe? Some kind of putty or plastic? Then she touched one, and it gave a tiny high-pitched squeal.

Mice.

Babies—hairless, blind, grayish pink. The flashlight illuminated a fragile web of blue veins beneath their skin, the faintest throb of a pulse, their clawless feet pawing the air. Bill shook the Corvette again, and three more of them fell, making small craters in the dust. Somewhere in the hidden recesses of the car she heard more squealing, the *skritch* of claws. She picked up one of them, no bigger than a cashew. Bill shook the car again; two more mice dropped down in a scattering of rust.

"Bill . . . stop." She cupped the mouse in her hand and stood.

"You know that rust," Bill was saying, "they call it car cancer, and if you—"

"Look." She held out the mouse to them. It had stopped moving.

"I'll be damned," Bill said.

"I saw at least half a dozen more of them under there," Alison said. "Babies."

"God, it's like a clown car, with rodents," Sarah said. "Now I know we're junking this thing."

"No, you're not . . ." Alison started to say.

"Hon?" Bill said. "Your dancers are here in twenty minutes. We gotta straighten the house. And where in heck is Mr. Kesler?"

"I want the car," Alison said. "I want to fix it."

"Oh, late late late, always," Sarah said. "Like he has to tack on ten minutes to his lateness every time. Break his own record. The late Mr. Kesler."

Alison bent to place the dead mouse back under the car, among the other mice and the islands of rust. "Did you guys even hear me?" she said louder. "I want to fix this car." She looked up in time to see Bill and Sarah trading looks.

"Ali . . . what are you talking about?" Sarah said.

Twenty-three months now since the fire, since her spirit unhoused itself. She should be better now, over it, moving on. The two of them press for signs. They talk about Marty in her presence, try to convert him into memory—even his aimlessness, his sulky temper. She says nothing back. They take her to parties, introduce her to men. They ask about her plans for the house, for the job she abandoned, for her life. But right then, with the tiny curled bodies of mice lit in the arc of her flashlight, with those shadows of decay in the sweep of its beam, she knew only this: She would fix this ruined car.

Sarah stomped around the living room, stuffing magazines into end tables, pushing the furniture back, rolling up the rug. Alison sorted through the compact discs, loading the player with backup music for tonight's lesson: Basic Swing. Just in case Mr. Kesler didn't show.

Finally, Sarah stopped and stood with her hands on her hips. "Can I ask you one question?" she said.

"You just did," Alison said.

Sarah ignored her. "I'll bet you don't even know how to *drive* a stick shift, much less fix one," Sarah said, "and now you think you can just up and repair this entire broken-down rodent car. I mean, I don't understand what you think you're doing."

Alison put a discount-bin Glenn Miller into the CD player, then

*The Best of Artie Shaw,* a Benny Goodman. "Ooh, so sorry. You forgot to state your rant in the form of a question."

Sarah frowned at her. "I'm sorry we even showed you the thing."

"Would you stop, Sarah? I'll *buy* the damn car if you want, but I'm going to fix it, okay? For a year now, you've been telling me— what? That I ought to get out and do something, right?"

Sarah shook her head, her face flushed sweaty from pushing back the furniture. "That filthy garage is not *out.* I want you to get a new job, go back to teaching. I want you to meet someone."

"Thanks for the suggestions. I want to fix the car."

"What are you trying to prove? This is like—what, some big symbolic *act*?"

"Yeah, exactly," Alison said. "I promise when it's finished, I'll drive off into the sunset. You can film me."

"Why are you acting like this? What's the point? I mean, really, explain it to me."

This is how Sarah always argued, pelting her opponents with unanswerable questions. And what could Alison say? She didn't really have any answer that worked very well. The car *needed* her, maybe? She knew how pathetic that would sound, echoes of Charlie Brown and his sad little Christmas tree. And it was a lie, too. She needed the car at least as much as it needed her. If nothing else, it gave her something to do while she wasn't getting better. It gave her order, the work of her hands. It gave her dirt and grit and progression.

Sarah prowled the room, gearing up for another barrage. Alison loaded the last slot of the CD player with *Kiss Alive* (Bill kept the same music he'd liked in high school—Led Zeppelin, Jethro Tull, Pink Floyd—the way he kept his alligator shirts and S-10 pickup, his peanut butter sandwiches and football trophies). Sarah turned and pointed at her.

"Listen to me, Alison," she said. "I really think—"

Before she could finish, Alison cranked the volume to ten, punched the play button for disc five, and let the collision of bass and guitar and drums drown her sister out. The walls shook as

Alison walked past Sarah, smirking at her, out into the dark toward the lake. Under the noise of the music, she heard Sarah shouting, *"Very funny, Al. Really hilarious."*

The lake lay spread out before her, slowly draining away under the eyes of the city fathers. Bill had explained it to her a few weeks back, when the lake level was still high enough to conceal the muddy banks. The county had decided to drain the lake just long enough to kill the algae which was choking out the fish which fed the egrets that spent summers slinking along the shore. Something like that. It reminded her of that rhyme from childhood, about the woman who ate the cat to kill the mouse and ate the dog to kill the cat . . . something. She mouthed the words but couldn't remember.

In the moonlight, the exposed banks looked oily, slick. The few other houses surrounding the lake were mostly dark, except for the blue throb of TV sets. She had hardly watched TV for these months, except for a video of the two of them on a trip to Ocean City, Marty displaying his new Orioles T-shirt, mock-ogling the women on the boardwalk, pulling the shark's tooth necklace from the gift bag while he hummed the *Jaws* theme. Goofy boy, she called him, hamming it up for her until she gave in and laughed. The bridge of his nose was sunburned, a white sunglasses mask around his eyes which she'd teased him over, telling him he looked like some cave fish washed from the basement and into the light. She would click pause on the remote, his face held still and flickering, a slight blur around the eyes, his mouth opening to speak. This was how her house had felt when she left it, all of the rooms, everything in them, on pause—the progression of wrinkles in Marty's work boots; his necktie, hanging in the closet, preknotted for church; the Visa card he had bent back and forth for an hour one night, determined to break it despite her offers of scissors. It was still there, she guessed, on the little corner desk in their bedroom atop a pile of old check stubs he'd been going through, organizing them into shoe boxes, tossing the wadded rejects on the floor. His fishing reel, apart for oiling, the tiny springs and clips scattered across a newspaper on a folding TV tray in the den. The Epiphone guitar he'd bought and the learn-to-play tapes, neither of which he ever got around to. All of it on pause, in a kind of blurred stasis, hinting of a next frame and a next and a next.

A pair of headlights swung into the gravel drive, the van from Seven Springs Retirement Village dropping off the dancers for their lessons. Gordon Kesler, the late Mr. Kesler, was first out of the sliding door, all business with his boxed set of LPs and the little kit he used for maintaining them. So for that night, they wouldn't need the Glen Miller ("total cliché," Mr. Kesler once said of him), or the Artie Shaw ("a thug"). Mr. Kesler didn't much like CDs anyway. Behind him, Tyra Wallace stepped from the van, wearing bright thumbprints of rouge on her cheeks, carrying her leather cigarette case, and waving to Alison. Following her were the Harmons, with their matching white hair and teeth, like televangelists. Then Mrs. Skidmore, the only one in the group who was a lifelong resident of Wiley Ford, whose husband had been a coal miner and onetime pole vaulter for the Wiley Ford Lions. She had grown up not half a mile from the rest home where she now lived, and the thought of this sometimes struck Alison, that a whole life could be as boundaried and safe as a day hike in a state park. Mrs. Skidmore walked toward the house arm in arm with Lila Montgomery, who always wore Levi's and penny loafers to her lessons, as though she imagined herself, at seventy-seven, still a cheerleader. Finally was Arthur Rossi, following his own large stomach from the van, decked out in a wide denim vest with chromed buttons that matched the heavy steel-framed glasses he wore and his thick shank of silver hair. Once he decided to take the floor, he would dance with abandon, fling himself at it until his broad face brightened and his hair and glasses shone with perspiration. He had retired as a science adviser for some defense contractor a dozen years earlier, and had used his leftover time (Alison's expression for retirement) to become an expert in trivia. He often drove to Baltimore for contests in some trivia-based board game, and had even written a book called *Funny Facts,* though he'd never found a publisher for it. Most of the group avoided him because he spouted trivia constantly, could turn the most innocent greeting into an excuse for another volley of arcana. But Alison didn't mind it much and could even act interested (if you really listened, it *was* interesting), partly because he amazed her with his store of facts, when her own was so shaky and unsure, but mostly because she understood his fits of trivia for what they really were—clumsy attempts at conversation from an awkward, lonely man. After she first moved to Wiley Ford, she had felt more comfortable around awkwardness than anything else. At least it always afforded you, right in the middle of a conversation, a place to hide out.

Alison left the lake (the air around it, she noticed, smelled increasingly of creosote) and walked toward the house. Sarah liked to have her help out with the lessons, changing the CDs when Mr. Kesler failed to show, or just coaching the students through the steps, guiding elbows and offering compliments, deserved or not. This was the third group of students that Sarah had taught in the time that Alison had lived there, so she was used to it by now. And she enjoyed watching Sarah, never happier than when she was dancing.

Mr. Kesler prepped his records, drawing each from its plastic sleeve, his hands hidden in white cotton gloves. He sprayed each album with a mixture of denatured alcohol and water, wiped it with a cotton diaper, dried it with compressed air. Alison always marveled at this ritual; she'd never seen anyone so careful with anything. Bill was giving Mrs. Skidmore and Mrs. Harmon a refresher from last time, turning one and then the other in slow motion. Sarah waited for Mr. Kesler to finish, a coach's whistle around her neck. Arthur Rossi sidled up next to Alison, his cologne like some oversweet aura.

"And how might you be this evening, Miss Alison?" he said. He called all the women "Miss," like the sheriff on *Gunsmoke,* Alison thought.

"I'm okay, Arthur," she said. Just talking to him made his face shift to a deep pink.

"Thank goodness we aren't experiencing the kind of rain we had last week," he said. "I imagine you find yourself wondering which state in the union has the most rainfall."

"I do," Alison said. "Sometimes at night, I wake up wondering that very thing."

"Well, what would your guess be?" he asked, oblivious as always to her teasing.

"I would have to say Oregon. Maybe Washington."

He smiled. "The answer is Hawaii, if you can imagine that. Rain, instead of all that travel-brochure sunshine. Not near what you'd expect."

Alison smiled at this. He ended every eruption of trivia with this same phrase. "That's amazing," she said. He kept looking at her. "Hawaii, huh?" She remembered a student giving a presentation on how the Spanish first brought pineapples to Hawaii, in eighteen something. She couldn't remember the exact date or much of his talk, only that the boy brought in a fresh pineapple, and when he was done he'd cut it up with a pocketknife and they sat around eating it, juice running down their faces.

Sarah blew her whistle and Mr. Kesler let the needle drop to the vinyl. The speakers, mounted in the high corners of the room, bloomed with a lush, slow rhythm, Sinatra singing "It Happened in Monterey." Sarah always started with a slow one, to let the dancers take to the floor and gently sway, to get the feeling of movement in their bones. Alison watched their eyes close as they gave in to the music, watched the flashes of gold at the women's throats and wrists. Bill turned Sarah in a slow circle, whispering to her and laughing as she held both his hands. Arthur Rossi stood beside Alison, always too shy to dance at first. Mr. Kesler eyed the tracking of the stylus in the groove, wary of any imperfection.

Alison leaned toward Mr. Rossi to speak, and he bent down to hear her, his silver hair warm under the room's bright track lighting.

"You know pretty much everything, Arthur," she said. "What do you know about cars?"

He smiled and blushed all at once, happy to have his answers, for once, prompted by an actual question.

"Well, now, Miss Alison, let's check the memory banks. In 1939, Packard put the first air conditioner in a car, and that same year Oscar Meyer began touring the Weinermobile. Nationally, mind you. Same year the cheeseburger was invented, come to think of it."

"Well, but do you know any hands-on stuff? Like how to fix the motor?"

He looked suddenly defeated. "No, not really. That kind of thing . . . I'm sorry."

Alison touched his shoulder. "I love hearing all the facts you know. I really do. They put my teaching to shame."

He nodded. "Did you know that Henry Ford once wore a suit and tie made entirely of soybeans?"

"Man, you think you know someone . . ." she said. She smiled at him, but he missed it. By now the dancers were choosing up partners. "Really interesting, Arthur."

"Certainly is that," he said. "A man of his stature. Not near what you'd expect."

Sarah began by reviewing the three-step pattern and a simple under-arm turn. She kept blowing her whistle, smiling and clapping, taking hands with the dancers to show them in slow motion. Mr. Kesler stood next to his records in their varnished wooden box. He would never dance, even if someone asked him directly. Alison swayed to the music as the Harmons took to the floor, as Bill patiently turned Mrs. Skidmore again and again, as Tyra Wallace and Lila Montgomery danced together, their faces alert with color and dampness.

Alison leaned toward Mr. Rossi. "They always look younger on the dance floor," she said. A brief panic flashed across his face, his mind, she figured, searching for some tidbit of conversation to offer back. Finding nothing, he nodded. She watched the women move, how it seemed as if they could step out of their years sometimes, their bodies recalling a dim memory of muscles and flesh, of bones and sinews and skin—the way she could still feel Marty sometimes, his fingers on her face, the cold in the flats of his palms after he worked outside, the hairs along his wrists brushing her knuckles in a movie theater.

"You want to know about cars," Mr. Rossi said, interrupting her thoughts, "your man is right there." He pointed to Mr. Kesler.

"Him? Hard to see him getting his fingernails dirty."

"Did you know that the fingernails continue to grow a year after a person dies?" He smiled again.

Tiring of this, she pulled him by his sleeve over to Tyra and Lila, who were watching Bill slow-motion his way through a kick step.

"Mr. Rossi needs a partner," she told them, and they both smiled, looked at one another, while Mr. Rossi stood gaping like a fish. An awkward silence followed. "I noticed . . . your penny loafers, Lila," Alison said. "Have you ever wondered how that came about, sticking coins inside your shoes?"

Lila hesitated half a second. "Why, yes, now that you say it. That is an oddity, how a person would ever think to do such a thing."

"Well, it's not what you'd expect," Mr. Rossi said. "The loafer, or Weejun, of course, was named for the Norwegian aboriginals who first began hand-sewing the shoes—which follows from their generally smallish fingers—and by 1935 . . ."

Alison left them just as the music faded and Mr. Kesler crouched to put on another record. Sarah lined everyone up to demonstrate another move, some complicated series of arm twists she called "the window shade." Mr. Kesler concentrated as he dropped the needle, then folded away his white gloves. He looked as he always did, as though he maintained himself with the same care and economy he gave his records. He wore a light blue zippered jumpsuit with some fake coat of arms stitched over the breast, a flap of pocket opposite it. His prickly crew-cut hair was the shade of gray (nickel almost) that looked as if it had once been blond. His face was tan, cut with wrinkles around the mouth, dark eyes held in the lenses of thick black horn-rimmed glasses. He looked like a scientist from some fifties Martian movie. She walked over next to him, smiled as he nodded politely. There were little details about him she had never noticed from across the room: the almost pure white of his eyebrows, hidden by the glasses, his department-store sneakers with Velcro straps instead of laces, the brown bowl of a pipe sticking out of the breast pocket in his jumpsuit. The bowl pivoted with his movements, as if his heart had sent up a tiny periscope.

"I'm told you're the one to talk to about a car. I mean fixing a car." Alison jammed her hands into the pockets of her overalls.

He peered at her through his glasses, rocking on his toes, his pipe wagging. "Is someone setting you up? Yanking your chain?"

"What? No, not at all. I have an old car and I want to make it new. I heard you might be the person to talk to."

He licked his lips, which looked painfully dry and chapped. He wiped away her question with a motion of his hand, the fingertips of his white gloves inching out of the pocket of his jumpsuit. "My son, now he knows a thing or two from the army. Practically an expert. As for me, well . . ." He laughed. "Fix the brakes. Better know you can make it stop, before you make it go."

His rheumy eyes watched her, behind their thick frames, the lines in his mouth deepening, then disappearing. "That's it?" Alison said. "I have a whole car to . . . to redo, and the extent of your advice is 'fix the brakes'? Maybe somebody *was* yanking my chain." She felt echoes of the same frustration she'd felt with Sarah earlier, as though she couldn't understand why her desire to fix the car was not instantly contagious, had not become, in the last hour, a cause taken up by the whole community. And why not? There wasn't much else going on in Wiley Ford.

Mr. Kesler shrugged. "Take it to a mechanic. Or, like I say, Max will be here soon, helping out with the lake, and he'll know a thing or two." He bent long enough to snap the clasp on his record box, which looked homemade, a little bit crooked. He straightened. "That's a true puzzle, how I get the reputation for knowing the first thing about cars."

Sarah gave a short blast of her whistle as she showed the dancers what not to do as they practiced some move she called "the corkscrew."

"I guess, you know, you have a reputation for . . . meticulousness." She shrugged. "Maybe someone thought your careful maintenance extends to cars."

He made a pinched face, so his eyebrows drew together. "Meticulous? Careful?"

She tapped on his wooden record box. "Most people don't wear nuclear radiation gloves to handle Perry Como, Mr. Kesler."

"Oh, that. Well, listen, Alison . . ." This sounded strange; he had never said her name before, but everyone in Wiley Ford knew who she was by now. He rubbed the back of his neck. "Thing is, I had a collection of over a thousand LPs and twice that many seventy-eights and now, out of my own carelessness, this is all I have left. I'm a careless man." He nodded. "That I am."

He paused long enough to remove his glasses and hold them up to the light. He blew on them once, then replaced them. "The National Archives," he said.

She blinked. "Did I miss something?"

"That's where I get the gloves. They use them for handling documents." He hesitated. "As for my long-playing records . . . I used to leave them in piles around the hi-fi, just scattered around the floor, cats walking on them, spilled food." He stopped, wiped the tiny white flecks from his lips. "Just fix the brakes."

She nodded. "Well, thanks."

"Hey, Mr. Kesler," Sarah said. "That's your cue. Late again." Mr. Kesler slipped on his gloves to change the side, then lowered the needle until the room flooded with Count Basie. Alison started to move toward the couch, but Mr. Kesler took her arm, his grip a firm pinch. He drew her back.

"One more thing about cars, now that you mention it," he said. "There's one on the bottom of that lake." He tilted his head toward the front door. "I put it there."

She leaned back to look at him. "What are you talking about?"

"Just what I said. A 1939 Chrysler Crown Imperial. Put it straight down on the bottom." He nodded, looking away from her. "Damn near killed me, too."

She shook her head, confused. "Well . . . I mean, are you hurt? When did this happen?"

He looked at the ceiling, squinting. "1946."

She laughed. "I guess you'll live, then. Mind telling me *how* you put a Chrysler Imperial on the bottom of the lake?"

"Oh, the usual way, I suppose." He smiled, and after a few seconds, she realized that he'd made a joke. His teeth looked crowded, all bunched together and overlapping in the front of his mouth. She saw in those teeth something of the carelessness he spoke of, as though his messiness had settled in his mouth, shoved there by his neat jumpsuits, his white gloves, his flattop haircut. He took the pipe from his pocket, squinted to look into the bowl, then replaced it.

"Just a kid, maybe fourteen or so, and we had this freak winter, kind that kills all the oranges in Florida and makes it onto the nightly news. Anyway, the lake out here froze over and all any of us kids wanted to do was strap some wood blocks to our boots and head out to skate, but none of the parents around here would allow it, having no experience with serious ice. So I took the car from my Uncle Crawford about midnight one night, so cold it felt like my blood might freeze, and I rolled his car down the road and popped the clutch and aimed to drive it out across the ice, and in the morning I'd tell everyone what I did, and we could all go out and skate and I'd be your basic hometown hero. So. You know how this one ends. I got out to the middle, ice made a sound like somebody cracking a two-by-four. I stopped right there. Put my brakes on, then I was in the water." He shrugged.

Alison tried to get her mind around all of this. "You weren't all too bright at fourteen, were you?"

He shook his head. "Not the sharpest nail in the bin."

"So what did you do?"

"Do? Well, the last thing I remember was swimming up out of that hole, my arms stiff and cold, and I stuck my head back down in that water to look. I could see the headlights still shining out through the water, these two yellow cones getting dimmer and dimmer. Before I got out, the car filled up with water as high as the dash, and up floated this pint bottle of rye. Never forget that, had a cork in the neck and a rooster drawn on the label, and I remember realizing it was my uncle's and that he'd been hiding it under the seat. So here I was, half-drowned and frozen, and all I could think was, Damn, he's been hiding his liquor."

She shook her head. "How did you get out?"

"I reared back and kicked out the window. The whole world, seemed like, came gushing in."

Alison left the conversation for half a second, thinking of when Lem Kerns brought her the news, standing on her porch, stammering, twisting his shirttail, his glasses duct-taped, and when she understood him finally, it was just that: the whole world, gushing in. Mr. Kesler leaned in toward her. "I never told anyone about that. Until just now."

She let this sink in a moment. "You mean you never . . . The car is still *down* there?"

"Like I said, it's still there. Of course, probably under ten feet of mud by now, don't you think? That's a deep, deep lake. Had an anchor once on fifty feet of clothesline and couldn't touch bottom. Reported it stolen."

"What?"

"The car. My uncle reported it, collected insurance. He was happy enough, so I never felt too bad over it."

"And you never told *anyone*? Not your son? Your wife? Your therapist?"

"I was more than a little embarrassed for a long time, then I was embarrassed that I'd let so much time go by without saying anything."

"So then why tell me, if you're so embarrassed?"

He smiled again with his crowd of teeth. "I just got over it."

Alison laughed at this, but she was touched, too. It felt like some small offering from him, as though knowing her past (as everyone in Wiley Ford did) had caused him to dredge up his own story of loss, however far off and forgotten.

"Besides," he said, "what with them draining the lake, I might get exposed here soon."

She smiled. "Just say it's some *other* Chrysler Imperial down there. I'll back you up."

Late that night, after the dancing ended, after Mr. Kesler packed away his records and gave her a smile on the way out, after the ladies kept dancing in pairs without any music until the van honked for them outside, after Bill plugged in his portable floor polisher to take the scuff marks out of the floor, after quiet and stillness returned, Alison sat on the front porch, watching the lake, the puddles around the exposed bank shining like pot lids. Sometimes she thought she could detect a lowering of the water out of the corner of her eye, as if she could catch the level dropping. But she never did. It always looked the same, looked as if it had not changed a bit, until you could begin to think the city fathers had decided against draining it, and then one afternoon you would notice how much of the steep muddy bank was exposed, or the angle of the boat docks pointing down into the water, some mossy pile of exposed tires, a bundle of Christmas tree skeletons. Late at night, the migrant workers from the cornfields in Paw Paw would venture down through the muck with fishing tackle and lanterns to the retreating edge of the water. Already, the exposed bottom had started to give way to a second bank, a steep slope down into the deep, hidden middle, where Mr. Kesler had lost his uncle's car. The smaller that middle became, the more regularly the men arrived at night, as if the diminished size increased their chances of the big catch. Alison watched them, heard their echoed laughs and curses, hugged herself against the breeze. She imagined all the fish in the lake retreating to the deep bottom, finding refuge in Uncle Crawford's car, swimming around the floating rye bottle with the rooster on the label. But that picture was a lie, she knew. Closer, probably, was what Mr. Kesler had said, the car buried under ten feet of mud, the paper label long since disintegrated, the upholstery, the rubber tires, most of the metal itself a casualty of time, worse than her Corvette. She shook the idea from her head. She would not think about that, the whole idea of decay. It was the worst thing—a bad joke built into the design—the way everything wore out, rotted away. The thing to do was to refuse to give in, like Lila Montgomery in her jeans and penny loafers, a seventy-seven-year-old cheerleader dancing away from broken hips and portable oxygen tanks and varicose veins. Alison walked across the yard toward the garage, some part of her mind vaguely trying to remember if Gutenberg had invented the printing press before or after the birth of Leonardo da Vinci. The question had pestered her since her undergrad days, when she'd gotten it wrong on an exam.

She swung the garage door up and open, clicked on the coffee-can light. The Corvette gave a dull gleam under the shine of the bulb. She opened the door, heard the scratch of claws inside the frame. She sat in the driver's seat, something she'd forgotten to do earlier. It smelled like any old thing, like the projects Marty had rescued from the basements of friends, from the county dump. Marty, always so hopeful about worn-out things. She put her hands on the wheel and looked out over the long expanse of silver hood, like a little kid pretending to drive. And she did pretend, closing her eyes, imagining what it would feel like to have this car clamor to life beneath her, to sense in her hands, in her bones, the synchronization of gears, of fuel and spark and burning and motion, slipping the pull of the earth, too fast for rust, too swift for wearing out, launching herself—why not?—into the sunset, into the bright, pure blade of the wind.

—from the *Haynes Automotive Repair Manual:*
*Chevrolet Corvette, 1968 thru 1982*

The newcomer to practical mechanics should start off with
the minor repair tool kit, which is adequate. Then, as confidence and experience grow, the owner can tackle more
difficult tasks, buying additional tools as needed.

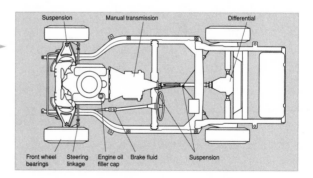

# 2

After breakfast on the porch (today, a shopping cart was visible along the banks of the lake), Alison walked toward town, letting her mind tumble through its snarl of dates and places and names. She'd found the address she needed in the Wiley Ford Yellow Pages, AAAA Auto Parts—an attempt, apparently, to best the competition alphabetically. But in Wiley Ford, there *was* no competition; AAAA was the only auto-parts place listed.

The front third of the store was nearly empty, a few parts and shrink-wrapped tools hanging on Peg-Board islands. Alison looked around, pretending she belonged there. The names of the tools sounded odd: *impact driver . . . torque wrench . . . valve reamer.* Punch lines to dirty jokes. The walls of the shop hung in loops of rubber fan belts, like the fringe around a tablecloth. The owner, Mr. Beachy, stood behind a counter that ran the width of the store, the front of it papered with out-of-date calendars and posters of bikini-clad women with inflated breasts, posing beside heavy machinery. A cowbell rang behind her as the door swung closed, and Mr. Beachy put his finger in a thick book to mark his place before looking up at her.

She knew him from the Thursday-morning farmers' market held at the high school track, where he sold organic cucumbers. He was also a deacon at the Baptist church, and each one of his cucumbers came with a religious tract rubber-banded around it, dozens of them in a bushel basket on the bed of his pickup, the corners of the tracts fluttering in the wind. He spent time between customers attaching the tracts to the cukes, the pile of pamphlets and rubber bands sitting beside him on the tailgate, weighted with a rock. All of the tracts had titles like WHERE DOES YOUR ROAD END? or WHICH WAY IS UP? This most recent one had a drawing on the front of a crying man riding an escalator out of puffy clouds and down into a sea of flames. Sarah would keep the tracts and trim them into shopping lists, and at dinner, whenever she was about to add cucumber to salads, she would always ask, "Christian or heathen?"

Right after the accident, whenever Mr. Beachy saw Alison approaching, he would quickly slip the tracts off her cucumbers before he sacked them up. She'd seen this same reluctance at Marty's church back home in Maryland, all those offers of casseroles and Mass cards, a drowning swell of niceness, but no one who actually wanted to face her, just to talk about what had happened. Like Mr. Beachy—embarrassed at the point where faith intersected a tangible death.

"Alison!" he said now. "Very surprised to see you in here."

"Well, you might be seeing a lot of me here," she told him.

She explained that she had a '76 Corvette that needed fixing. "Really *big* fixing," she said, jamming her hands in her pockets. He nodded, leaning on the wooden countertop, where pale elbow rests had worn into the surface. He didn't say anything, and she felt herself blush. "Everything," she said, shrugging. "The whole car."

"So," he said, "Bill's finally saving that Corvette." She smiled at his choice of words—*saving*—as if he saw the entire world in terms of redemption and salvation, all the way down to cucumbers and cars.

"Not Bill, me," she told him. "I'm planning to fix the car." This phrase was rapidly becoming some odd mantra for her.

He raised his eyebrows, pushed his reading glasses up on his forehead. "Well, that's just fine," he said, nodding. "That's terrific." She felt like a kindergartner showing off a plaster handprint. Mr. Beachy looked around the sparse storefront, as if wondering what his next move should be. She could sympathize. "How much do you know about cars?" he asked.

"Zip," she told him. "Where do I start?"

Mr. Beachy lifted his finger, asking her to wait, then disappeared into the back of the store. She leaned against the counter, looked around at all the strange parts, dug a penny from the Styrofoam cup atop the register and dropped it in the Lion's Club gum-ball machine. She got a piece made to look like a baseball, painted with perfect tiny red stitches. How did they ever manage such a thing? She bit it, finding it hollow inside, then picked up from a cardboard display box a small screwdriverlike tool named the "Lil' Wonder All-N-One," which advertised that it was actually eighteen tools in one. It could be opened and folded and twisted, different attachments and blades carried in the handle for cutting wire, turning screws, and pulling nails. She turned it over, opened it, pulled off the tip, unscrewed the bottom, and let the attachments spill out. This was at least as good as the Swiss army knives all the junior high boys used to carry. She chewed her gum, blew a bubble, then carved a small *A* in the surface of the counter. Maybe there should be a list of lesser inventions, the ones that are overshadowed by the printing press, the steam engine, the cotton gin—all the hotshot ones. And this seemed like a pretty good start on that list: painted gum balls and the Lil' Wonder All-N-One. She reassembled it and put it on the counter, her first purchase.

Mr. Beachy walked out of the back, whistling "The Yellow Rose of Texas" and carrying a shrink-wrapped book, which he tore open. The cover showed an intricate drawing of a Corvette in cutaway, the frame and engine and seats, the smallest wire or fuse rendered in meticulous pen-and-ink lines. She imagined that if she squinted hard enough, she could make out the baby mice curled into fleshy balls, drawn no bigger than the period at the end of a sentence. She opened the manual and turned the new pages, looking over the black-and-white photos of men in lab coats dismantling and reassembling every part of the car.

"This here is the bible of shop manuals," Mr. Beachy told her. She nodded, and the two of them leaned in together while he showed her all the divisions of the manual, the different section titles—emissions, braking, electrical, clutch, and driveline—the entire car, those ten thousand parts on the cover, neatly divided and parceled out. Her eyes drifted to the stack of tracts on the counter beside her elbow, pushed in behind the gum-ball machine. The one on top showed a drawing of a man crying (they were always crying) as he stood beside a Mercedes and a wheelbarrow full of money, the crucified Jesus, rendered in cartoon lines of light, towering above him. The title was WHERE WILL YOU STORE YOUR TREASURES? Maybe for Mr. Beachy these tracts were just another kind of instruction manual, a detailed explanation of how to solve eternity, how to fix your broken afterlife. They made it all seem so easy—birth, sin, rebirth, forgiveness, death, eternal reward. When she used to go with Marty to St. Luke's, she'd sit there wishing it *could* be that easy, that bread and wine could absorb all your sin. She could see the appeal, the desire to believe that all the disarray and breaking down and decay of a life could be repaired by ten pages of a cartoon man purging his regret, by a quick handful of Bible verses and a prewritten "Sinner's Prayer." Everybody wanted to impose a little order on all this mess. It's why someone went to the bother to print up religious tracts or shop manuals for broken cars. And why not? Slip on your white lab coat, find some space in which to work, and go through your existence part by part. It might even run when you finished, or at least make sense. So, okay then, she decided—let the Corvette be her religion for a while. She bought the Haynes manual and the Lil' Wonder All-N-One, and then, just to make Mr. Beachy happy, she picked up a handful of tracts and dropped them into the paper bag.

The plan was that after lessons that night, Sarah's students would stay for snacks and drinks. Alison was supposed to be helping her with chocolate-chip cookies and pigs-in-a-blanket, but instead spent all afternoon in her garage. She cleaned the small, high windows, filled four garbage bags for the curb, cleared off the workbench in the corner, and hung up the assortment of hand tools that Bill had left scattered around the floor. She placed her new Lil' Wonder All-N-One on the bench next to her shop manual. In the attic, she found a dusty kitchen radio, which she plugged in and hung from the Peg-Board above the bench, to let its old songs and talk shows keep her company. While she was at it, she washed the Corvette with a bucket of suds and sprayed away some of the muck underneath with the hose. At least it looked better. Once or twice, she looked at the drawing of the engine in the manual, and then at the engine itself, finding almost no correspondence between the two, the drawing like some foreign road map in a hilly, complicated land.

Toward evening, Sarah brought her a glass of iced tea, a plate of pigs-in-a-blanket, and the cordless phone. "Some guy," she said, handing it over.

"Me? Who would call me?" she whispered.

"Want me to ask?" Sarah said.

Alison shook her head as she took the phone. "Hello?"

"Al, how you doing?" The loud voice belonged to Ernie Holloway, her department chair from the community college. She heard a *clack clack clack* in the background, and immediately could see him sitting in his windowless office, desk cluttered with his executive desk toys, a tiny putting green and gold putter, a ball meant to be squeezed as a stress reliever, a yo-yo, and—the source of the background noise—a set of ball bearings that swung inside their frame, dangling from fish line and hitting into one another as some experiment in momentum.

"Ernie, you sound like you're a thousand miles away," she told him.

"I might as well be, as much as we ever see of you. The Invisible Woman." He laughed, and she could see the way his face flushed when he laughed, his thinning hair sprayed into place and his freckled scalp visible beneath it.

"Yeah, well I can hear you there, Ernie, still playing with your balls."

"Hey, hey, let the world know they're *steel* ones, okay? Grant me that much."

Alison started grinning. These were long-standing jokes between them. "As if there were any doubt. The way you stood up to the dean last fall? You want new ice trays for the lounge, and by God you get them." Sarah pretended to be suddenly absorbed in the Haynes manual, when Alison knew she was only waiting around to hear how this conversation turned out.

Ernie laughed again. "Hey, I don't take 'Whatever' for an answer. But listen, Al, that was *two* falls ago I got the ice trays. Remember?"

She was quiet a moment, reluctant to remember that so much time had gone by. "Well," she said, "I still miss everybody there." This was only partly true. Cumberland Valley Community College tended to treat its faculty like the teenage employees of some fast-food burger outlet, and turnover was high. Truth be told, she had known the names of only half the other instructors when she left.

"You don't have to. Matter of fact, if you have your handy Gregorian pocket calendar in front of you at the moment, you will note that today is the twentieth of August." She heard the clacking stop, then resume again, louder than before.

"Very good, Ernie. Wanna try to guess the year now?"

"Well, I think that one might be left to you." He sighed. "We have a line in the cafeteria right now. And do you know why?"

"A sale on corn dogs?"

"You know perfectly well it's late registration. Classes start Monday. A little dodging and rope-a-dope, and I've managed to keep your sections open for you. For now."

She didn't speak for a moment.

"Well, those are going to be popular sections," she finally said. "What with no teacher."

"We need you back here, Al. How else are all those welders and dental assistants going to learn about the Battle of Wippedesfleot or the spread of Celtic monasticism?"

"You can handle it," she said, thinking how she'd always envied Ernie his easy, off-hand mastery of the whole chronology of world civilization. He always shrugged off her admiration, treating history as a given chain of cause and effect that was as easy to understand as a crossword puzzle. He taught all his classes without notes, without videos lifted from the History Channel, without an overhead projector, just him and his vast and effortless understanding of the past. A few years back, an evaluation committee had taken him to task for not using audiovisual equipment in his teaching, and he'd stood up and said, "*I* am audio. *I* am visual." Alison had to use outlines and notes for every lecture. The problem was, had always been, rote memorization—dates and names, the ordering of history—which they still expected of students. In grad school, she began her habit of clicking off the lists in her head, carrying history around with her and worrying it like a hangnail. The dates and names didn't want to stay still in her head—would not *behave* was how she thought of it. She admitted this once to Ernie, and he hadn't let her forget it since. He told her once that they ought to offer a course called Approximate History of the World. The last Christmas she'd lived in Cumberland, he gave her a T-shirt with the words DOOMED TO REPEAT IT printed across the front.

The balls stop clacking on the other end, and after a moment came the whirring of the tiny motorized train on Ernie's desk, around and around its circular track.

"So, how about it, Al? Say the word, I'll head down to your office right now and warm up your chair until you get back."

Alison glanced at Sarah, who was now studying the index. "Ernie, I really have missed you, Lord help me. But, I'm just . . . I'm not ready to be back there yet. I know that sounds lame. Plus, I have a project going."

"What kind of project?"

She thought for a second. "It's a surprise."

She heard him cluck his tongue on the other end, the whirring stop. "The thing is . . . ." He hesitated. "The provost wants to take your position. We could lose the slot. And to *English* on top of it, those greedy bastards. They want to hire a 'developmental person.' I keep asking them why they don't just go ahead and hire a fully formed person."

"Hey, you might have just put your finger on *my* problem."

"You're fully formed. You just had a few holes punched through you is all."

"I'm sorry, Ernie." She suddenly found herself blinking back tears.

"Listen. You still have until Tuesday before registration ends. Don't give any final say right now, okay? Give me a shout Monday evening and let me know."

She said good-bye and clicked the phone off, then turned in time to see Sarah looking at her, biting her lip. Sarah opened her mouth to speak, then shook her head. She still held the plate of food, which she tossed on the workbench, a tiny corner of the stoneware chipping off. She stared at it a minute, then turned back toward the house. Alison watched until she rounded the corner, then lifted one of the pigs-in-a-blanket. She hadn't eaten all day, but the food had gone cold, the ring of dough grown stale and hard.

The dancers, still flushed and sweaty, sat in the living room, knees locked together, plates balanced in their laps. They took polite bites of the microwaved pigs-in-a-blanket and cookies. Mr. Kesler kept a stack of Oreos on his stereo table, using the social hour to clean and box his record collection. He had arrived earlier that evening, not driving the van from the retirement home, but riding in a battered yellow pickup truck. Alison had been on the porch, half-watching the lake and studying the grease that traced the whorls and loops of her fingertips, already dirty after so little work. He'd eased out of the truck, and someone—his son, the car expert, she guessed—waved to him out the window. Mr. Kesler kept trying to coax him out of the truck and into the house, motioning with his arms. She'd never seen him so animated.

From where she sat the son looked like a college yearbook photo of Mr. Kesler—the same face, only thicker, the same close-cropped graying-blond hair. His glasses were not Mr. Kesler's thick horn-rims, but tiny wires that could barely be seen beyond the flashes of light when he turned his head. He looked not like Mr. Kesler's mad scientist, but more like a real scientist, someone who collided atoms for a living. He kept letting the truck roll forward and back while he resisted being talked inside to meet everyone. "No, no. Go on, Dad," he said in a clipped, thin voice. His arm hung out the window, his hand patting the dented door.

"Just to meet everyone?" Mr. Kesler said.

"Dad—"

"Just for a few?"

"Maybe next time," he said. Finally, Mr. Kesler gave up, and his son waved and drove off. Mr. Kesler looked defeated, and Alison felt a twinge of anger. What had been so important he couldn't do this little thing for his father? It had surprised her as well to hear Mr. Kesler wanting his son to meet everyone. His involvement in the dances rarely extended beyond his record collection.

Now Mrs. Skidmore sat talking about the slow disappearance of the lake, about the outboard motors that had been found, along with the two sets of golf clubs (even though the nearest course was fifteen miles away). Her radar for gossip swept in a low, steady arc over all of Mineral County, carefully attuned to both fact and rumor. She said that the mosquitoes around the lake were carrying encephalitis, that there were two cases already over in Garrett County, and *that* was the real reason for draining the lake.

"You know," Mr. Rossi said, his mouth stained with mustard, "it's not the mosquito's sting that causes the bump, it's the insect's saliva pumped under your skin. She spits into you."

Several of the others put down their napkins and stared at their plates, while Mr. Rossi looked around at them and said that this was not what you'd expect. Mrs. Skidmore cleared her throat, allowing the interruption to fall away from her. Carrying with her this decades-old mix of rumor and fact, she was, Alison thought, the closest thing Wiley Ford had to a museum. She talked in her shrunken, scratchy voice, pausing to take sips of the beer she always insisted on drinking straight from the can.

"Now the funniest part—is that a word, *funniest?*—of this business with the lake is that the intent of the geniuses in charge—of course, the leader of that pack was Newton Hauser, whose idea of an original thought was to put out a fire using a bucket of water—anyway, the whole plan when they built it was to make it a *tourist* attraction. Can you imagine? Out here about seventy-five miles from anywhere, and they think they can just plunk down a water hole and suddenly people are going to drive out from Hagerstown and Washington—this is 1932, did I say that?—just to soak their toes in West Virginia and get eaten by a bear or a wild boar. Maybe that should have been on the brochures: 'See West Virginia—Get Eaten by a Bear or Wild Boar.' Anyway"—she took a sip of beer, wiped the corners of her mouth—"we didn't even need the lake, not for water supply nor nothing, and all along the state wanted to make it hydro-electric and put it over in Gad, only of course the Baptists put a stop to that."

Alison interrupted. "The Baptists? I thought they liked water."

She laughed, took a drink. "Ordinarily. But they didn't want the dam put up over in Gad and having people running around the state saying, 'They almost finished the Gad dam,' or 'Let's go visit the Gad dam.' Afraid everyone would be thinking, The goddamn *what*? Said we'd get a reputation for profane language and stupidity all at once. Like that's news for West Virginia."

Everyone laughed.

"So," she continued, "thanks to the Baptists, all of Coalville ended up getting baptized. Of course, none of the people, so I guess it doesn't count. Near miss for the holy rollers, they almost converted three hundred in one shot."

Alison took a sip of her beer. "What do you mean? What's Coalville?"

"Well, we kids used to call it Coca-Colaville and really it never had a real name, just some mining shacks and a company store and a church and a bar or two was about all. The mine stopped producing, so they went and flooded Colaville."

"The shape of the Coke bottle is modeled on the cocoa bean itself," Mr. Rossi tossed in while he had the chance.

"Flooded?" Alison said. "The whole town?" The others nodded.

"Like I said, weren't much to it," Mrs. Skidmore explained. "It happened a lot around here, all those forgotten coal burgs, worth-less once the ground was empty. So they filled it up, waited for the tourists to arrive." She laughed and drank. "The tourist mine came up empty, too, I guess."

Alison pictured the miners standing around with their wives and children, watching their cellars and kitchens and attics fill up with water. She thought, too, of Mr. Kesler's Chrysler down there, could see it settling in along some narrow water-filled street, the car parked forever in front of the flooded company store, as though its owner had merely popped in—left the engine running—for sugar and lamp oil. She imagined the watery ghosts of that old life gathering to gawk at the wide tires and shiny paint job, while around them dropped the slow accumulation of years—fishing tackle and outboard motors and golf clubs and abandoned shopping carts, maybe someone's wedding ring or a gunnysack of kittens, and then her own stack of self-help books floating down out of the murky water, pages fluttering, the people in the watery town picking them up to read phrases that had not yet been invented, words designed to steer them past the kind of grief that must have been as much a part of their lives as wash day or the evening meal.

She shook the thought away and turned to Mr. Kesler, who was just starting his food, after the other plates had been cleared away. "The person you were with tonight, your son? He's here about the lake?"

He nodded, swallowing. "Max, yes. Living with me for the time being."

"Well, then, it attracted *one* tourist," Alison said, and all of them laughed.

"Little Max Kesler," Mrs. Skidmore said.

"Actually," Mr. Kesler said, "the town honchos figured that as long as the lake is drained, they should take down the old dam and rebuild it."

"I didn't know there *was* a dam," Alison said.

Mr. Rossi spoke up. "Only three natural lakes in all of West Virginia."

"So Max is going to build the new dam?" Mr. Harmon asked.

Mr. Kesler folded his napkin in thirds, put it on his plate. "Demolish the old one, take it down and clear it out. He can have it down in about five seconds, after all the prep is done." He leaned in conspiratorially. "Works with dynamite." There arose a chorus of approval at this bit of information.

Mr. Rossi held up his index finger, his face bright pink.

"Invented, ironically enough, by Alfred Nobel, of Nobel Prize fame? Not what—"

"What do they call someone like that, who knows about using dynamite and such?" Lila Montgomery asked.

"Around West Virginia," Mr. Harmon said, "they're known as 'fishermen.'" His wife gave him a playful slap on his arm.

Mr. Kesler smiled. "Well, Max likes to call himself a percussionist, but I think the term is munitions expert. That's his company, Kesler Munitions, Inc. Just last month, he took down a thirty-six-story building in Brazil." He smiled. "Amazing work."

"But you mean he's just going to blow it up? Isn't it historical?" Alison said. As she said it, Bill began sliding away the glass of wine Sarah had poured for herself, edging it away from her reach. Weird, Alison thought. Earlier, when Sarah had asked for wine, he'd brought her ice water.

Mr. Kesler clucked his tongue. "If by 'historical' you mean dilapidated, yes."

"Historical *always* means dilapidated," Lila said. "Just look at us."

The evening had grown late, the conversation quieted to a trickle. It was hard to top a munitions-expert son assigned to dynamite part of the town, though Mr. Rossi kept batting around his trivia ball, trying to entice someone to play. Alison was the only one who ever took him up on it, and she nodded at him now, half-listening as he talked about the weight of the Hoover Dam and the distance record for hand-walking. Soon even he stopped talking, and Mr. Kesler left as a horn honked for him outside; then the others moved slowly toward the door, the postdance stiffness seeping into their bones. They gave Sarah and Alison and Bill hugs and handshakes, then left, the van's headlights sweeping across the lake as they pulled out, illuminating the men down in the mud, fishing the lake's shrinking center.

Bill piled plates in the sink, kicked the rug back into place, kissed Sarah good night, and excused himself off to bed.

Sarah and Alison worked in silence, rinsing and stacking plates, sealing leftovers in plastic wrap, handing things back and forth as they did growing up, the easy, old rhythm of any Saturday-night dinner. Alison kept trying to catch her sister's eye, though Sarah resisted looking in her direction. Finally, Alison spoke.

"Sar? Bill was acting kind of strange tonight, did you notice?"

Sarah paused. "More than usual?"

"Well, you know . . . He kept pushing away your drinks, scooting the wine bottle away from you. I mean, if there's any-thing—"

"Oh, *that*."

Alison shrugged. "If there's some kind of problem or, I don't know . . ."

"Ah, shit." She shook her head. "Okay, the story is, Bill wants us to get pregnant. I want that, too, but Bill wants it in the sense that he wants to keep breathing. For a year and a half now, we've been trying and just . . . *nothing*. So this is his new plan."

"A year and a *half*? You never said anything."

"Well, you've been occupied, haven't you?" She turned away from Alison and busied herself dropping forks into the dishwasher.

"Yeah, but . . ." She thought for a second. "How does cutting you off from the liquor supply get you pregnant? It's been a while, but that's not how I remember it."

"This is Bill's idea, that we aren't thinking about it the right way. We aren't *visualizing,* he says. He got the idea from the Olympics, for godsakes. Some javelin thrower talking about how he visualizes a toss. Sees it fly through the air and it does and he wins, and some-how this translates into us having a baby. You know Bill, ready to believe in anything."

"You've tried doctors, I take it?"

Sarah took her rings off her soapy hands and put them into the seashell beside the sink. "We have had every test they can toss our way and passed them all without even studying." She puffed her cheeks, blew out a long, low breath. "We've been poked and scraped and injected with dye. 'Just one of those things,' I think was the official diagnosis."

"They have drugs," Alison said.

Sarah looked at the dish towel in her hands, shook her head. "Not if they don't know what's causing it."

"So, the tried-and-true javelin approach," Alison said.

Sarah nodded, ran a glass under the hot water, her jaw working stiffly. "We visualize how it will be if we are pregnant, or little sperms backstroking into little eggs. Or Bill does. Mostly I visualize how much I would like to catch a wine buzz and smoke cigarettes again. But I go along, right? Poor Bill. He just intends to . . . *will* it so. He talks to my stomach. Our favorite sex toy is now a thermometer."

Alison laughed a little and Sarah smiled. "What does he say to your stomach?"

"He kneels down and says, 'Hi in there. Daddy's here.'" She swallowed. "Things like that."

"Oh, man." Alison glanced down at her sister's stomach, imagining the words vibrating inside. "You know you should have told me all of this."

Sarah stiffened. "Yeah, that would've been nice. Too bad, huh?" She pinched her lips together and banged the water faucet off, then wheeled on Alison. "That is *exactly* what I wanted. To pick up the phone some afternoon and call you up and picture you sitting in your kitchen, leaning on the butcher block and putting the ends of your hair in your mouth the way you do, and I could just spill the whole damn thing. Instead, we sneak around to doctor's appointments, not wanting to burden you with anything else."

Her face flushed, and she flinched a little under Alison's touch, and Alison saw all at once that Sarah was not upset, not verging on tears, just angry.

Sarah shook her head. "But you weren't there, Ali. You were here. Do you see? You were here sitting on the porch and here crying by the lake and here pacing the halls at night and so I couldn't tell you, not any of it. You were just *too* here, in this house. Too unavailable."

Alison didn't know what to say. She let all of this sink in for a minute. "You want me to apologize because my husband died?"

"No, Ali. I want you to go home. Five months ago, I wanted you to stay here forever. Now I want you home. That phone call from Ernie today . . . I really thought you would just take a deep breath and say, 'Okay.' I mean, you have a *'project'* going? How about having a *life* going? Like the rest of us."

Alison eyes started to burn. "A year was supposed to be the deadline, right? That's what all those stupid books say. 'Sorry, time's up. Feel all better now.'" Alison stopped talking, waved her hand in front of her face. She wondered how many times Sarah and Bill had talked about this. Or Sarah and Ernie, for all she knew. Maybe the whole town and everyone she knew, wondering when she would finally buck up and stand strong and pull herself up by her bootlaces and all those other phrases that were supposed to have kicked in by now. Problem was, she didn't feel any of it.

"A year? Year and a half?" Sarah said. "I don't know how much is enough time. If there's ever enough." She wiped her hands on her jeans. "It's not a deadline. It's just . . . You miss Marty, and we do, too, okay? But we have to miss *you* on top of it. And you aren't gone for good, that's what's so frustrating. I just want to know when you'll be back. *If* you'll be back."

Alison looked at Sarah, at their reflections in the narrow, darkened window above the sink, and felt nearly pulled under by the weight of longing. She missed it, too, those Tuesday mornings when Sarah would call and tell her everything about the latest batch of dancers, about who had said what or fallen ill, about some elderly man hitting on her, about Bill asking her to read another book on angels or ESP, and they would laugh as her coffee cup slowly heated a white ring into the surface of the butcher block, and time passed so easily. How had it gotten so far out of her grasp? All of it gone now, not just Marty. When, Sarah had asked, would she be back?

"I'll be back when I finish the Corvette," Alison said.

Sarah was squeezing out the sponge, wiping the area around the sink. She scrubbed harder, shaking her head. "You have a job, students, a house, *us*. But you're pinning everything on that damn stupid car." Just when it seemed she was gathering herself up for another barrage, she sagged back against the counter. She looked, Alison thought, tired. Just tired. "Then you'd better get busy," Sarah told her. "That thing is a disaster area."

There are a number of techniques involved in maintenance and repair that will be referred to throughout the
manual. We hope you use the manual to tackle the work
yourself. Doing it yourself will usually be quicker and much
less expensive than arranging to get the vehicle into a
repair shop. An added benefit is the sense of satisfaction
and accomplishment that you feel after doing the job
yourself.

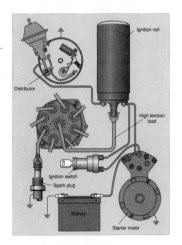

# 3

Even after she and Bill installed a new battery, nothing—not the engine or the headlights or the radio—worked.

"Electrical," Bill said, nodding. "You got those mice in there, they chew the wires."

Alison looked at him, then back at the exposed engine of the car. A wad of twigs and paper scraps lay tangled in one corner, and on top of the big iron block, oil puddled in the depressions. The bundles of wires were everywhere. Wires, belts, hoses. It bore almost no resemblance to those careful drawings in her manual.

"Mice eat *wires?*" She hadn't heard the clawing noises since that first night. "Why would they do such a thing?"

"Well, I don't think they have any particular motivation." He shrugged. "Their nature. Mice chew up our phone lines all the time."

"That's not fair," she said. Bill laughed and so did she, but in a way, she meant it. For the past three nights she'd stayed up late, sitting on a stepladder in the garage, reading her new manual, trying to absorb all the instructions and procedures. But there was no mention anywhere of *mice,* no photos showing teeth marks in wires. Her problem already was in figuring out where to jump into all the mess, some way to get a handle on it. How much harder would that be if she had to worry about mice destroying the car from the inside out? She took comfort in thinking of the men with the white lab coats, imagining them as benevolent doctors, restoration scientists. She wanted to be like them, the way they made it all look so effortless, how they smiled in every photo.

Late that afternoon, unannounced, Mr. Kesler dropped by with his son, Max. She heard them before she saw them, their low voices as they walked toward the garage. Mr. Kesler knocked on one of the rough boards.

"Alison? I'd like to introduce you to Max here." He indicated his son with a pat on the shoulder, as if she might have missed him standing there. She shook his hand.

"The percussionist, right?" she said. "Gene Krupa minus the heroin." He laughed, his tiny glasses angled down his nose.

"Yeah, according to Dad. I call myself a freelance munitionist." He dug around in his jeans pocket and handed her one of his cards, which had his name and a PO box number, along with a little cartoon of Yosemite Sam igniting a powder keg.

"Freelance, huh?" she said. "I'd guess most of your work is commissioned." She stuck the card in her pocket.

"Except when I'm practicing. Then it's just vandalism." He had one of those narrow smiles, she couldn't tell if he were joking or not.

"I'm going inside to set up," Mr. Kesler said, his white gloves tucked into the pocket of his jumpsuit.

"The dance isn't for another hour, Gordon," she said.

He shrugged. "I'm here now. Records could stand a cleaning."

She smiled at him. "The early Mr. Kesler." He paused a moment, looking at the two of them, then turned to go inside.

"He seems really proud," Alison said. "A son who blows things up."

"He'd be prouder if I were a forty-five of Shorty Rogers," he said. "And anyway, I don't really blow them up." As he spoke he moved around the car. He had his father's habit of nervously licking his lips. "I just take out the base, the supports or foundation for whatever structure, hold my breath, and let it fall. I just teach things about gravity."

"What a coincidence. I teach students about history," she said, though it wasn't exactly true anymore.

He nodded, then pulled out a crumpled pack of Marlboros and lit one. "Good for you."

"You know, I've seen your work on TV," she said. "Buildings and bridges coming down. Your father told us about the skyscraper in Brazil."

He leaned into the engine bay, cigarette in his mouth. "I wish," he said. He bounced the car on its shocks, and Alison noticed on his upper arm a tattoo of the same Yosemite Sam drawing he had on his business card. "That's the Alfonsi family," he said. "They did the Caldera Building in Brazil, thirty-six stories. I just do silos, a few stone bridges, small-town stuff. I did the library in Charleston two years ago. Came down in three and a half seconds. Laid it down like a little baby."

"So, your father's confused."

He laughed, flicked ashes away from the car. "Yeah, I guess you could put it that way."

She wondered what he meant by this, but probably it was none of her business. "And now you get to teach the Wiley Ford dam about gravity?"

He bent down to look beneath the car, his blond crew cut shimmering and angled, like hammered metal.

He straightened, grinned. "That," he said, "I'm just going to blow up." Before she could ask, he said, "No supports as such. It's just a big stone wall. Just, boom—down."

She nodded, wondering suddenly what he was *doing* here, if this was Sarah's awkward stab at some kind of blind date. "So, where did you get your munitionist's degree?"

He pulled a bandanna from his pocket and wiped his fingers, stamped out his cigarette on the dirt floor, then picked up the butt and put it in his pocket. "Fort Dix. I wanted to be a photographer when I was growing up. Won a Brownie camera in a contest for picking best name for the Munsters' car. Second place. After that, I took photos of every neighbor, the neighbors' dogs, the dogs' fleas. *Every* damn thing. I wanted to work for *National Geographic* and take pictures of the first man to cross the Arctic Circle on foot, or whatever." He wiped each finger carefully, like his father wiping his record albums. "You ever think about that? If that guy is supposed to be the first across, but the photographer is there to take his picture doing it, then he's really the *second* one across, right?" He stopped, as if he really wanted her to answer this.

"Second. I guess you're right. He should only win the Brownie camera."

"So the captions are bullshit, right? Anyway, the recruiter told me the U.S. Army has the best photography schools in the world." Max shrugged. "He was less than truthful."

She laughed. "And you were more than gullible."

"I was eighteen. After my discharge, I kicked around for a while. Sold my darkroom equipment, wanted to be an inventor, own my own business. Lived with a woman who didn't like me very much. A string of bad ideas."

Alison looked away, thinking of all those weekend projects Marty had done with Lem, the folding ladder they'd tried to invent, the welding cart half-finished, all their plans that came, finally, to nothing. Blown money. Dead ends. A short life wasted in a damp basement.

"So, what'd you name it?" she asked.

"What?"

"The Munsters' car."

"Oh, that. I called it the Ghoul Mobile."

"That won second? How many entries were there, two?"

Max smirked. "Hey, listen," he said. "Three hundred bucks."

"What?"

"Sorry it's not more, but in all honesty, I'll just sell parts, then scrap the rest."

She looked at him a moment. "This car isn't for sale. I don't know where you got the idea . . ."

Max shook his head and looked at the garage ceiling. "My 'confused' father, that's where," he said. "He said he wanted me to see about your car. I just thought . . ." He spread his hands open before him.

"Well, sorry, but this one I'm restoring. I just started."

"You're restoring *this* car?"

His tone annoyed her. "No, one of the other cars in here. The blue one in the third row."

He half-laughed. "Hey, good luck is all I have to say on that. I hope you have a big fat bank account. And the patience of Job teaching PE in junior high. You're going to need it."

"Why do you say that?"

"Well . . . Alison, right? This car . . . it's a goner. It's terminal. It's on life support. I mean, call in the priest, okay? The money you're going to have to spend, you could buy a nice *running* Vette. A better model, too, a more desirable year."

*A more desirable year?* This sounded so strange, she nearly forgot her annoyance. "What do you know about it anyway?" she said. "Have you blown up Corvettes in your time?"

He ran his hand along his crew cut, pushed up his glasses. "I've spent a little time working on cars. I think that's what Dad must've meant. Help you out some."

"Tell him I said great idea. So far you've been a godsend."

"Hey, sorry. Just trying to save you a little bother and money."

Alison felt her face warming. She imagined the ride home for the two of them, Max describing in detail the car's ruin, the piles of rust, the torn interior. She saw them laughing over her stupid plan, pitying her futility. And she saw herself never finishing the car. What would she tell Sarah then? What would she tell herself? Maybe his description of the car fit her, as well: a goner, a terminal case.

"Listen," Max said. "Get yourself some jack stands, raise the car up so you can get to it. And start with the brakes. Better know it can stop before—"

"—before you make it go. Your father told me the exact same thing. You two must sit around memorizing little adages together."

He laughed. "Maybe we should try that. It would give us something to say to each other—you know, besides 'The Orioles need pitching,' or 'Get me a beer.' Liven things up some."

She busied herself, straightening up the sparse tools on her workbench, the Lil' Wonder All-N-One and the manual (still clean, the pages crisp), the set of wrenches she'd found on the floor. The whole collection of them must look pathetic, held up against the condition of the car. "What's the matter?" she said. "You don't talk to each other?"

Max shrugged. "Sure. We talk about his record collection, TV, work. We get along."

"He *really* talks to me," Alison said. This wasn't exactly true, but she wanted to get back at him for making her feel so stupid. "He tells me about his past."

"Yeah, I suppose he told you about losing the car in the lake."

She looked at him. "Is your father genuinely confused, or just a liar?"

Max smiled and lit another cigarette. "He's a liar. To the core."

"You mean the whole thing? There is no Chrysler in the lake?"

"Nope. You and I are probably the only ones in Mineral County who know that."

She sighed. "Okay, so your father's a convincing liar. You don't seem too bothered."

Max sucked on the cigarette, then looked at it. "You got one good lie from him, and I've had . . . God knows. Thousands. He's a liar, Alison, that's what he does."

Alison shook her head. She thought of all those times when Marty was in the basement, gone for hours, for whole Saturdays and Sundays down there, and at night in their bed she would ask him why. Why was he avoiding her? He would lie, too, tell her how much work he had left on some project, how he was going to make some real money this time, how Lem was counting on him to be there. He'd smile and shake his head, would never tell her what was wrong. They had argued about it the night before he died, after he'd spent that entire day at Lem's and was planning to head back the next day. It had been this way for the last few years, his almost constant avoidance of her. *Why?* she wanted to know. Why?

She looked at him, absently thumbing the pages of her manual. "But why me?"

He blinked behind his tiny glasses. "He's recruiting you."

"He wants me to lie, too?"

"To cover his back. Help him out when that lake turns up empty and his famous car story turns up bullshit. You're from the *college,* after all. It carries weight if you say the car is buried under mud. He keeps trying to convince me, too."

She shook her head. "I'm not a geologist. I teach Western civ."

"Around here? They don't care. He just needs corroboration. You're it."

She sat on the hood of the Corvette. "How do you know all this?"

"It's his MO." He shook the red cigarette pack, then crumpled it up and tossed it into the corner. "One time when I was a kid, he gave me a baseball signed by Lou Gehrig, for a birthday present. Came in this glass display box. I cleared off a whole bookshelf to make room for the 'Lou Gehrig ball,' right? Later on, I was maybe sixteen, I took it to a collector's show in Morgantown, just to see what it was worth."

"And?"

He smirked. "Total fake. The guy showed me how the ball was all but brand-new, how the signature didn't match. Dad just bought a ball and signed it."

"What did he do when you called him on it?"

"He recruited somebody. His boss at Celanese comes over for dinner, admires the ball, starts telling me how those collectors are con artists, how they will tell you anything just to steal your stuff. He was convincing. I think because Dad had convinced *him*."

"That doesn't sound so terrible. Really, it's kind of sweet if you think about it."

"It wasn't sweet." He shook his head. "And that was nothing. There was much worse." He said this with such foreboding that she didn't want to ask. Max looked at his cigarette, flicked it out into the gravel drive.

"So now he wants to convince me. To lie to you."

"Not me. He *knows* I'm onto him. He wants you to convince Wiley Ford. He's pretty famous around here for that story."

"Well, if he asks," she said, "tell your dad I'm not interested in being his little fib partner, okay?"

Max nodded as he stood in the doorway of the garage, looking around for a minute. "Good luck with the car, I guess."

Two days later, the *Wiley Ford Press-Republican* ran a story on the draining of the lake, Colaville, the new dam replacing the old one.

The article talked about Kesler Munitions as if it were some big company, instead of just one guy with a tattoo. There was a sidebar about the lake itself, its history, most of the things that Mrs. Skidmore had spoken of at the last dance lesson. And when Alison turned the page, her eyes fell on an accompanying photo of an old Chrysler, though not Mr. Kesler's (the caption said "Photo courtesy of Flow Motors"), and two paragraphs in the middle about "the Kesler Chrysler," about young Gordon Kesler and the frozen lake, how he was anticipating finding the car again and bringing it out. They even quoted him, telling the lie over again. Alison folded the paper, didn't bother reading the rest.

The old joke in Wiley Ford was that at 7:00 every evening they *wanted* to roll up the sidewalks, but everyone was asleep. This was not quite true, though you would never mistake it for anything other than an American small town, as if you might turn a corner and find Norman Rockwell sitting in a chair with his pipe and sketch pad. Cumberland, where she'd lived with Marty, was small, but not this small, and nothing like the Baltimore suburbs where she'd grown up. The worst thing about a small town was also the best thing: Everywhere you went, you saw the same people. Every church gathering or bar or ball game or parade, you would turn around and see the same ten people you'd just seen that morning, or yesterday, at the market or the Laundromat or at the fire hall, buying fried chicken to raise money for new uniforms. Like a high school play where the same actors play three or four different parts. It was comforting, this familiarity, and claustrophobic, all at once. Tonight, feeling it closing in on her, Alison walked alone through the streets downtown, away from the lake, away from the dance lessons. Five minutes into the dancing, she'd had her fill. Five minutes of watching Mr. Kesler clean and reclean his records, five minutes of Tyra Wallace complaining about the new library committee, of Sarah blasting her coach's whistle, of Mr. Rossi talking about some tiny country where fruit was used as currency. So she'd left.

Now she sat on the low brick wall that surrounded the square at the end of Main Street, next to a store that sold sandwiches and frozen yogurt. Across the street was the Discount Beverage Center, which had found a place in her heart during her time here, not for the liquor they sold but because at night their neon sign lit up to read DISCOUNT RAGE CENTER, a few of the red tubes burned out. Every time she came this way, she imagined a long line of the timid and shy, waiting their turn to purchase hostility, to stock up on anger. The thought made her think about her own rage right after Marty's accident, long since subsided, discounted by nothing more than time.

Next to DISCOUNT RAGE was the Red Bird Cafe, all lit up and filtered pale green through the plastic window film. Inside, the waitresses slid around on their crepe-soled shoes, carrying coffeepots and trays. As she walked closer, she could make out Mr. Beachy in a corner booth, a book spread open before him, next to his pie and coffee. She pushed open the door and walked inside, sat on the stool opposite him.

"Evening, Mr. Beachy." She swiveled around to face him, after ordering coffee. He looked up from his book and then politely closed it. The title was *Rangers of the Lone Star,* a Zane Grey novel.

"Well, Alison, how are you tonight? How's the work coming along on that Corvette?"

She carried her saucer and cup to his booth and sat down across from him, grateful for innocuous company, for small talk.

"Slow, I guess. I don't know what I'm doing. But I've decided to fix the brakes first."

The corners of his mouth turned down, as if he were giving this careful thought. "That's fine, you have to start somewhere. Just jump right in. Come by the store tomorrow, I'll fix you up with parts."

"I'll need jack stands," she told him. She had no idea what these were, but now that she was learning some of the jargon, she wanted to try it out. She wanted to throw it around like a pro, like a restoration scientist.

He nodded, chewing his coconut pie. "Yes, of course. Plus new lines if they're cracked. And a master cylinder, or will you rebuild yours?"

She mentally leafed through the pages of the manual, trying to remember "master cylinder." Nothing came to her. "Oh, definitely a new one. Absolutely."

He smiled. "No reason to be penny-wise and pound-foolish, right?"

They were quiet a moment, and suddenly the whole thing felt awkward; Mr. Beachy seemed exposed, almost frail, without the long counter in front of him. She stirred her coffee, drank it. The waitress refilled her cup. She tried to think of something else she could say about the car without sounding like an idiot.

"It's not a very desirable year, is it?"

"Well," he said quietly, "I don't think anyone would wish on themselves the kind of year you've had. But things can only get better is how I feel."

"Oh, no, I meant—" She groped for words. "I meant the car, Mr. Beachy. Not a good year for Corvettes."

He flushed deep red. "Oh, *that.*" He wiped his mouth with a paper napkin. "You see, customers ask me all the time about blue-book value, and what this or that might be worth. I tell them, if you love the car, then it's priceless."

She smiled and nodded. "You should be a diplomat, Mr. Beachy. Or a marriage counselor."

"Alison, I do wonder if during . . . during the year or so you've been through, has the church been much of a comfort to you?"

Oh, *man.* The last thing she wanted was to have Mr. Beachy trying to convert her. She wanted suddenly to get out of there, to be back sitting at the edge of the lake in the quiet and the dark, or in her garage, tinkering.

"A few Mass cards, some flowers from Marty's church, but really, Mr. Beachy—"

"Oh, so you're Catholic, then? My late wife was Catholic. I never did join up, though. Never had much use for any religion until after my surgery. I guess I'm not too original in that, am I?"

"Hey, that is the very same with Marty and me," she said. "He grew up in the church, and I just kind of went along."

Mr. Beachy smiled, his teeth small and white, like baby teeth. "Well, that would be me, too. I liked the pageantry of it, I suppose, but could never get behind following a priest or any kind of preacher, really. I wanted to chart my own course."

"Marty used to tell me that Mass was like obedience school—you know, stand, sit, kneel. If you don't learn young, you'll never get it. I was just an old dog, or a bad dog, I guess."

He laughed again, and she felt her face warm. "But not too bad. You went, didn't you?"

"Every Sunday, every day of obligation."

"So, why did you?"

She thought about this, sipping her coffee. "Marty liked dressing up for church. Some Sundays, they asked him to do the collection baskets, and he just *loved* that. He was so happy. The only time I ever saw him in a tie was at church." This was the same tie that still hung knotted in the closet at home.

"Wearing it some other place would've spoiled the whole effect."

"Exactly. So, how could I not be there?"

He nodded. "You couldn't."

She patted him on the arm, put a dollar on the table. "I should get back, before I'm missed."

"Okay, Alison. Just remember that all the answers you need are in the book." He gave a solemn nod, and it took her a good five seconds to realize he was talking about the Bible—*that* book, not her Haynes manual. Her silence made him blush.

"I don't mean to proselytize. You come on by tomorrow, and we'll get you fixed up."

As she walked out of the diner, she turned to see him back reading his Zane Grey novel where he'd left off, his finger shaking a little as it followed slowly along each word, the next, and the next.

————

When she got home the dancers had left, and the little window light was out in the kitchen, which meant Sarah had gone to bed. Alison walked to the house in the slight chill of a summer night, anticipating having the quiet house, the porch, the lake to herself. Instead, she found Bill in his bathrobe and slippers, standing in the shadows under the front windows, tossing handfuls of Uncle Ben's rice onto the roof of the house.

"Bill?"

"Alison! You scared the heck out of me. I thought you were upstairs." He stood holding the orange box as if it were the most natural thing in the world.

"I just got in. I was downtown."

"Oh. Well. Good night, then."

"You know I'm going to ask, Bill." She leaned on the porch rail, looking down at him.

He held up the box and studied it, as if just realizing what it was. She could tell from the way he held his arms that he was embarrassed. "This?" He nodded at the box. "I know Sarah told you about the javelin throwers, right?"

"Yes. Why the javelin? Some kind of phallic thing?"

He waved away the question. "You know why they throw rice at weddings?"

"As opposed to javelins?"

"No, really. Do you?"

She shrugged. "For good luck?"

"Rice is a crop, grows abundantly and all that. It's for fertility." He shrugged.

"And less subject to litigation than, say, cabbages." To her relief, he laughed at this, as she knew he would. She had always liked Bill for his sense of humor, not the kind that caused him to say funny things, but more the kind that let him laugh at anything worthy of it that crossed his path.

"Bill," she said, "this really is sweet, what you're doing. But . . . *rice?*"

He pressed his lips together, looked toward his feet. "I want more than anything else for us to be pregnant. Well, Sarah, I mean. Guys at work come in saying, 'I'm going to be a Daddy,' and they act all like they will be so broke now and no more fun and no more poker games and nothing but worries from here on. But at the same time, everybody is slapping them on the back, shaking their hands, and they just smile." He picked a grain of rice off his bathrobe sleeve. "We go through it again and again, this letdown every month. I guess that sounds strange. . . ."

Alison smiled. "And throwing rice on your house doesn't?"

"No . . . yeah, it does." He nodded at the orange box. "It sure does. Strange and odd, I know. But we've tried everything, Al. Every thing. So I'm going to try everything *else*. I don't care if it makes sense or not."

She thought of her Corvette, of her need to see it finished and working. "I hear you, bro," she said.

"Will you help me?"

She shrugged again. "Sure, I can throw rice if you like. Want me to throw some around back?"

"Nah, not that. Just help me . . . get the momentum moving. That's what we need, the big mo."

"But how?"

He looked at her. "Beats heck out of me. But I'll think on it and let you know. Fair enough?"

"Yeah, fair enough." She walked back down the steps to give him a hug, told him good night, and then went into the house. From the kitchen, she heard the quiet *shush* of more rice hitting the shingles and trickling down into the gutters. She sat at the darkened table, sipping wine and eating a leftover cheese puff from the dance, listening as if to a rainstorm, until the noise quit and she heard Bill make his way upstairs.

Instead of heading off to bed, she decided to check on the car. She could start making a list of what she would need in the morning from Mr. Beachy. Maybe circle the parts in the diagrams. By this time tomorrow, she could have made real progress, have some little piece of the job done. When Marty and Lem got involved in a big

project—repairing a sump pump or constructing a go-cart or building their own computer from a kit—Lem used to take such satisfaction in finishing part of it. He'd walk into the kitchen, flushed and
sweaty, tugging his shirttail, and dig a beer from the fridge. "We're
eating that elephant," he'd say, "one bite at a time."

As she snapped on the coffee-can light, she nearly tripped over
the bag at her feet, from Wal-Mart. Inside were two cardboard
boxes, each containing a pair of jack stands. On top was a note
scrawled on the back of the receipt and weighted down with a piece
of gravel:

*Alison,*
*Didn't mean to insult your project. Sometimes I am not very good*
*at making myself understood the way I want to be (all that army*
*sensitivity training did me no good). Hope these help, I can show*
*you how they set up if you need. I'm headed out to Tygart to blow a*
*silo tomorrow. Want to come?*
                    *Max*

She slid the note into her jeans pocket and picked up one of the
boxes. The nearest Wal-Mart was across the river in Cumberland,
which meant he'd driven over and driven back before he had to
pick up his father. She tried to picture him doing it, carrying the
two heavy boxes in his hands, walking into the middle of the dance
practice and asking for her. Strange, it was hard for her to remember exactly what he looked like; she could see only his hammered-
metal haircut, the tiny flashes of light his frameless lenses made. But
how tall was he? What was the texture of his skin? His smell? These
were the same questions she asked her students in Western civ
when they talked about da Gama or Karl Marx. How to pull the person out of a boldface name in a textbook, how to give back to them
their profanity and lust, their bald spots and infidelities, the sound
of their breathing or their coughing when they suffered a head cold.
And this was her worry with Marty, too—that the little details of
him would start to fade, that his small clutters and messes in the

house would be neatened into extinction, her anger and impatience with him swept away, her memory of him transformed into merely the memory of her memory, like a photo in an album, trimmed and aligned, held under plastic.

So tomorrow Max was blowing up a silo. Three seconds, he'd told her, for the library in Charleston. Laid it down like a baby, he'd said. And when the dust settled, that bit of the town was gone for good. Some part of her wanted to know what that looked like—something coming to its end so suddenly and so violently. The thought of it made her breathing subside for a moment, but at the same time, she wanted to see this.

Component disassembly should be done with care and purpose to ensure that the parts go back together properly. Always keep track of the sequence in which parts are removed, and make note of special characteristics or marks on parts that can be reinstalled in more than one way.

Front Suspension

Rear Suspension

# 4

They were met at the silo by a balding man named Donald, who was in shirtsleeves, wore a tie, and carried a clipboard full of pink permits. He stood next to a pickup truck with state seals on the doors, its two-way radio squawking noisily. Max shook hands, then walked around the base of the silo, sometimes stopping to kick it, causing a powdery spill of brick and mortar. He kept muttering to himself, lighting cigarettes and then dropping them, picking up a few grass blades and tossing them in the air, like golfers on TV. She and Donald watched him. All around them was nothing but a sloping expanse of red dirt, tiny pink flags stuck on rusty wires here and there into the ground. The county had recently condemned the property to make way for a new bypass. The silo itself leaned a little (almost as bad as her garage), brown bricks scattered around its base. Stored inside, according to Donald, were thousands of plastic gallon milk jugs, some of them spilling through the rotted doors at the base.

"Let me ask you," he said. "What would someone have in mind to do with maybe five thousand milk jugs?"

Max struck the base of the silo once with a hammer, then shouted, "Wrong, wrong, *wrong*."

"I just don't get all those milk jugs," Donald said.

Alison shrugged, pushed a stray curl away from her face. "I don't know," she said. "What's your theory?"

Donald looked puzzled by the array of possibilities. Alison got the impression that a silo filled with milk jugs was the most exciting thing that had happened on his job in ten years. He frowned and scratched his head, then suggested that maybe the owner had a big trotline catfishing operation going.

"Or maybe he was a moonshiner," Alison said. "They use jugs, I think."

Donald snapped his fingers and pointed at her. "Hey, that's exactly right. I read that somewhere. In some book." When he said the word *book,* she realized—she'd missed her Monday-night deadline to call Ernie back and keep her spot in the fall semester. They would not need her again until mid-January.

Donald gave up on solving the mystery of the milk jugs (this sounded like one of the Hardy Boys books she and Sarah had traded as kids, preferring them to prissy Nancy Drew), saying this was cutting into his lunch hour. He sat in his white county truck, said something into the mike, and drove off. Max walked over and drew some rough sketches on the back of a fast-food sack he found in his truck. He jotted math problems in the corners, as if he were balancing his checkbook instead of readying to blow something up. Finally, he took a stick and traced in the dirt a set of parallel lines leading out from the base of the silo.

"You do such precision work," she said. "I would've just used my finger."

He looked at her, and seemed to tear himself loose from the wild concentration that had held him the last twenty minutes. "I tell you what, if we were the Alfonsis, we'd be doing all this by computer model," he said. He stuck his pencil behind his ear. "But if you're me, the dirt-and-stick method works fine. Want to help with the dynamite?"

"Just like that?" Her hands were shaking a little, and she was half-hoping Donald might come back to watch. "You mean . . . *now*?"

He smiled. "We could wait around a few years, see if it falls down all by itself."

They walked to the back of the truck, where he pulled from under the camper top a cardboard box of dynamite. He handed her one of the sticks, which felt heavier than it looked, the outside covered in waxy red paper.

"Hey, you know, this looks just like dynamite," she said.

"It *is* dynamite." He pulled other, smaller boxes from the truck.

"I know, but it *looks* like dynamite, in bad-guy movies. Like Wile

E. Coyote dynamite. I expected, I don't know, something more high tech."

"I have plastics and emulsions for special jobs, cutting steel cable and such. But mostly I just use good old TNT. Nitroglycerin and wood pulp and paper. Nothing beats it for velocity." Max tossed the box of dynamite on the ground, and she jumped. "Relax," he told her. "Until we connect the caps and cord, it's harmless as a box of pencils. Just don't get the stuff inside the sticks on your hands."

She looked at her fingers. "Why not?"

"The nitro is what's called a vasodilator. Gets under your skin and gives you one hell of a headache."

"All these years, I never knew my sister was a vasodilator." Max smiled as he continued to count and make notes. She was nervous, making dumb jokes. She tried to think of something else to say, but all that would come to her were the kind of things Mr. Rossi might have said had he been here—Marco Polo's introduction to gunpowder in Asia, Alfred Nobel's invention of dynamite, and so on. She used to mention all of these to her students, impressing them with easy ironies while they sat in the dark watching World War II documentaries.

"You ever go to Ocean City?" Max asked.

She put the stick back in the box. "Every summer when we were kids in Baltimore. Us and about seven million others." She thought of her trips there with Marty, of the obsessive way she'd watched their videos after his accident, watched as if they were the Zapruder film and could be made to reveal some truth about what had been wrong with them.

"In 1922, a dead whale washed up on the beach there," Max said. "Huge thing. The rescue station towed it out to sea, and it came back in on the next tide. You know what they decided to do with it?"

"Turn it into a funnel-cake stand?"

He looked at her. "They blew it up. Fifty pounds of dynamite. Newspapers said it rained blubber and blood for five minutes."

"That's pretty gross."

He nodded slowly, as if he'd never considered this angle of the story. "Yeah, I guess it is."

He turned to his work, motioning her back as he fired up a gas generator from the truck bed and ran a long extension cord over to the silo. He hooked up a huge drill all coated in white dust, and handed her safety glasses and foam earplugs. She put them on, and he clicked on the drill and leaned into it, his arm muscles making Yosemite Sam twitch. He bored a series of holes into the brick around the base of the silo. On one side, the holes formed what looked like a snowman's face, button eyes and a wide smile. Max turned off the drill, wiped his forehead.

"You need to add a nose," she said, pointing to the face. Her ears buzzed.

Max lifted his safety goggles over his glasses, the ghost of the goggles still on his face where the white dust hadn't reached. "Listen, I'm really awkward with this kind of thing." He paused, and she thought for a second he was talking about the drill. "You're not married or . . . involved or anything, are you?" He busied himself with dismantling the drill. "That's the word these days, *involved,* like you're a calculus problem."

She looked at him, the top of his head bent toward his work, the dust on his shirt, on the hairs of his arms. He didn't know. Somehow, he hadn't heard the gossip, or hadn't been around enough to find out, or maybe it had faded away by now. Why in the world hadn't his father told him? He had to be the only person in Wiley Ford unaware of what had brought her there, unaware that she'd become, for a time, the town's official Grieving Widow. She felt her mouth opening and closing.

"I think I'm more like long division," she said. *Dumb.*

"Well, are you? Involved?"

"The thing is . . ." she said. He looked up at her then, and her vision fell away, so that she saw the two of them crouching before this broken-down silo with its snowman face of holes, the foam plugs muffling their words to each other, the dust settling out around them. Max waited for her to speak, the safety goggles resting at his hairline, his face sweaty. She felt the two of them preserved in this moment somehow, a snapshot held by the corners of his not knowing and her not being known. She thought of how she'd imagined Mr. Kesler's Chrysler Imperial slipping down into Colaville, and its presence there, also preserved, the burning of its headlights and the shine of its paint. A lie, yes, but a pretty lie.

"The truth is, no, I'm not married. I was." She let it go at that, hoping that he would not, God help her, ask her out, that he wouldn't make her *say* it. He waited for her to continue, then turned to his boxes.

"Hey, you don't have to tell me your private business," he said, and right then she *wanted* to, to set him straight, knowing what he must imagine her private business to be: an ex-husband in another state, a messy divorce, the usual cynicism and wariness of so many women she knew. Old story, he must be thinking.

Max set to work, explaining as he went along. He opened the ends of the dynamite sticks with his pocketknife, eased the blasting caps into place, tamped the sticks into the holes with a piece of broom handle, then packed plastic lunch bags of sand in behind them. "To keep our nice little explosion in the hole," he said. He spoke quickly—overexplaining, smoking as he worked—and she knew he must have mistaken her hesitation for aversion. She didn't know how to tell him otherwise without draping herself in black and spilling the whole sad story. She couldn't take a fresh round of pity.

"This silo is like taking down a tree with a chain saw," he told her. "We blow out a wedge, cut through the base, and the whole thing lays right down. County brings out a loader and it's gone in two hours." As he spoke, he finished packing the last of the holes, wired up the caps, then wrapped the base of the silo in chicken wire to prevent pieces of brick from flying out. He spooled cord along the ground until they were behind the truck, where he connected the wires to a worn plastic box with thumbscrew connectors and a push button in the middle, a keyed ignition switch mounted on top.

"Well, that's a letdown," Alison said. "I wanted a little more Wile E. Coyote, one of those wooden boxes with a big plunger handle."

"They had to go invent batteries," he said. "Ruined the whole thing. Are you ready?"

"That's it? We're—you're going to blow it up right *now*?"

"You keep asking that. What is wrong with right now?" This seemed to be the question—the same one Sarah had been asking her, Ernie, everyone. She had no answer for it.

They crouched in the packed dirt behind the truck, to shield themselves when the silo fell. As she tried to think of what exactly *was* wrong with right now, Max interrupted her thoughts.

"Besides, it's you that's going to blow it up. Alison Durst, honorary button pusher."

She shook her head. "No, no way. I couldn't."

He smiled. "What the hell. Pretend it's a piano with Daffy Duck inside."

"Really, I can't."

"Why not?" The sweat on his face mixed with the mortar, running along his cheeks in thin white streams.

*Because I've done enough damage,* she might have said, but didn't. In the five thousand times she'd been through it in her brain, she knew that she had not killed Marty. The acetone that soaked his sweater had killed him, the gusts of wind, Lem's new welder, or the fact that it hadn't rained that day or that it was July instead of June or November . . . a spark had killed him, or a million sparks, or the place he was standing when the wind stirred the sparks or earlier when the acetone had tipped off the porch rail and spilled. All of it had killed him—a thousand intersecting moments. But all during the funeral, while the organ music played and the funeral home men stood beside his closed casket in all their polished sorrow and everyone she knew took her hands and held her, a voice inside her repeated *please . . . please . . . please,* repeated over the days that followed, a habit of repetition like the lists of history she carried around, until finally she thought to ask the voice, *please what?* And the voice drew back a thin curtain of memory and showed her herself, the night before the accident, yelling at Marty for another wasted day at Lem's, for coming home late and missing dinner, and the next morning in bed, whispering to him to hurry home, to not be away so long this time. *Please . . .* the voice asked, let it not be that he had rushed because of her. Let it not be that his own impatience had made his movements jerky and hurried. Let it not be that he had failed to change his soaked clothes because the slant of afternoon was already upon him, the hour late. Now those empty, negative prayers echoed across twenty-three months, her anger and pleas drawn down into a small hard knot of doubt.

"I'll just watch you, Yosemite Sam," she told Max. She forced a smile. "Maybe next time."

He shrugged, then leaned up over the hood of the truck to shout at the silo. "ANY LAST REQUESTS?" he said. "CIGARETTE OR A BLINDFOLD?" He paused, head cocked, as if waiting for it to answer. He looked at her. "Guess not."

Without another word he turned the key in the switch and pushed the green button. She knelt lower behind the truck, hands on the fender, peeking over, and saw the base of the silo cut through with fire and beige puffs of sand and smoke, saw the snowman's face erupt a split second before the explosions sounded. Max had wired in delays, he'd told her, but she could not distinguish them, so the sound came all at once, muffled and deep through the earplugs, more a tremor in the cavity of her chest, a rumble in the ground beneath her knees. She tasted the grit of mortar and sand blown toward them, blinking it from her eyes as the silo quivered on its base. It shifted and was changed somehow but did not fall for what felt like seconds, long enough for her to look at Max and for him to nod quickly at her, his eyes wild, telling her *just watch, just watch,* and as she turned a crack sounded from inside, like boards splintering, and the silo slowly twisted, the domed tin top of it cantered and tipping, the silo falling and almost whole in the air but with white spaces between the bricks, like a paint-by-numbers half-completed, spaces of light where the silo's destruction pressed in, expanded, filled it up, and lengthened. There followed a short space of silence, then the ground beneath her shook as if the earth rested on thin boards. The impact spewed up a cloud of red dust rolling skyward, and then the dust boiled away to reveal how the ground held the broken bricks and wood and tin still almost in the shape of the silo, but flattened and spread, a shadow of a structure that was no longer there, the five thousand milk jugs spilling out like fish eggs, rolling away with the breeze or crushed into piles. Stillness rose behind the cloud of dust, marked by the noise of random bits of brick or wood dropping and shifting inside the ruins.

"Like the wrath of God on high," Max said, nodding. Alison slumped back on her haunches—crying and shaking, unable to breathe, her stomach tight, dust drying the inside of her mouth. He looked up at her, and she saw that he was shaking, too, his hands quivering.

"Hey, listen." He touched her arm. "First time I shot something bigger than a stump, I had to excuse myself from the site and go throw up. Did not exactly instill confidence in the people who hired me."

She laughed and wiped her eyes with her thumb. "That really was . . . amazing," she said to him, only because she had to say something. He nodded, awkward in the face of her crying, and began to pack up his supplies. She helped him, the two of them stepping around the ruins of the silo, slapping the dust from their jeans, working in all that stillness they'd made.


In late afternoon they started for Sarah's house, and Alison leaned against the window, looking out at nothing in particular, at the trees and the car lots and front lawns. Max filled the quiet in the truck by digging around on the cluttered floorboard for cassette tapes, until he found one that featured arias from different operas. He hummed along, sometimes making little conducting motions with his fingers along the top of the steering wheel, pointing at streetlights or mail-boxes as if they were the string or woodwind sections.

"I had you pegged for more of a rock-and-roll type," she said. "Kind of aging and cool."

"Thanks a lot," he said. "I know, like, zero about this music." He angled his mouth toward her but kept his eyes on the road. "I ended up taking music appreciation at the community college after the army, and just decided I liked this. Don't ask me why. I mean, I grew up on Lynyrd Skynyrd and the Stones. So you were mostly right." She recognized the tape as a packaged "greatest hits" of arias by Puccini, Mozart, and Verdi, the kind of opera sold in the checkout line of the grocery store. Really, this about exhausted her knowledge of it, too.

"I thought you grew up on Count Basie and Lionel Hampton and . . . whoever."

"You mean Dad's stuff?" He laughed. "Back then, it was pretty much the way it is now—his record collection was totally off-limits. When I was a little-little kid, for the longest time I thought 'Don't touch' meant hearing it. Like if I listened to the music, I was touching it. I used to walk around the house with my ears covered. My mom thought I just hated the songs."

She looked over at him. He was smiling at the memory, the corners of his eyes dovetailed with lines. "That's pretty sad, really," she said.

He shook his head. "Nah. No biggie."

Alison listened with him now as Pavarotti hit a high C. There was something oddly fitting about the way the music went with the rhythm of riding in this broken-down truck.

"I think you like this music because it's noisy," she said. "It reminds you of work."

He laughed and reached down to the floorboard, and somehow among the scatter of food wrappers and crumpled Marlboro packs brought up a brown bag full of pistachio nuts. He offered her some and she took them, eating and tossing the shells out her window while her fingertips slowly stained red. When she and Sarah were little, they would wedge the shells onto their fingertips for fancy nails. She tried it now but could no longer make them fit. For a long space of time, she and Max didn't speak, just chewed and listened to the music. Her mind went back to Max's earlier question. What *was* wrong with now? She'd told Sarah she would get her life moving when the Corvette could take her, and so far, what had she done? Bought a kitchen-drawer gadget and a manual and sat on a stool, looking at pictures of men in lab coats. She'd tried to undo the bolts on the hood, to lift it away as the manual told her to, but the nearest-size wrench she had kept slipping off and bloodying her knuckles. The car was no closer to restored than it had been a year ago, or the year before that. Up until Marty died, the whole idea of right now never carried much weight. All during her growing up she lived in the same house in the same neighborhood, which backed up to the shopping center where her mother bought groceries and her father got his hair cut. They lived there still, just outside Baltimore, older and slower, retired, but mostly unchanged. They watched TV and read biographies. They mowed the grass by taking turns walking the narrow lawn, and at Christmas decorated their dusty plastic tree. When Alison visited them, she ate off the same stoneware dishes she'd eaten off all her life. In the soft pine surface of their kitchen table she could trace the pencil imprints of her handwriting from fourth grade, or sixth, or tenth, loopy cursive describing the Spanish-American War or tallying square roots. And all the time of her childhood and teenage years, and even now, Sarah, always the look-alike, always two years and two months older, would point to herself and say, "This is what you'll look like at fifteen" . . . "This is what you'll look like with boobs" or with braces or a tan or a first swipe of graying hair. As if Sarah forged ahead over the next year and the next, tracking the landscape for her, beating down the path, showing Alison what *now* would look like when she finally got there.

But the last couple years had taught her how stupidly arbitrary now could be—a silo could stand for decades and then one day not, or she could find herself on a country road in a pickup truck spilling opera and pistachio shells. None of it meant anything. In her classes, she would spend more time covering the War of Jenkins's Ear than she spent on the War of 1812, only because she liked telling about it better, and it shook the boredom off her students and made them laugh. If she gave that war and its ridiculous cause more importance than some other war, who was to say it *wasn't* more important? The present was just a tangle of uncertainty, and history no more than stumbling through the tangle, looking backward, naming its random parts once they'd slid past. And everything could be named: love, anger, Corvettes, arias, pistachio nuts. Dynamite. A war fought over a severed ear. The newspaper had had words ready when Marty died. ACCIDENT CLAIMS LIFE OF LOCAL RESIDENT. Section B, page 1, below the fold, all the particulars stored in their inverted pyramid. This was the way of all history: If it could be named, delineated, it could be made to make sense. ACCIDENT CLAIMS (not TAKES or STEALS or ENDS) LIFE. The words could be cut out and filed away, kept, stored on microfiche. Her loss parceled out, labeled, gone through, and finished. All the books she'd thrown in the lake had said so, so it must be true. Alison held another shell out the window and gave it up to the wind, noticing how early twilight came these days.

Back at the house, the energy of music and dance spilled out of the narrow windows and across the lawn. They sat inside the truck in the dark, Max's finger poised over the eject button while they waited for the aria to end.

"You don't even have to understand the words, you can tell what they're saying anyway." He looked over at her. "Love, sex, heartbreak. These guys and Elvis are pretty much singing about the same things."

"Yeah, the big three," she said, and popped open her door, filling the truck cab with light. "Thanks for showing me the silo."

"I bet you're going to say you had a blast," Max said, and she laughed.

"Munitionist humor," she said. "Hey, thanks for the pistachios, and music, too." She slammed the door and hesitated, not wanting to go into the house, where she'd have to watch the dancers, or help with the food, or make conversation with Mr. Rossi or Mrs. Skidmore. Max must have sensed her hesitation.

"If you like," he said, "we can get that car up on the new jack stands; then you're all set to work tomorrow morning."

"Yeah, thanks again for those, by the way." She hesitated. "I'll let you help, if you promise not to blow anything up."

He nodded, opened his door. "I try to leave my work at the office."

Inside her garage, she tuned the radio to NPR, hoping to find some opera. Instead was a local call-in show about bond issues in West Virginia. She clicked it off and they worked in silence, getting one wheel at a time jacked up, taking turns working the scissors jack in the narrow confines of the garage, the car groaning under its own weight. As they lifted each wheel in turn, a cascade of rust fell from under the car, and each time Max clicked his tongue and shook his head, as he had the first time he looked at the car.

"Look," she told him, "if all you can do is cluck and sigh, then I don't need your help, okay?" She looked out the open door of the garage toward the lake, the small distant puddles glimmering like nickels. She heard the voices of the men fishing the deep middle.

Max stood with his hands on his hips, turning his head to wipe his face on his shoulder. "Have you even talked to a body shop? Asked about how bad that rust might be?"

"No, I haven't talked to anybody but Mr. Beachy at the parts store."

"And what did he say?"

"That he doesn't want me to spend eternity in hell. And I need a new master cylinder."

"Alison . . ." He kicked the bottom of the door, causing more rust to spill out from under the car. "You really ought to get an estimate, at least."

She bit her bottom lip. "I'm going to fix the brakes, then make the engine run. I'll worry about rust later on."

"Well, I think you ought to worry about it now. You might end up spending a lot more than the car is worth. Two or three times more. Thousands."

It surprised her how angry she felt. Of course, he was only trying to watch out for her, to keep her from throwing away her money. She didn't know how to tell him that, no matter the amount of money, this rusty car was the only thing she had in front of her, the only thing she could see.

"Listen," she said. "Thanks for your help."

"Alison, I'm just looking out for your best interest."

"Yeah, I know. That's why I said thanks."

"I mean, really, it's none of my—"

"Max—"

They both stopped talking, and the moment hung in the air between them. She knew that if he stayed to help, he would tell her again and again how far gone the car was, how impossible the whole idea was. She didn't want to hear it, would *not* hear it. If she had learned nothing else in these two years, she'd learned not to trust the practical, to put no faith in the expected.

"Really, Max. I'm not mad. Please just go." She looked at her hands, wiped the rust and dirt on her jeans.

He was quiet a minute. "I'll go, but I'll come back, too. Unless you say not to."

She looked at him. His face now, without its smirk or cigarette, seemed so open and guileless . . . unburdened in a way she nearly envied.

"I'm not saying not to, okay?"

He looked around the garage. "I'll be honest. . . . I'm not sure what just happened here."

That's just it, she wanted to say, it *didn't* just happen. It happened twenty-three months ago, and kept happening, over and over, and would keep happening for the rest of her life. Max stood in the door, waiting for her to say something else, then told her he would see her around. Then he walked out the door, heading up to the house.


Thirty minutes later the Seven Springs van pulled out of the long drive, and through the big front window she saw Bill and Sarah pushing the furniture back into place, saw Bill sometimes stopping Sarah from her work and patting her stomach, or talking to it, and Sarah playfully pushing him away. Alison smiled, listened for a few minutes to the radio playing some old Cat Stevens song, one of several that had seemed to float through the years of her stay in high school. She remembered reading somewhere that Cat Stevens had changed his name and was now Yusuf something or other, that he had converted to a sect of Islam that shunned all music. At last all the lights in the house were dark except for the hall light they left on for her. She clicked off the coffee-can bulb and looked out to where the men were fishing, their laughter rising and falling, their camp lanterns giving off a dull glow. She turned and studied the Corvette. Propped up on the jack stands, it looked almost as if it were levitating, the wheels hanging down. She knew practically nothing about the car, its own history, beyond the story of the deadbeat nephew. The car was just another deadbeat, a transient tired of the road, found sleeping in an old garage. Like most transients, it had no discernible past—cleaning it out, she'd found a few artifacts—a plastic package that had once held a beach ball, an old roach clip, an eight-track tape by Styx, some bobby pins, a receipt for a 1981 state inspection in Indiana. They might be assembled into a kind of narrative, but that story would always be, at best, a wild guess.

She had spread an old shower curtain liner under the car to make it easier to slide beneath, and she did so now, holding the orange trouble light Mr. Beachy had sold her. She liked the trouble light almost as much as the Lil Wonder All-N-One, the way the lightbulb was held inside its wire cage like a canary, the way you could swing open the door to remove the bulb when it burned out. The orange cord of the trouble light trailed behind her as she slid under the car. She shone the light on the underside of the Corvette and up into its recesses.

Ruin.

Everywhere she looked, everywhere the white beam reached, she saw nothing but patches of rust, ragged holes, wires hanging down.

She knew from the manual that every part she could see opened up with bolts or screws or gaskets and held another ten or fifty or a hundred parts inside. Parts inside of parts. And all of it would have to be replaced. Everything. She grabbed the widest part of the frame and shook it. A few parts clanked together, the hoses and wires swaying. The taste of rust bloomed in her mouth, like the taste of a pricked finger. Within that small space, she swung and hit the underside of the car with the cage of her trouble light, swearing as she did it. When it hit, the bulb gave a small metallic snap and went out.

She clicked the button off and on, put the light down, laid her head back on the shower curtain, looking out from under the car. Faint light from the town pulled a dull gray color from the walls, the light from the radio dial spilling a luminous green on the floor. Above her, the parts of the car were hard to see, the whole thing now just a looming murkiness. She felt her breath moving in and out, a sense of the working of her lungs in this compressed space. The shower curtain crinkled and puckered beneath her as she stretched out her arms to the sides, palms turned up, as if she imagined the car might break loose of its stands and fall on her in the dark and she would embrace the whole of it. It felt immense above her, massive and impossible. She brought up her hands and held them tented over her face, then balled them into fists and hit the bottom of the car—a dull, hollow *thunk*—then hit it again and again, the skin of her hands scraping, grit falling on her face and arms. Nothing was adequate. Nothing was enough. No work she could summon equaled the brokenness of the car, no memory equaled ten years of shared life, no damaged love could keep anyone from dying. A car disappears into rust, a town into the lake that swallows it, a silo into its parts, a man into fire, a marriage into the man, a woman into the marriage, into the absence of the man. What was the point of this world if the whole thing or any part of it could be wiped away by any brief, dumb accident, leaving no meaning in its wake, no dust to trail our fingers in? Alison held her hands over her face, her own breath grown metallic and rusting, the dull space inside her chest an urn made from some brittle alloy—bright, polished, and empty.


By 7:30 the next morning, she sat on the brick wall outside AAAA Auto Parts, waiting for Mr. Beachy to unlock the door. By 8:30, she had filled the back of Bill's truck with boxes and boxes of car parts, nearly twelve hundred dollars' worth—steel brake lines and a power-brake booster, rebuilt calipers and new rotors and pads, enough for all four wheels. Not everything she needed, Mr. Beachy said (some of it was special order), but enough to keep her out of trouble for a while. He smiled when he said this, and slipped two new tracts into her hand with the credit-card receipt.

Six hours later, her knuckles were bruised and bleeding, she had chipped the crystal on her watch, and she'd fully exercised her vocabulary of swearwords. But progress was definite. She'd managed to replace one brake line, install a new rotor, and repack the wheel bearing just the way the manual showed her, rubbing it into the grease on her palm. As she worked—prying away the crud, soaking the bolts in penetrating oil—the lightly oiled gleam of new metal slowly took the place of rot. When the first assembly was finally done, she put the wheel back on, gave the tire a slap with her palm to watch it spin, and listened to the faint hush it made. As it slowed, she looked at her greasy hands, marveling at what they had done, as if they possessed more skill than she ever could. Six hours earlier, this wheel, like all the others, had been encrusted with rust and mud; now it shone and spun. That's all this amounted to—taking away an old part, replacing it with the new. Piece by piece by piece. She could *do* this. She imagined finishing the job, replacing the last hose or clamp or wire, and having then *two* cars: the new one, shining and perfect, and the old one, dismantled in a heap of cast-off parts, as though its wearing out were nothing more than a shell peeled away and discarded.

The manual said that the next job, after finishing all four wheels, would be to bleed the brakes. *Bleed* them? She thought of poor

George Washington, killed after doctors drew his blood five times in one day for nothing worse than a sore throat. As for bleeding the car, though, she had no idea, but could glean enough from the manual to know it was a two-person job. She hoped she didn't kill it completely, when the time came.

By afternoon, the next day's ache had already begun to settle into her bones. She packed up her tools, put away her now-dirty manual, clicked off the radio, and headed to the house. She glanced toward what remained of the lake (as everyone in the town did, making checkout-line talk over its progress) and noticed something new: the top of an arched bridge sticking up above the water, the stone arches as sloped and knobby as a backbone. Mrs. Skidmore had described the stone bridge across the river, which separated the mine from the town it had created. Also visible now was the long, dark wall of the dam, the top of it tapering down and meeting itself in the water's surface.

Tonight, there was a dance lesson, and inside the house, Sarah busied herself making Toll House cookies and lemonade. For all her desire to think of herself as a gifted cook and hostess, most of Sarah's attempts at cooking and party-throwing, like Alison's own, ended in disarray and a dozen tiny disasters; neither of them had ever gotten along with housework all that well, just like their mother, who many nights gave up and ordered Chinese. Their father always insisted that the best cook in the house was the telephone.

"*Damn* it," Sarah shouted, her face streaked with cookie dough. The cookies broke in half as she tried to spatula them from the baking sheet. She looked up at Alison. "This *sucks.* 'Pardon me, would you care for a chocolate-chip shard?' Just great."

Alison took the pan and spatula away from her. "Let them cool off first, the same way we handle you." She set it aside. "Let me go clean up, then I'll help."

Sarah blinked. "You will? We get to see you tonight?"

She smiled. "I might even dance, if you're lucky."

Sarah ate one of the cookie pieces. "Boy, somebody must've had a good time at the silo explosion yesterday."

"It's not *that*. I finished a wheel on the car. You should see, it's like new." She calculated that by sometime Saturday, she could have the other three wheels finished.

Sarah nodded, took a breath. "I love seeing you like this, Ali. I do. But that car . . . What if you don't finish it? Then what?"

Alison shrugged without answering, not wanting Sarah to get started. Finishing one wheel really didn't prove anything, she knew. Her mind kept going back to the night before, the decay she'd seen under the car, creeping like tendrils into all its darkened corners.

After she'd showered (her fingernails impossibly dirty) and dressed, she went out to her garage to take a look at her work, at the newness of all that clean steel. Soon after, the van from Seven Springs swung into the drive, Mr. Harmon at the wheel, and a little while later Mr. Kesler arrived, riding in Max's truck. When Mr. Kesler opened the door, she heard the aria spill out of the pickup, then silence after he slammed the door closed. As Max started to back out of the drive, he spotted Alison and stopped, his brake lights turning the grass and gravel bright red. He waved at her, smiling, and she waved back. She felt the impulse to walk over to the truck and talk to him. He'd said he'd be back, but not this soon. Too soon. She didn't know what to say, didn't know what thread was left from yesterday's conversation. He hesitated, too, lifted his hand a second time to wave, and she waved again as well, and then she saw him decide to leave. The taillights dimmed as the truck rolled backward. She thought of the lifeguards at Ocean City, communicating over long distances, waving semaphore flags in the wind.

Since she'd last seen him, Mr. Rossi had placed first in a trivia contest sponsored by a Cumberland radio station, and the event had recharged him. He began spouting trivia without any kind of segue at all. Near the beginning of the evening, Sarah and Bill demonstrated a new move, which Sarah called "shuffling the deck," with lots of leg kicks and movement. After a couple of slow walk-throughs, Sarah asked if there were any questions.

"Did you know," Mr. Rossi said, "that the king of hearts is alone in not having a mustache?"

Everyone stopped and looked at him for a second, the record player needle caught in the groove and making a low *thump-hiss* through the speakers. Sarah nodded. "I wasn't really after rhetorical questions, but thanks, Mr. Rossi."

He nodded and smiled, gave a little wave to the room. "Nothing more than a medieval copying error," he said. Alison patted his arm.

Mr. Kesler made his way back from the soft drinks, lifted the needle, and put on another side. Benny Goodman's "King Porter Stomp" crackled through the room and the dancers all took to the floor to practice shuffling the deck. Mrs. Skidmore danced with Bill, Mr. Rossi with Lila, who didn't much mind his paroxysms of trivia. The Harmons danced in matching golf clothes, their movements practiced and smooth, Mr. Harmon reaching out his hand without even looking at it, finding his wife's hand, her fingers slotted into his, her weight falling against him. Through long familiarity they'd worn grooves and depressions in one another, the years rubbing smooth the edges of their differences. One of the things Alison used to think about most in the first months after the accident was how Marty would always remain thirty-four years old—a young man in photos, in the videos from Ocean City, in the memory of everyone who'd known him. She would go off and wrinkle and decline without him, would draw down into an old age that he had simply side-stepped. It felt almost like a betrayal of him, or him of her. The idea had made her think of eleventh grade, Mr. Loggin's natural science class, and the film strips they had watched to learn Einstein's general theory of relativity. One of the filmstrips showed a cartoon of twins, young red-haired men with big drawn-on freckles, one of whom boarded a rocket and flew through space at the speed of light, gone for seventy years or so before returning to earth. In the last frame (flipped to after the accompanying record gave its loud *ping*), the door of the rocket was open, with a stepladder leading down, and the earthbound twin, now an old man with a cane and wire glasses, was there to meet his astronaut brother, who had aged only a minute or so, his red hair still thick and wavy. Years later, Alison remembered nothing about Einstein's theories, but still saw in her mind the expressions on both brothers' faces, the exclamation points drawn above their heads, the shock of their recognition, or their lack of it.

Alison sidled over by Mr. Kesler just as he bent down to his record collection, and the pipe stuck in the pocket of his jumpsuit fell out and clattered across the floor. As he retrieved it and straightened up, he looked startled to find her next to him.

"You know," she said, "you could have briefed him a little bit before you brought him over."

He looked around the room. "Who . . . what?"

"Your son, about my husband's accident."

He flushed and began fingering the bowl of his pipe, as Max had busied himself with the drill yesterday.

"Well, Alison. That's your business to tell him or not tell him. I'm no gossip."

"I wish you were a gossip. The whole thing was awkward as hell, for me at least."

Mr. Kesler nodded. "He put his foot in it, did he?" He snorted a little.

"Yeah, and by the way, I thought I was the only one you ever told the car story to."

He tucked the pipe away in his pocket and wrinkled his brow thoughtfully, looking for all the world like one of her freshman students trying to explain a plagiarized paper. "No, if you think back, the part I told just to you was about Uncle Crawford's bottle of rye." He winked at her. "Don't want to sully the family name."

For half a second, given her usual doubt of her own memory, she believed him. But no.

"You're good," she told him. "I'll give you that."

"Well, I suppose you read about my exploits in the paper. That story has been making the rounds for fifty-odd years, if you can believe that." He shook his head sadly, grimacing theatrically. "Thing is, I hate to see so many folks around here disappointed."

"How so?"

"Well, if—just if—that car sank so far in the mud it isn't there to be found anymore, it would be a letdown for everyone, once the lake drains."

She smiled, amazed at how accurately Max had his father figured. "Think of the children, right?"

"Just talking to Rossi earlier," he continued. "He was telling me about sinkholes in Florida. Half a minute, an entire house gone. God knows how far under that Chrysler is by now. Could be twenty feet under, don't you think?"

"Oh, I don't know about that," she said. "Just today I saw people hauling a grocery cart out of there. I saw part of a *pool* table, of all things." So, maybe she wanted to see him squirm a little, too. Whether out of sympathy for Max or for some other reason, she couldn't say.

He shook his head, licked his lips, adjusted his glasses. "Well, sure, a cart, or some recent thing. But we're talking about a *car.* We're talking fifty-plus years. You're a smart girl; I don't have to explain the physics."

They both became aware of the *thump-hiss* of the needle again, and he crouched to change the record. By now, the dancers had reached that stage Alison liked so much, their clothes lightly damp with sweat, their faces bright pink, mouths open as they guzzled water, their bodies shedding years, reclaiming their heat and blood. Mr. Rossi, in particular, was deep red in the face, his skin glistening with sweat he wiped away with a checked bandanna.

Alison turned back to Mr. Kesler. "You know, it could be nobody even cares about that car anymore."

He reached in his pocket and pulled out the newspaper article. He had laminated it by pressing it between two pieces of clear shelf paper. "Right there," he said, pointing to his own printed name. "They care. A town like this, about all we have is our old stories, wars and heroes, a fire, a flood, a scandal or two."

"Well, I guess you're right," she said. "And you must be the king of old stories."

"Yesterday afternoon, Vern Macy called me and offered free towing to drag it out of there." He kept nervously readjusting his glasses, and Alison felt a surge of sympathy for him, a slight anger toward Max for wanting to watch his father's public embarrassment.

"Then damn all that mud, if it took your car," she said. He nodded, seemed to relax a little. Maybe it was the best thing, to let herself be recruited, as Max called it.

The evening slowly wound down, Sarah and Bill dancing with a straggler or two, going over the new moves, no music behind them. The others drank water. Mr. Kesler put on his cotton gloves to rebox his record collection. Alison walked over to Mr. Rossi, beside the cookie table.

"So, Mr. Rossi, you ever hear about the War of Jenkins's Ear?"

"Why, yes, Alison. As a matter of fact, I have." His face was impossibly pink, his ears almost glowing.

She smiled. Of course he had.

"At least six people have entered the history books because of ear loss," he told her. "There was, most famously, van Gogh, of course, but no one remembers—"

Just then, the phone on the table rang loudly, and Alison answered it. The voice on the other end, a man's, was awkward and stumbling, asking for "Mrs. Sarah Michaels" as if reading it off a card. The voice was familiar somehow, like she'd heard it on the radio in the background of some kitchen.

"Sorry," she said, "Sarah can't come to the phone, and if you're selling something, it is after nine o'clock at—"

"Who I need to speak to," he said, "is a Mrs. Alison Durst, if she's there. I gotta talk to her." He said this with a stiffness and bulky formality that made her recognize the voice the way she would recognize a stomach punch: That quiet, stumbling voice belonged to Lem Kerns, the same voice that had echoed through the worst of her dreams, when she saw him forever on her front porch, tugging the flaps of his shirttails, bringing her the bad news.

**—from the *Haynes Automotive Repair Manual: Chevrolet Corvette, 1968 thru 1982***

Repair of major damage cannot be readily carried out by the home mechanic. Damage to a major part is a job either for your Corvette dealer or a body repair shop.

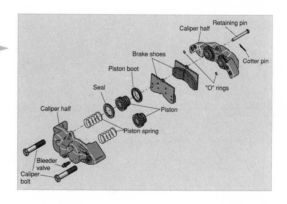

# 5

From the top of Holland Street, she recognized Lem's battered blue station wagon sitting, as it so often had, in front of their house, the front wheels angled against the curb in case he forgot to set the brake again. The house itself, the cracked driveway, the side alleys and surrounding houses all looked strange and unfamiliar, the lawns overgrown more than she remembered, the faded stop sign on the corner replaced with a new one. Even the street seemed too narrow, the houses crowding one another for space. Her hands shook, her chest almost too tight for breathing.

"You look like you need three or four drinks," Max said. He pulled the truck to the side of the road, letting it ease slowly down the block. "Are you okay?"

"Yeah. Well, no. Not exactly. Two drinks might do it."

"This whole deal is pretty weird, huh?" He lit a cigarette and tossed the match out the window.

She nodded, tugged the ends of her hair. "To say the least."

"Afraid you might run into him?"

"Who?"

"Your ex. He probably got the same phone call, right?"

Her stomach tightened. "I don't think he's here," she said.

Eventually, she would tell him. She *had* to. The poor guy—already she was somebody else who had trouble delivering the straight truth to him. But she knew, too, that the thing she liked best about Max right now was that he *didn't* know about her the way the rest of Wiley Ford did. And so she had called him that morning, apologizing for what happened in her garage two days ago, asking him for a ride to Cumberland, asking him to come back. It all felt so clean, having no real past in the eyes of this person. She could lose herself in her newness to him, fold herself into the void of her presence with him. Clean, bright, uncomplicated. All the mess of herself hacked away and hidden, no blood, no dripping guilt. Like a magic trick, her weighty past gone in the flash of his gaze. And she allowed that gaze, felt it lingering on her face, on her breasts when he thought she wasn't looking. He flirted with her in his own blunt way, brought the heat of sex into the room with him, when everyone else she knew brought only the chill of politeness. How could she think of ending that with confession?

They were close enough now that she could see her old house, the rusted roof bracket meant to hold the cutout Santa Claus Marty had made, the forsythia under the front windows overgrown and tangled, the fake alarm-system stickers peeling in the corners of the windows. Their car, an old Honda Civic that Marty had bought at an auction, sat at the back of the driveway, hidden under a green tarp.

"Why don't I come with you?" Max said. "See what all the fuss is about?"

Actually, she wondered, too, what all the fuss was about. Lem didn't say much in person, and even less on the phone. And last night when he'd called, the only thing she could get out of him was that there "was trouble with the house," that she'd "best come see." She'd told him she would try to make it out the next day.

"Try?" Sarah had said. "This is your *home* we're talking about. You have to go."

"Lem can take care of it," she said. Lem had watched the house for her all this time, had mowed the grass once or twice in the summer, adjusted the heat when a freeze threatened the pipes. There was no mortgage; the house had belonged to Marty's parents, who'd bought it in 1947 for two thousand dollars.

But Sarah wouldn't drop the idea, had kept hounding Alison, telling her she could not turn her back on her own home, could not turn her back on Lem. And in this she was right, Alison knew, as much as she did not want to go back there. Finally, she'd agreed to let Max take her the short hop across the river and back into Maryland, then pick her up a few hours later. Enough, she figured, to satisfy Sarah.

But now she wasn't so sure. She looked out the truck window at the house, her hand frozen on the door handle. Lem sat on the front stoop, looking at his fingernails as he chewed them down to nothing.

"Three hours?" she asked Max.

He shook his head. "Told you on the phone, I'm headed to Hagerstown. It'll be five at least. I'll hurry if you want."

She nodded, drew a long breath. "Yeah, I want."


Everyone she had ever come into contact with, it occurred to her once, was known mostly for one thing, identified that way. Mr. Beachy was a devout Christian. Sarah loved dance. Bill believed in most anything unexplained or unproven. Marty had liked to repair and build. Her father flew radio-controlled airplanes. Her mother organized all the local blood drives. Mr. Rossi knew trivia. Even herself . . . she was the Tragic Widow for a long while; by now she'd probably graduated to the Corvette Lady. Lem was no exception. People in Cumberland who had no idea of his name had known him for twenty-plus years as the *Star Wars* Guy. In 1978, he was in the newspaper for seeing the movie 129 times, a record in all of Maryland. He still carried that identity around with him, still kept old movie posters and framed articles on the wall of his house trailer, still wore *Star Wars* T-shirts and hats. He wore one now, with Darth Vader on the front, half-hidden under his work shirt.

"Hello, Lem," Alison said as he stood. He slicked his hair back with his hand and nodded at her. She felt suddenly embarrassed that she'd been away so long. Like she had just run from everything, while Lem—good, dependable Lem—stayed here and dealt with it.

"We missed you around here," he said, and she saw how nervous he was, pulling at his shirt, rocking from foot to foot.

"How're Pammy and Marshall?"

"Oh, can't complain," he said. "Or I could, but nobody'd listen. Marshall is seventeen now."

Alison smiled. This was pretty much the same conversation—the *only* conversation—they'd had several hundred times.

"We figure it was kids," he said now, adjusting his glasses. They stood in some mirror-image version of two years earlier, he standing on the porch, she below, looking up.

"What? What was kids?"

"Aw shit, Alison. Some kids got in. They tore the place up pretty bad."

She shook her head, then saw the open door of her own house beyond his shoulder and understood. She started past him and he took her arm in his big claw of a hand, held her there a second, then let go.

The graffiti covered most of the living room wall. No serious stuff, nothing threatening, not in Cumberland—just a drawing of Kilroy, the name of some rock band, the words *fuck* and *suck* repeated a couple of times in fuzzy red paint, the drips dried in pools along the baseboards. In the middle of the room, her over-turned coffee table held the abandoned spray cans, a torn bag of beer bottles, several condom wrappers, half a fast-food hamburger, and one of her china cups spilling cigarette butts. A series of holes had been kicked or punched in the walls and her glass bookcase had been shot full of BB holes. She moved slowly through the room, touching the edges of things. Lem followed her, futilely straightening and picking up as he went along. There was no graffiti in the kitchen, but the faucet had been left on at some point, and the water had overflowed on the linoleum, which was swollen and peeling. Alison stopped, took a breath. She turned and faced Lem.

"More of the same all the way through," Lem said. "Sheriff says he could name you the kids that did it, but he don't have proof."

"Ah God, Lem. What the hell is wrong with people?"

"I wish I knew," Lem said. "Listen, me and Pammy will put everything back right. It looks bad, but we can do it." Alison remembered hearing him saying this to Marty, no matter how easy or difficult the task that faced them.

She looked around, noticing for the first time the smell—urine and spilled beer, and beneath that an attic smell of neglect and limbo. "Maybe, I don't know, I should just hire somebody."

"They wouldn't do it right. They wouldn't care all that much. Listen, why don't you come and stay with us until the work gets done?"

"Thanks, Lem. But I don't think I'll be staying."

He blinked, pushed his glasses up. "Well, but you have to," he said. "You can't just leave things like *this*." She looked at him. Never before had she heard anger in his voice, but it was unmistakable now.

"I just meant—"

"I should've been watching better." He twisted his shirt. "Same when Marty died. Every two years, I have to apologize for not watching better. Difference this time is, I get to put it back right."

He wouldn't look at her. She walked over to him and patted his arm, as thick as one of her own thighs. "Okay, Lem. We'll do that. We'll put it back right."


Later that afternoon, she stood in her ruined kitchen, dialing Sarah's number. So much time had passed that she had to look it up in her address book, which she found heaped with other books at the bottom of the stairs, the pages singed by matches. The phone still worked for the same reason the water and electric did: She'd never bothered to have them turned off; the bills were paid through the bank.

Sarah answered the phone, and Alison slowly described the destruction to the house.

"Those damn kids," she said. "I can't believe it."

"I can't, either," Alison said. She leaned on the butcher-block table, which had had one of its corners hacked away by a large knife. The duck decoy that Marty had carved from a kit sat on the stove, blackened with burn marks.

"Is Lem there now? Somebody should be there."

"He's home making dinner until Pammy gets off work. Max will be back in a few hours."

"Listen, do you want me to come there? I can cancel dance."

"No, don't worry about it. I'll be home by this evening."

"Alison . . ."

"What?"

"You *are* home. For the first time in two years."

"Yeah, how about that?" she said. But looking around, it felt wrong. It felt like—what? Like a monument. Like a trip to the cemetery. Like anything but home.


They had ruined the bed, torched a hole in the middle of it and urinated on the floor all around it. In the bathroom, pieces of the mirror lay shattered in the sink. As she walked through the house, her mind tried to draw Marty out of every corner, to assemble him out of scraps of moments, half phrases, dimly lit mornings and sleepy conversations, a dropped button or a hunt for socks. But this was the wrong house, all of it broken and ruined and misplaced, as if her own neglect had done this, had dismantled everything through the violence of trying to forget. Violence had taken him, and now none of the violence that lay before her would hold him.

Through the bedroom window she noticed Marty's sagging tent still set up in the backyard, where some weekends he and Lem, like a pair of ten-year-olds, would camp out while she slept in their empty bed. She walked outside and opened the tent, thinking of all those mornings when he'd come into the kitchen smelling of beer and no sleep, mornings when she wouldn't talk to him. The tent was an old boxy army-type that staked down with pegs, something Marty'd found at a yard sale. She wondered what had made her so angry about those nights, about all those days he'd spent with Lem in the basement, or at Lem's house, or off somewhere in the car. Neglect, maybe. But strange as this sounded to her now, she knew that at least part of it had been jealousy—jealous that she'd never had that kind of time with him, that he hadn't taken her on his random jobs or into his tent or down to the basement. But why would he have? She'd disapproved of all of it, was how it must've seemed to him. The things he loved she'd equated with negligence. If she didn't like his life, why *wouldn't* he keep it hidden from her? It made sense. And why had she been so rigid? Marty had been that kind of man—he lived inside his skin and inside his moments and hobbies and casual friendships, and the quiet strength that at first attracted her so had slowly twisted itself into a secret unwillingness. Unwilling to make his life into the kind of vessel that would hold children and a future, the kind that is warm and narrow enough to incubate the intimacy she'd thought she wanted.

When they met, he was painting the apartment complex where she lived her first year of grad school. She found him one day in June when she'd gone to the pool for a swim and instead found the water all emptied, Marty down in the deep end with a long roller and a metal pan full of pale blue paint. His shorts and T-shirt were a collage of smears, his legs strong and tan. He stopped his work and told her to jump on in, the water was fine. She stood there, conscious of her pale stomach, of the baggy puckers of last year's suit. She had a hangover and an overdue paper. She sat and opened her book while he muttered to himself and painted, interrupting his work and hers by trying to draw her attention. He puffed out his jaws and pretended to swim, bug-eyed. He pretended to paddle a boat all the way around the walls of the pool, his roller an oar. Finally, she gave in and laughed.

Their differences were what she loved most about them, what gave them dimension and edges—the things she saw lacking in the academic couples she knew, who stood together at parties and drank wine and traded off their worry about teaching jobs. Marty had been all muscle and work and the sweet odors of paint and sweat and gasoline. She imagined that for him she seemed like someone serious enough to whisk him into a real life, though when she asked, he would only say she was the prettiest girl he'd ever been able to talk to. For a long time, she worried that it went no deeper than that. Once or twice, she dressed him up and took him to those parties, where he stood next to the sink in his corduroy jacket, drinking beer and trying to catch her eye, begging her with his gaze to leave. And the leaving excited her, making thin excuses and taking off on his strong arm into his narrow basement apartment, into sex, into the world outside grad school, followed by what she imagined to be the envious stares of her colleagues. She'd made a prop of him then, she knew, and the differences between them gave her the sense that she could belong to her world and another, could orbit two spheres. She was bigger that way. *Her* version of love would not be safe and planned, not tenured and worried.

And then—time. The sediment of years weighed on them, pressing down their differences until they became flattened and one-dimensional, abstractions drawn on different parts of a page, no lines intersecting, no edges overlapping. Space became just the forced-air heat in the house, occupying the areas between his life in the basement and hers at the college. Just a blank expanse of nothing. And time, she knew, might have cured those differences as well, might have drawn them into one another through the slow gravitation of aging, the tectonics of children or long familiarity. But they would never have that chance, all that space filled with the dark matter of remorse and guilt.

Just then, she heard the squeak and slam of the doors on Lem's car, a sound that used to mean those two big men tumbling through her front door, filling her house with mud and profanity and sawdust, with another stupid argument over the right way to cut a board or a pipe. Now she heard Lem knocking at the front door, and Pammy's small voice saying, "Maybe she left, honey," until Alison walked around the corner of the house and called to them.

Lem's wife had always felt to Alison exactly like the sound of her name: *Pammy.* Cute and little but also somehow hard and no-nonsense. She was all of these, a native of Cumberland, a former drill squad cocaptain for the Franklin Falcons twenty years ago, who had moved from pom-poms and go-go boots to flannel shirts and work gloves and a pickup truck. Not quite five feet tall, she worked for the state park, grooming and shoeing horses that little kids rode around the dirt ring.

She found Alison in the backyard and gave her a quick, muscled hug, not even glancing at the tent, which looked so odd in the daylight.

"Been a while," she said, cinching on her work gloves. She looked up, her eyes a flinty gray. "Let's go knock this place back into shape."

Already, Lem had emptied the back of the station wagon into the middle of the living room and hallway: paint-spattered tools, sections of drywall, and paint and plastic bags from the building-supply store. They set to work, Lem measuring the wall, locating the studs, using a saw to cut squares around the holes that had been punched, a trickle of dust covering the toes of his work boots. Pammy set all the furniture back into place and began scrubbing at the stains on the carpet. Alison felt a little lost. What was she supposed to do? She wanted them to give her a job, like some little kid on an allowance, but they seemed to have forgotten her presence there. Lem hummed a mindless tune as he worked, and Pammy just worked, her face flushed, long hair held back by a bandanna around her head. Finally, Alison poured paint into the tray and went to work with a roller, going over the wall that had been spray-painted but not otherwise damaged.

She had forgotten the odor of this kind of labor, of paint and caulk and paste. A clean, familiar smell. All at once, she realized she'd also forgotten to put a tarp down, and already she had spattered the carpet some, but she didn't mind. She could clean it up later; for now, she didn't want to stop, wanted to keep going over the red spray paint and making those words disappear, making the attack itself disappear. She moved the roller in neat, straight swaths, listening to the wet *shush* it made against the background of Lem's humming.

The words came back. Almost as soon as she'd finished the wall, the red paint began seeping through, the words *fuck* and *suck* becoming faintly visible.

"Unless you seal it," Lem said, watching her, "they'll keep coming back. Just give it three, maybe four coats. That should do it."

She left the wall to dry and went downstairs to the den, stepping over the torched books at the foot of the stairs. Thank God those on the shelves hadn't been touched, only this pile which had sat on the coffee table. How could anyone do that? To a book? A few semesters back, she'd taught Western civ II, and she spent a whole class period talking about the Nazi book-burning campaigns, coupling it with newspaper articles about recent efforts to ban *Huck Finn* and a handful of kids' books. Her students responded with blank stares and yawns. They didn't care the least about books or what books meant. For the first time ever, she raised her voice to a class and sent them away before the period ended. The next day, in an attempt to get through to them, she showed the movie *Fahrenheit 451,* which she remembered having scared her to death as a teenager. As it happened, it was also the day Ernie picked to do his yearly surprise observation of faculty. Later, in his office, she'd tried to explain while he sat grinning at her, telling her he liked the idea of a history course that covered future events.

"In fact," he said, "when you get around to your proposal for that approximate history course—"

"Shut *up,*" she said, smiling.

"No, really, you ought to do a whole unit on the future. The fun part, you know, will be the pop quizzes on stuff that hasn't happened yet."

She smiled now remembering it, wondering how the new semester was going, who they'd gotten to take her sections. The shelf above the TV slowly filled as she reshelved the books, trying to remember what order they'd been in. All the trash went into the fireplace, and then she ran the vacuum over the rug. Back upstairs, Lem and Pammy were taping over the joints of the new wallboard they'd installed, and Alison gave the graffiti another coat of latex. Pammy went with her to the kitchen, where they worked on their hands and knees, pulling up the ruined linoleum. As they worked, she couldn't help but notice how strong Pammy was, her arms hard and sinewy, biceps like small oranges stitched under her skin.

They finally took a break to eat from the cooler Pammy had packed, pimento cheese sandwiches, peanut butter crackers, and Gatorade. They didn't talk while they ate; they just sat looking out the window or at the work they had finished. Conversation used to flow easily with the four of them together, out on the deck on a Saturday evening, Pammy and Lem's son, still little, asleep on the couch inside, Marty cooking fish on the grill while Lem sat holding bottle rockets in his fingertips and lighting them with Pammy's cigarette to shoot them into the treetops, and the evening would smell like citronella candles and beer. Now they sat mostly in silence, commenting occasionally on how cool this summer had been, or how paint could brighten up a place.

By early evening, the living room was roughly back into shape, and the curse words were finally covered. If only progress on her car could happen this fast. Lem stood with his hands on his wide hips, looking all around the room and nodding his approval of their work.

"Why don't you let us finish up tomorrow?" Lem said, winding one of the extension cords around his elbow. "We'll go on, and you can take it easy."

This sounded good, in fact, and she took him up on it. She had been here a little more than five hours, and she reassured Pammy that Max would be there soon to pick her up. She saw them exchanging looks, and figured they had decided that she needed this, some time alone in her house. She gave them each an awkward hug. How to tell them that Marty no longer existed here for her, that her old life felt as broken and burned as all her belongings? She went upstairs to shower and change, finding some of her old clothes, sweatpants and an Orioles T-shirt, packed in her dresser. By the time she got out, Lem and Pammy were gone, the house quiet.

She remembered some of the things left in their basement, things that she had ignored or resented at the time, Marty hauling in yet another bag from Lowe's or Sears. But now that she thought of it, many of those tools might be useful for her Corvette—screwdrivers, pliers, socket wrenches, electrical tape. She clicked on the switches at the top of the landing and started down the wobbly stairs into the gloom. Her fingers rode the slick banister, and as she moved down past the narrow stairwell walls, she leaned over and squinted through the prickly light toward the corner workbench, and there was Marty.

It was a relief, really, to see him. All day, she'd chastised herself as heartless and empty, unable to draw him up in her memory. But there he sat, as full and real in her mind, in this undisturbed part of the house, as if he'd never left, as if the past two years had been some minor disturbance not worth bothering him with. She saw the tight creases of his dirty jeans as he sat, legs splayed, at his bar stool, leaning over his work, a thin tassel of smoke rising from his soldering iron into the light, some ruined old radio gutted on the bench, that one unruly shock of hair dangling across his forehead and into his vision. Of course this is where she would see him. Of course she hadn't found him in the rest of the house; he'd barely lived there. Now he was clear enough for her to see every detail: the strips of black tape he stuck to his forearm when he worked, keeping them within reach; the ragged neck of his T-shirt; the stripe of his boxer shorts peeking out over his jeans; the muscle in his back; the way he spoke to the radio as he worked on it, urging it to cooperate. Memory animated him, brought his fingers to the controls of the tape player hung from the Peg-Board, brought the rough curve of his hand to his coffee mug, made the dusty tip of his boot move in time with the music which she heard now, too, the old rock songs about women and love. Other sounds spooled out through memory, her feet on the floorboards overhead, her voice calling Marty upstairs to dinner, telling him the food was getting cold, or asking him when he might come to bed. She watched him lean back far enough to shout at the joists, then bend forward again, muttering words she still could not hear.

Her hands shook as she closed the door at the top of the stairs and clicked off the lights. She wiped her eyes and leaned against the closed door.

Outside, the street was awash in the pale yellow-purple of evening. Where was Max? Why was he taking so long? On the living room wall, the faded words had begun to reappear through the paint. She could not stay in this house. That had been true two years ago, and it was still true. *More* true now. She left and paced up and down the street, trying to calm her hands, letting her mind run through everything she could remember about Chaucer: born in thirteen something. Thirty? Forty? Around the time that the Black Death killed just about everyone, she remembered. He began *Canterbury Tales* the same year he was robbed twice. What year? Which happened first? She couldn't recall, and didn't much care anymore. Instead, she ran through a list of parts she needed from Mr. Beachy. This was easier—all she had to do was think of the drawings in her manual. She needed brake lines coming off the master cylinder (stainless steel, he'd recommended), new shocks and springs, a spring compressor, bushings for the trailing arm ends, rear spring mounts. She surprised herself with how much she knew, just from reading and crawling around under the car. Maybe it *had* soaked in, the way she'd wanted it to. Down the street, some of the neighbors were out in their yards, raking grass clippings, washing window screens. The last thing she needed was for some old neighborhood acquaintance to recognize her and start asking a hundred questions. She turned back, walked around the house and toward the tent.

Inside, things were just as Marty and Lem had left them two years before—a six-pack of empties, potato chip bags, a damp sleeping bag spread across the floor—everything coated in a dusting of yellow pollen. Alison sat and unlaced her sneakers, then tied open the front flaps to let in the light. In the corner sat a battered spiral notebook, the pages swollen with moisture. She turned through the mostly blank pages, some of them filled with lists of building materials or tools, one with a checklist for a camping trip he'd taken. Near the middle, Marty had written "NEW YEARS 1996," and underneath he'd included a list of resolutions:

1. More situps (flabby)
2. Get a <u>real</u> job
3. Fishing with Lem
4. Make A. happy
5. No more shit.

She felt the words with her fingertips, reading over them again. *Make A. happy.* You poor thing, Marty, she thought. All his plans so abstract, so . . . ungrounded. *No more shit.* His whole problem had been that he never understood the happiness or the shit, where they came from, how they played out in the marriage. Near the back of the book she found rough drawings and notes in Marty's handwriting, some of the drawings crossed out and redone in what she guessed was Lem's hand. The drawings were odd— boxes, circles, arrows. Finally, she figured it out: These were plans for some kind of perpetual-motion machine. Magnets spun on a turntable, a series of interlocking wheels. She looked them over, shaking her head.

She thought about them, these two grown-up little boys excited over the impossible, dreaming of the unattainable, and the thought of it made her cry. The boyishness that at first had so attracted her and later made her push him away now just seemed sad—a missed chance, a lost opportunity. She cried now for the same reason she had in class once, when she was lecturing on the meeting between the leader of the peasant revolt and fourteen-year-old King Richard. She'd taught this the same year as the Gulf War, when even some of her youngest students were snatched up by their reserve commit-ments and scuttled off to the desert, and suddenly the weight of all that and the thought of this boy-king, like some king in a fairy tale, made her break down in front of her class, her voice quavering. (Later, Ernie had told her, "You can't laugh or cry in front of stu-dents, it just confuses them too much.")

But that is what she felt now, for her husband. That somehow he'd gotten stuck in seeing the world as a boy would, and she had pushed him away for not growing up. He had even died because he'd been playing. Playing with Lem, using the new toys in the backyard. She'd hated it then and maybe she would hate it now, but in his absence, she at least understood it. The past rose up to debate the present for meaning, but both of them lied and meaning was lost. The future leaned in the corner, knowing everything but unable to speak.

She still carried with her the vinyl telephone book she'd used to look up Sarah's number, and she thumbed through the pages, the

numbers for businesses Marty had worked for or with, always cob-
bling together his living as if it were another of his projects built
from scraps in the basement. Just before the accident, he and Lem
had a weekend kiosk at the mall, making wooden plaques carved
with peoples' names or the names of their boats or beach houses or
dogs, making barely enough to pay rent on the kiosk. They did odd
jobs they found with flyers stapled to telephone poles and tacked
up on the bulletin board at Food Lion. In the fall, they would sweep
out chimneys, using a brush set they'd bought at Sears. Marty
always had big plans: getting insured and bonded, placing an ad in
the Yellow Pages, hiring a work crew, starting his own contracting
business—*get a real job . . . no more shit.* None of it ever happened,
and she used to tell him he was throwing away his life, squandering
his skills on make-work. Sometimes it hit her that his whole existence had been a patchwork of unfinished things, but then she felt
mean for thinking this and tamped it out of her mind. It wasn't his
fault the years were snatched away from him. Lem now worked for
someone else's contracting business, even though, he said, he
would not climb a ladder any higher than his own head or use a
radial arm saw, afraid of some accident, some terrible little slip.

Alison pushed the buttons on her cell phone, and Sarah
answered on the third ring. In the background were the sounds of
big-band music and the murmur of half a dozen voices. Of course,
the dance lessons.

"Hey, I have a couple messages for you," Sarah said after hearing
about the progress with the house. "Max called and wanted me—oh
crap, hold on a sec, okay?" Sarah muffled the phone, and Alison
heard her telling Mr. Kesler that they were waiting for music, and in
the background was Mr. Rossi's voice and the sound of water pouring into paper cups, and those sounds felt as though they contained
all the other sounds of Wiley Ford, the men talking in low voices as
they fished the lake, or the creak of her garage door, or the buzzy
lights of the Discount Rage Center, or the hiss of the coffee machines
at the Red Bird, or the jangly bells behind Mr. Beachy's front door at
AAAA Auto.

"Anyway," Sarah was saying, "Max got held up by something. He's on his way."

Alison nodded. "Good. I need to get out of here." She'd noticed that she'd left a light on in the basement.

"But you're going back, right? To finish?"

She stiffened. "I'm not sure."

"You're not *sure*? Alison, that's your *house* we're talking about."

"Yeah, I know. I'm looking right at it."

"You can't just dump the whole thing and—"

"Just shut *up*, Sarah."

"Don't you say that to me. God . . ."

That was part of the problem: all the things she hadn't ever said to Sarah. How her marriage had never been bad, not abusive or angry, but just a quiet disappointment, all that passion and hope shrinking down to a small hole through which they would speak in the daytime and touch briefly at night, through which their years and days would pass. What could she have said about a marriage where nothing was really wrong, aside from the way it slowly drained feeling from her? How could she explain her mourning, which stayed with her not because of its depth but because of its shallowness? Because she never felt like she'd been engulfed by it, never covered by it, never porous with loss? She'd loved Marty and missed him now, but she had also lied, and the love and the missing were never what she'd made them out to be, never filled up the shape she'd made for them, never matched the long shadow of guilt they created. And the house now, fixed or not, was only some left-over thing, the unfilled shape of her missing life. She thought of their work throughout the afternoon, how Lem and Pammy had wanted everything back exactly the way it was, how they'd tossed Marty's boots into the entrance hall, where Alison had always tripped over them, and put his dismantled fishing reel back on the folding tray, as he'd left it. A museum was what they wanted, a diorama of some earlier, happier life, all painted and shoe-boxed. But it just didn't work that way; teenagers broke into your diorama and trashed it, a dammed-up stream flooded it, neglect let it rust. Time, as a thousand clichés had it, marched on, a stoic soldier, armed and deadly. But she preferred to imagine time as some grimy little kid just scuffing down the road, kicking a tin can along the gutter, ignorant of all those people in the houses that lined the street. Two years unfurled and dragged behind her, tethered to this empty house. In those two years, Lem had turned forty, Ernie's daughter had left for college, the Orioles had built a new stadium, one of Sarah's ex-students had died, a war had been fought in Eastern Europe, a president had been involved in a scandal, her Corvette had decayed into ruin, and Bill had discovered the need to procreate. It never ended. The tin can kept rattling.

She made quick half apologies and see-you-laters with Sarah then put away her phone and left the tent, standing in the yard with the cool of night on her bare arms. When she peeked in through the glass square of the basement door, of course all she saw was the dusty bench, the harsh light, the scattered tools.

Soon she heard the truck turn into the drive, saw the lights in the tops of the pine trees. She ran as hard as she could, popped open the door, settled herself into the soft green light from the dash, the aria floating up out of the speakers. Max turned to her, shaking his head.

"I am so sorry. I tried to get a message—"

"Let's go," she told him, her breath shallow. "Get me out of here."

"Whoa, what happened?"

She looked at him, studied his face. "My husband died," she said.

—from the *Haynes Automotive Repair Manual: Chevrolet Corvette, 1968 thru 1982*

Some sort of suitable work area is essential. It is understood, and appreciated, that many home mechanics do not have a good workshop or garage available, and end up doing major repairs outside. It is recommended, however, that the overhaul be completed under the cover of a roof.

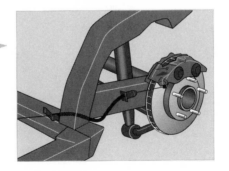

# 6

Back in town, all of Wiley Ford was festooned with flags and pennants and plastic banners hung across the bars, everyone ready for the start of the upcoming Founders' Day Celebration, and the parade, the culmination of the week's activities. The town had the parade every year, along with ones for Halloween and Arbor Day, but none for Christmas or Columbus Day or the Fourth of July, all the ones Alison was used to growing up. It was like some discount store had run a special on irregular holiday parades, and Wiley Ford had snapped them all up.

The Founders' Day Parade was a big deal for Sarah. She and her students would dress up in costumes from the forties (though Alison imagined that for many it wasn't so much a costume as it was just back-of-the-closet clothes) and ride on a flatbed hay truck, stopping every block to play swing music through a boom box and put on a dance demonstration, using the truck bed for a stage. They billed themselves as the Try to Remember Dancers, named for the line in the old song, but as Alison had watched them last year, following along, whistling and clapping for them at every stop, she heard people in the crowd saying that the dancers were trying to remember the steps, trying to remember where they'd put their car keys, trying to remember to take their medication.

But now it was quiet and dark, the streets empty, flags stirring lazily in the night air as she and Max rolled through town. She'd told him as they drove home, and it had all tumbled out so quickly that it surprised her, as if the weight of it deserved a bigger story. He didn't react much, and neither did she, her voice flat, as if she were delivering some lecture on history she'd been through a thousand times before. And really, it was that. Exactly that. Max grimaced some as she told it, almost flinching, then he told her simply that he was sorry. She nodded, then shrugged.

They rode in silence for a while, the awkwardness like helium filling the cab of the truck, threatening to lift them from the ground. She sat back in the corner of her seat and studied the side of his face, the thin gold wire of his glasses along his temple, the mica flash of his blond stubble in the dash light, the bundle of smile lines at the corner of his eye. He glanced at her.

"My father made me take a Dale Carnegie course one time, right out of high school." He stopped, hesitating.

"Is there more to this story?"

"A little, yeah. I remember they taught us that if someone tells you a story of loss, you're supposed to tell one back. They called it 'commiserative reinforcement.'"

"Well, that's robotic of them. So, you have one to tell?"

"That's just it. I don't really. All my sad stories are stories of stupidity."

She laughed. What a relief, to tell him and not have to endure his pity. "Then tell me one of those," she said. "I can take it."

He nodded, turned down the stereo volume. "Right out of the army, my friend Keith and I had this plan to open a business raising beef cattle and chickens for vegetarians."

She held up her hand, as if in class. "I think I detect a teeny flaw in your thinking."

He frowned. "No, just listen. This is back when vegetarianism was this huge *fad*. Everyone running around saying, 'It's bad to kill a cow,' or whatever."

"They have such a complex philosophy."

"Well, I might be leaving something out. Anyhow, we decided that most vegetarians *want* to eat meat, but don't for ethical reasons."

"Chicken murder."

"Exactly. So we had the idea to raise them like pets, treat them nice, give them names, let them die of old age, and *then* sell them as meat. We called it the Natural Causes Ranch."

She covered her mouth with her hand. "You're making this up."

He shook his head. "We had eight acres of pasture down near Ripley, plus two chicken houses. We raised the cows and chickens, put out some advertising in health-food stores. We didn't have a clue. We did learn one thing, though."

"What?"

"Cows and chickens live a *long* damn time. My idiot friend was always trying to *scare* them, hoping to give them heart attacks. When we finally did have one die, man, that was the worst, toughest meat you ever ate."

At this, she started laughing.

"Twenty-four years old, an honorable discharge from the army, and this is what I'm doing with my life. Took me an hour to decide to bail."

"I have to say, that's the saddest tale of stupidity I ever heard."

He shrugged, then turned to look at her. She could just make out a gray silhouette of him, his face drawn by shadows.

He shifted and stretched his legs. "My foot's asleep," he said, squeezing his calf.

"If it sleeps now, it'll be awake all night," she said.

"Have you always been a comic?" He lit a cigarette, the coil of the lighter oranging his face.

She felt her own face warm, as if lighting up all by itself. "I'm sorry. It's nervous habit. I should borrow some of your cigarettes instead." She wondered what he'd do if she told him her *real* impulse right then—not to smoke or make jokes, but to start ruminating on Galileo or the Industrial Revolution. Probably he'd drop her off here, on the dark end of the lake, and not look back. And who could blame him?

Instead, she told him a little of her own history, going back to high school, when she had crammed herself into a mold formed by big sister Sarah before her: class clown and softball jock, goofing her way to a diploma by way of boyfriends and sneaking out of the house, nights of beer and cigarettes up by the cliffs, of giving up her virginity piecemeal, and days of *C* averages, ball games, and riding in cars. This had gotten her through college, skimming along a familiar life, when suddenly friends started marrying themselves off into real lives, slipping into suits and dental plans, and one day there was no more class for the clown. So she'd tried to shed that by turning up the volume on her good brain, forcing herself into grad school, cramming the lists into her memory, marrying her vo-tech sweetheart, with his pretty religion. She wanted to be known as smart, the kind of smart where someone much like the person she wanted to be would stand around at cocktail parties sipping martinis and tossing off names and dates and whole histories, only the grown-up world had cheated by not caring all that much, by no longer having time for cocktail parties. So, by default, she'd ended up teaching all those other class-clown jocks and was never very good at it, not any better than Marty had been in all his failings.

She looked at him. "So now you know. Typical clown, yawning on the inside. Bored with her own pretensions."

He took this in, thought about it. "Listen, if you aren't pretentious in your teens and twenties, you have a genetic defect. Don't be so hard on yourself. Now, if you're like my father, pretentious at sixty-eight, you have a problem."

"He's not really pretentious. He just likes to pretend."

Max finished the cigarette and flicked it out the window. "Yeah, well, we'll see how much he likes it when he falls on his ass in front of eight thousand people."

There was an edge to the way he said this that bothered her, so she said nothing.

"You said a nervous habit," Max said. "What are you nervous about?"

"Well, number one, that I've spent an entire truck ride pretty much spilling, down to my very last gut."

"And number two?"

"Is there a number two?"

"You tell me, professor. You divide your answer into a part one, there has to be a part two, right?"

They pulled into the driveway and sat in the dark with the engine idling. She noticed Bill standing on a stepladder at the front door, in his bathrobe again, a flashlight propped on the ground behind him throwing his big loopy shadow over the front of the house.

Alison pointed. "Wonder what he's doing now?"

"Who?"

"My brother-in-law, the mystic. He's trying to use magic to get my sister pregnant."

Max thought about this. "Maybe you should tell him that's not how it works."

"Oh, they're using the tried-and-true method, too; this is just . . . a backup."

"So what's he doing?"

"I have no idea. Last time, he threw rice on the house."

"Well, now I *have* to know what he's doing. After you tell me what number two is."

"Number two is, I think there's a good chance that I'm going to kiss you sometime in the next few hours, and that makes me nervous."

He nodded. "It's supposed to do that. That's part of the point."

She popped the handle on the truck, all that harsh overhead light blasting the fragile moment back into reality. Max's fair skin was etched in color, his eyes dark-rimmed under the light. The lake, as she turned toward it, looked alarmingly low, as if her day in Cumberland had given it a chance to speed up its own draining away. Several buildings of Colaville were fully exposed now, vague, dark shapes, stone cubes tilted in the mud.

Bill worked as quietly as possible, nailing rows of fruit around the front door. Splatters of red juice ran down his pale forearms, disappearing into the sleeves of his robe, seeds and liquid dripping down the painted frame and pooling on the landing. He paused long enough to wave at them.

"What *are* those?" Alison said.

Bill stepped down and took the nails from his mouth. "Pomegranates." He reached in the pocket of his robe and handed her one, then shook hands with Max, his wrist streaked red.

"I should know what they mean, but I don't," Alison said.

He pulled another one from his pocket, a birthday magician performing tricks. He hefted the fruit in his hand, tossed it in the air. "Ancient fertility symbols, all those seeds in there. You know King

Solomon? From the Bible? Threw this party one time for his bride, and decorated his temple with two hundred pomegranates and lilies. He dressed up like a phallic god."

"Well, Halloween is right around the corner," Max said.

"So what about the lilies?" Alison asked.

Bill shrugged. "Food Lion was sold out."

Max dipped the toe of his boot in the pooled juice. "Is everyone in this family a history teacher?"

"Nah, I'm a telephone installer," Bill said. "I get this stuff off the Internet, a few books here and there." He shrugged, smiled, and, having nothing else to say, took the fruit from Alison and turned back to his quiet voodoo.

They left him to his careful tapping and made their way into the garage. A fast, warm lump jelled in Alison's stomach, her heart thudding in her chest. This all seemed too quick—confront Marty's ghost at the house, and then tell some near stranger she's about to kiss him? And she'd *announced* it, for godsakes, like he'd won a raffle or something. Then again, her brain argued back, no one could say that two years was quick. In fact, everyone had said just the opposite, until they'd gotten bored of saying it and given up. It was high time she kissed someone, wasn't it? And Max was pretty much the only candidate in the running right now. Maybe she'd lied in the truck, had not spilled down to her very last gut. The very last was her loneliness, her aloneness. It was the nights under a comforter in her sister's guest bed, listening to the drone of the TV downstairs or the buzzy murmur of voices down the hall, staring up at the watery reflections off the lake pulsing across her ceiling, letting her finger-tips move over the heat of her skin, her mind slipping into blue-colored half dreams that became the angled light in the bedroom of her old grad-school apartment, or the seats of parked cars in high school, all the places where the touch of men had settled in her memory. She could hear the sounds that Marty would make in the dark, his long sigh when he shifted in the bed and turned to her, full of want, and felt the way his fingers always traced the same path along her stomach, stopping at the waistband of her underwear, feeling along the seams and stitching, as if the needlework had worn grooves that his fingertips followed like water, his calluses pulling at the threads. Then she would open her eyes, excited and frustrated, her dream thwarted by sadness, the guest room filling up with its darkness. So now what? Was she supposed to think that just because she'd recognized some of her guilt over Marty, had found it stored in the basement of her house, that she had somehow absolved it? She thought of all those times she'd mocked him for making his way into that draped confessional booth on Saturday mornings, and here she was, confessing and absolving all by herself. Her hand quivered as she snapped on the coffee-can light. She told herself to calm down; infidelity to the deceased was not betrayal, and the promise of one kiss didn't exactly make her a slut.

"Look at all this stuff," she said, waving at the latest pile of parts she'd bought from Mr. Beachy, all of them boxed or shrink-wrapped.

"Hey, pretty nice job on the wheels," he said, bending.

"Do you have any idea what they mean by 'bleed the brakes'?"

"They who?"

She pointed at the manual on the workbench. "The book guys."

He nodded. "I know what the book guys mean. It's a two-person job."

She pointed at him and then herself. "One, two. Let's get to work."

"*Tonight*? It's nearly midnight."

"Now you're Cinderella? So what?"

"Besides, you can't bleed the brakes until you finish all the wheels, and it wouldn't hurt to replace the parking-brake cable while you're at it."

Now she remembered—one of the lab-coat guys had suggested exactly the same thing. "Let's do something, then. Let's work on the brake lines."

"Listen, tomorrow we'll get whatever else parts you need and spend the whole day on the car, I promise. I still think you're throwing good money after bad."

"How long did you say those cows and chickens lived again?" She smiled.

"Okay, okay. It's your Visa bill, not mine."

Actually, he was right to be worried about her Visa bill, without even knowing it. She had not collected a paycheck in nearly two years now, living off the modest life-insurance payment and the tiny bit of money they'd saved. Since the start, she'd bought groceries for Sarah (the only way Sarah would let her contribute anything), but the last two times, she'd had to put them on her credit card. Now she was buying car parts, expensive parts for an expensive car, with no way of paying for them. Maybe Mr. Beachy would hire her and give her an employee discount, or, better yet, pay her in parts. Selling the car once it was all done seemed pointless, like those game-show contestants who sell their new boats to pay for the taxes on them. Anyway, if Max was right about the rust, the car wouldn't be worth half of what she'd put into it. So now she'd put herself into the same kind of predicament that she'd always bitched at Marty about—throwing away money on some big plan, on the next perpetual-motion machine. In the morning she would be back at Mr. Beachy's, running up her bill again, her own impossible project taking on the kind of meaning that Marty's must have held for him. The dead indict us, over and over, guilt by association.

She was distracted by the noise of the men who fished the lake and turned to look out at the circle of them gathered at the lake's center. The laughing rose up hollow, almost wooden-sounding. Already they had occupied the two small stone buildings left exposed along the bottom, the square windows filled with yellow lamplight. They moved in and out of the buildings, faint shadows of men.

"Looks like they've settled in," Max said. He stood behind her, close enough that she felt the aura of heat that surrounded him. She let herself float into that heat, leaning back into him until her shoulders were against his chest. Then she leaned forward and back again, bumping him. Then again, as if it were only a game, only playground flirting, instead of what it really felt like at the warm center of her chest: a need for touch that rivaled, just then, her need for air.

"I don't want to jinx it," Max said, "but I might have a job coming up in Morgantown soon. A big job. If it materializes, I want you to come with me."

"What are you dynamiting this time?"

"Something big. Puts grain silos to shame."

"A whale?"

"Bigger."

She bumped him again, and he put his hands on her shoulders and held her there, keeping her against him. His chin rested atop her head.

"Are all our dates going to involve blowing something up?" she asked him. "Not that I'm complaining." She settled back, leaning against him fully.

"Are we dating?"

"Aren't we?"

"Then will you go with me? We'll have to be there a few days. You can be my good luck."

"Gee, you sure know how to make a girl feel like a rabbit's foot. When did you get so superstitious?"

He slipped his arms down around her, pressing her arms to her sides. She loved to be held that way, all wrapped up. She'd forgotten how much. "If you're working with dynamite," he said, "superstition kind of goes with the job."

"You told me it was safe as a box of pencils."

"Yeah, well, *exploding* pencils. I left that part out." She felt his chin moving as he spoke, the vibration of his throat against the back of her neck.

"You're as bad as your father."

He was quiet a minute, then let out a long sigh, his breath stirring her hair. "I'm not like my father in any way, Alison, okay?"

Her face heated up. "Fine, I'm sorry. But for the record, I happen to like your father."

"That makes one of us."

"You know, Max, you make it sound like he was some crackhead who used to beat you with a board, instead of this harmless guy who likes to tell stories."

"And make a career out of bullshitting his son. And tell enough lies to drive his wife away. He's done damage."

"Who hasn't?" She found herself widening her eyes to prevent tears from forming. Max nodded in answer, making her own head nod with his. She turned inside his arms and faced him, leaning back a little to look up at him. He was shorter than Marty, his shoulders wider. He had a different smell, different angles to his body. He tightened his grip and bent to kiss her, her heart stretching out like drum skin across her chest, the fronts of their thighs touching and trading warmth, and at the last second she turned her head, so that his kiss landed clumsily at the corner of her mouth, a moist smear, the lens of his glasses tipped by her cheek. They were quiet a few moments, his forehead resting against her temple.

"It's been a while for me, too," he said. "But I don't think my aim has gotten that bad."

She nodded. "No, that was me. I'm sorry."

"You're sorry and what?" He let her go and leaned against the Corvette's fender. "You want me to leave again? So you can call me back here tomorrow?"

She looked at him, thinking of the way she'd imagined Marty in the basement of their house, a ghost-man rebuilding some old radio, willing it to work, the footsteps of his wife above him falling like hammer blows of accusation, the hard rhythm of all they had missed, all the ways he'd failed her. And now there remained only the rhythm of absence, the quiet tick of months and years passing, some wordless song about time running out. Grass grew under her feet like a million tiny hammers, landing their own blows. Marty was dust now, long in the ground and gone, the wisp of smoke from that soldering iron curling itself into outer space. Max shifted his weight on the Corvette, and something inside it clanked, some part that she would have to fix in a week or two or ten. We restore our radios, our cars, our dams, and all the while our bodies keep failing us, refusing to restore themselves except in the trick of sex, or childbirth, or some sad weight-loss plan. Or a kiss.

"No, don't leave," she said. "Sorry I flinched."

He looked at her, thinking. "You know, the real Cinderella got her kiss, eventually," he said. "And I was promised."

"First off, it wasn't a promise, more like a statistical probability, and second, I can't believe you're really going to use that Cinderella thing."

He shrugged. "Hey, whatever works."

"Typical man," she said, "pretending to be a fairy-tale princess just to get to first base. I don't suppose you know the origin of the Cinderella story?"

He looked at the ceiling, squinting. "Not offhand."

"It's Chinese . . . eighth century, maybe? Ninth?"

"Don't ask me. Those two always run together in my mind."

"Hush, and you'll learn something." She thought a minute, pulling together the details of the story. "The girl in the Chinese version is named Yeh-shen." Alison drew nearer to Max, slipped her arms around him, and kissed the whiskered skin along his jaw. "The fairy godmother appears as an enormous fish with golden eyes, swimming at the edge of a pond. Yeh-shen's evil stepmother kills the fish, but the bones are magic and continue to live in the water." Her voice dropped down to a whisper, punctuated by tiny kisses that traced the boundaries of his face. He held still, listening, she thought, or not wanting to scare her away. Skittish, he must think of her, or just odd. "Yeh-shen visits the bones every day, talking to them, but mourning them, too, that they are no longer her beautiful golden fish." She kissed his mouth then, his lips dry a moment until he drew them in to moisten them, her hands moving up to hold his face, her lips moving against his again, their tongues briefly touching. She tasted on him the cigarettes he'd smoked earlier, the taste like the smell of a campfire caught in clothing. "Yeh-shen wanted to go to the spring festival," she whispered, her mouth beside his, "but had nothing to wear until the magic bones gave her a gown, azure, with a cloak of kingfisher feathers sewn with silver thread." She kissed him harder and his mouth softened, their bodies touching where her hipbones knifed against the flat planes of his body, holding him like hands, triangulated by his own hardness jutting between them. She pressed against him, his arms drawing her in, his hands delineating her skinny curves, the arch at the small of her back, the cant of her rib cage—places on her body she hadn't given any thought to for a long time.

When she drew her mouth away to whisper again, she felt the small thread of saliva that anchored their mouths an inch apart, imagined it as silver under the lightbulb, as if illustrating the story of the azure dress, and as she thought that, she felt herself slipping out of the moment, pulling back from it as though she were watching not only that fragile wet thread but the two of them under the light, her awkward hands on his face, her angled hips, and as soon as she saw them that way, she was not thinking of the kiss or of being in the near dark with a man again, finally, but of the fairy tale. Of all fairy tales, and how they tell lies about happily ever after and the presence of magic in the world. Instead, how about one that explains that life is a spoiled five-year-old, an Indian giver that, in the end, wants itself back? A few nights before, Tyra Wallace had shown up for the dance partnered, Alison couldn't help but think, with the chrome-and-green oxygen tank she drew behind her on a small stainless dolly. She spent the evening sitting and watching, drawing ragged breaths through the filmy plastic mask. Somehow—either slowly or all at once—life slipped in its thin needle and sucked away its own essence, a lunatic mosquito, feeding on itself. And if you avoided the kinds of accidents that had taken Marty away, then you ended up like Tyra Wallace, the body doing itself in, and you with it. A double-crosser, planning an inside job all along.

Just as she felt Max pull back from her, just as he began to ask her what was wrong, a flash of orange lit up the walls of the garage, and she turned in time to see a fireball curl upward and disappear in the dark air above the lake. The noise of the men grew more excited, louder, and then settled back into quiet.

"Cousin of yours?" Alison said, her voice unsteady.

Max smiled but seemed worried as well, moving to the window and cupping his hands to look out. He told her he didn't really like the idea of anything exploding when it wasn't supposed to. He insisted on walking down to make sure that everything was okay, that no one was hurt. Alison shrugged. Men were always like this, wanting to mother the whole world of strangers, then acting like strangers themselves. She clicked off the light and followed him out.

Some of the other people who lived in the houses around the lake stood on their front porches, clutching bathrobes to themselves, trying to see what all the commotion was about. She and Max stepped down into the cracked mud along the bank, Max holding her hand, their feet oozing into soft spots. She'd thought enough to bring her new flashlight, the one Mr. Beachy had sold her, and fanned its light out as they walked, picking up broken bottles, pull tabs, muddied scraps of paper. All of them seemed like souvenirs of the night, insistent little reminders that she had just kissed a man for the first time in two years, had her tongue inside his wet mouth. And the first man other than Marty in more than ten years. She tried to convince herself of that old Humphrey Bogart song—what was the line, a kiss was just a kiss? Still a kiss?

Alison looked back toward the house, where the rows of pomegranates made blotchy shadows in the dark. Bill had given up for the night and disappeared inside. Just then a pair of headlights swung into the gravel drive, and the Seven Springs van lurched to a halt, then sat idling, dust spinning in the air around it. "What the hell?" Alison said. For a few seconds her mind did a little time jog, thinking it was early evening and time for the dancers to arrive. She looked at Max and he shrugged, and both of them walked back out of the lake.

Mr. Kesler sat behind the wheel, looking at the dark house, slowly turning his attention to the two of them as they approached the van.

"Dad?" Max said. "What's going on?"

"Gordon, is something wrong?" Alison asked. He sat in his powder blue jumpsuit, both hands in his lap.

"I must have the wrong night," he said. He looked at his watch and shook his wrist, then looked at the house a few more times.

"Dad, it's after midnight. What are you *doing* out here?"

"I . . ." He opened his mouth, closed it. "I think this watch is faulty. Cheaply made and all that." He looked stung by his own confusion, his eyes old and a little panicked behind his scientist glasses.

Alison and Max quickly looked at each other. Alison thought, but didn't bother pointing out, that if this *had* been the right time, he'd brought the van and no riders.

"I guess I made a big mistake," Mr. Kesler said, his voice overly loud.

Max's jaws worked with either impatience or worry, his temples throbbing as if he had gum in his mouth. "Yeah, I guess you *did,*" he said, which struck Alison as a harsh thing to say, given the circumstances. Just then, the porch light clicked on and Sarah came out of the house, hopping two steps to look at what it was she'd stepped in on her own front porch, never guessing in a million years, Alison thought, that it was pomegranate juice. She walked out into the harsh cones of the headlights, clutching her faded bathrobe, legs exposed and almost pale blue in the light. Her hair tumbled over to one side of her head, half of it in her face.

"It is one-*thirty* in the morning," she said in a loud hiss. "I heard an explosion, which I guess was *you*—" she looked at Max "—and now we're having a little party out in my driveway." She had walked just past the reach of the headlights, and Alison could see that her sister was naked under her threadbare bathrobe. She felt awful; all of Bill's King Solomon preparations, and here they'd likely interrupted their lovemaking, their latest attempt to form a baby out of superstition and abandoned hope. She imagined Bill upstairs in some makeshift phallic god costume, peeking out from behind the curtains.

"My father is putting on a little show," Max said. "I apologize for both of us." He tapped a cigarette from the pack and lit it. "And the explosion wasn't mine, I'm off the clock."

"Max was just about to drive his father home," Alison said. She tilted her head, trying to indicate in sister-code that something was wrong with Mr. Kesler. Even now, he kept shaking his watch and tapping its face, holding it to his ear, muttering about having the wrong night. Sarah was too angry to break the code, and just stood watching everything in her dark confusion.

"He can drive himself home," Max said.

"Well, no, I really think you should," Alison said. "He's probably tired." She heard herself using the composed voice that nurses always employ with difficult patients. Hard to say who was the difficult one here.

Max shrugged. "One of us worked today, and it wasn't him. Go on, Pop. Just go out the way you came in." This reminded Alison of a phrase repeated on nearly every page of her Haynes manual: *Reassembly is the reverse of disassembly.*

"Max, don't you think—"

Alison was interrupted by another flash of orange, another hollow *whoosh* of flame shooting up into the night, the reflection of it caught in the front bay window of Sarah's house.

"I'm going down there," Max said. "Those dumb bastards are going to kill themselves." As he turned away from the truck, his eyes locked with Alison's, and he gripped her forearm to lean in toward her. "Don't buy it," he whispered, then strode off, over the lip of the bank and into the bowl of the lake. So strange it looked, a lake with no water, a man walking in over his head into nothingness. Finally, Alison convinced Mr. Kesler to drive back home, after assuring him that there would be a dance lesson the next night, assuring herself that he was okay. When he started the van, Alison heard the insistent *ping ping* of some warning device, and noticed as he backed out that Mr. Kesler's own seat belt swung free, though his record collection was strapped in tight, a passenger beside him.

"While you were out here playing with your car, or whatever," Sarah said, "Lem called about nineteen times. Wants to know if you want latex or oil on the front door. Wants to know if you want to keep the carpet leftovers. Wants to know why the hell you've left *him* to do all the work on *your* house."

"He never said that," Alison said. She'd never heard Lem curse at anyone, much less her.

"No, that last part was me," Sarah said. "You can't even be bothered with your own home?" She shook her head, as if she wanted to say more but decided not to.

"I know Lem is working—"

Sarah pushed the hair off her face. "And while we're on the subject, Ernie called and said they had to give up your slot. They'll replace you with adjuncts." She said this so as to hit hard on "replace" and "adjuncts," small, sharp daggers to throw at her sister. They landed, too, so that Alison felt a warm thickness in the back of her throat that could quickly become tears if she let it. She'd been replaced, or worse, just phased out. A whole chunk of her previous existence canceled. Sarah backed off a bit.

"Hey, I'm glad to see you getting along with . . . what is it, Max?"

"Yes, Max. Thanks."

"That is, you know, if he's okay and all that."

"Why wouldn't he be?"

"Well, I don't know. He just seems a little strange, is all. And he should be talking you out of this car thing, not helping you with it."

"He tried. And as for the strange part, maybe I should find a nice normal boy who nails fruit to my house." She immediately regretted saying this, for letting Sarah, as usual, turn Alison into a version of herself. A little too mean, a little too mouthy. "Listen," Alison said, "go to bed. I'm going to catch up to Max." Sarah nodded and went back inside, stepping over the pomegranates, which by now were pulling loose of their nails and plopping onto the porch, the passing hour like some invisible Nebuchadnezzar, tearing down the temple walls.

A **caution** provides a special procedure or special steps which must be taken. Not heeding a **caution** can result in damage to the assembly. A **warning** provides a special procedure or special steps which must be taken. Not heeding a **warning** can result in personal injury.

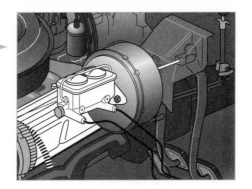

# 7

Mr. Kesler's phantom Chrysler was again featured in the *Press-Republican*. A local woman named Frieda Landry wrote a column called "Out-n-About," which dealt, apparently, with whatever was on her mind the day she wrote it. One week, she'd write about the family of chipmunks living in her Christmas wreath, and the next, she'd make an earnest appeal for peace in Northern Ireland. Today's column, though, asked "Where Oh Where Can Our Little Car Be?" They ran the same Flow Motor's photo of a Chrysler similar to Uncle Crawford's, and Frieda Landry retold the entire story, embellishing the cold ("bone-numbing"), and the severity of the ice storm that had hit Wiley Ford that winter of 1946 ("a glacial tempest"), and fourteen-year-old Gordon Kesler's struggle to make it out of the freezing water ("a frantic skirmish with death"). Mr. Kesler was quoted, saying he wasn't sure exactly where the car went under, and Frieda herself speculated that the car might have rolled along the sloped bottom and could be anywhere, most likely it had settled in the "bottomless crevasse" of the middle (Alison pictured Frieda writing her column with a thesaurus open on her lap). The article also quoted Max, who explained the very small breach he'd cut in the dam, saying that the middle of the lake would be drained within a couple of weeks and couldn't be rushed because of structural weaknesses in the dam. The thought occurred to Alison that Max was purposely holding things up, so as to prolong his father's agony, but she didn't want to dwell on that possibility. There were other quotes as well, a woman from the National Register of Historic Places, who noted, gently, that while the buildings of Colaville certainly were historically *interesting,* they held no intrinsic historical value. Tanner Miltenberger, who made his living scuba diving golf course ponds and selling the drowned balls he raked from the bottom, said he planned to dive in the middle and see what he could see, as soon as his bad back felt better.

The night before last, those buildings of Colaville had looked like toy blocks scattered around a rug. She had tramped out into the cracked mud after Mr. Kesler had driven off in the van and Sarah had disappeared inside the house. Max was waiting for her, sitting splay-legged on a stump, smoking a cigarette.

"I thought you went to see what was wrong with those poor bastards," she said, giving her words enough edge to register her annoyance that he'd lacked equal concern for his father. "Make sure the poor bastards weren't killing themselves."

"Well, they were, but slowly. Eating fish they were cooking over a Sterno fire. That was the big explosion, throwing Sterno cans on the campfire. Besides, they were mean."

"Did they threaten you?"

"No. They ate my fairy godmother."

She punched him on the shoulder with her knee. "You only need the bones anyway, remember?"

"I think they ate those, too."

She sat beside him, and he extinguished his cigarette by pushing it into the mud.

"Has your father had any other episodes like that?"

"Oh, maybe a thousand, going back to 1965, at least."

"You think *that* was more pretending? That he's nuts? Or senile? What would be the point?"

"I think you know." Max squinted and bent over, affecting an old man's voice: "There was a car? What car? I can't remember anything. Poor me."

"God, are you cynical. Maybe he's really sick."

"If I'm cynical, then you're gullible."

Alison bit her lip. "Okay, I already told you about Yeh-shen, maybe we have to move on to Aesop's fables? The Boy Who Cried Wolf?"

"Yeah, and when you get to the end, you'll recall that the idea of the story isn't that we end up feeling bad for that lying little shit, is it? The idea is supposed to be 'Don't lie.'"

Her face heated up. "So someday your father actually dies, and you sit home watching Oprah while the rest of us are at the funeral crying, because you don't believe it really happened. Is that how you want it to end up?"

"Well, no." He lit another cigarette. "I don't really want to watch Oprah."

"I'm serious. At least take your father to a doctor."

He shook his head, blew smoke at the night sky. "Alison, at home he rattles off Cal Ripken's batting averages for the last fifteen years. He keeps a mental catalog of seventy-eights he doesn't yet own, who recorded it, what orchestra, what label, and so on. His brain is better than both of ours put together."

She had taken his hand then, laced her fingers through his, which they both took as an end to the conversation, cutting it off before it spoiled the night. They'd sat in the quiet, the only sound the few men left at the lake's center, the crackle of paper from Max's cigarette. Maybe Max was right about his father; she had known him for only a couple months, and Max had known him his entire life. And, since Marty, she was too careful about everything, too worried. Besides, after only one kiss, she could still tell herself that it was none of her business, that she wasn't really involved.

She and Max had spent half the previous day in her garage, working on the last two wheel assemblies. Max did most of the work, without effort, ignoring the Haynes manual, while she stood behind him and watched. After her late night with Mr. Kesler, a gauze of sleepiness had settled behind her eyes, but she cleared it away with coffee and the small quickening of her breath that came when she thought about the night before, the feel of Max's whiskered jaw under her lips, his tongue alive against hers. They worked by way of silences and occasional touches, brief glances. Progress was quick; Max knew what he was doing. He'd offered to come back again today to help with the master cylinder rebuild, but she'd declined. They'd already finished up the last two wheels, so that now all four spun with that smooth hiss of newness. She was glad, but what good was undertaking the whole project if she ended up letting Max do all the work? She'd felt a little foolish telling him, "I want to do it myself," sounding like an eight-year-old fixing a peanut butter sandwich. But still, that *was* what she wanted, and besides, underneath everything we were all probably eight years old anyway.

After leaning for a full hour under the hood, banging her head on it twice, fitting her hand and a ratchet under and in between everything, and dropping three bolts down somewhere into the bowels of the car, she finally had everything disconnected and had labeled all the hoses and wires with little flags of masking tape, to make sure she put it all back right. The master cylinder now sat on the bench, clamped in the vise. She loved the size of it, smaller than her own two hands, and the way it was all of a piece, so self-contained. It came apart easily, a jumble of springs, retainers, and pistons that dumped out on her bench. The rebuild kit went in just the way the diagram showed it, every piece right there. Too bad they didn't make a kit for the entire car. All of the new parts had to be bathed in brake fluid, like bathing a baby in a washbasin. The fluid was a bright, pale yellow, almost fluorescent, and covered her hands so thickly, it felt as though she'd slipped on a wet pair of woolen gloves. When she finished and everything was back together, she reinstalled the master cylinder, connected it to the brake booster, reconnected the lines, and finally filled the reservoir with fresh fluid. The brakes, she realized as she wiped her hands, were done, except for the bleeding, which Max had promised to help with. *Better know you can make it stop before you make it go.* Well, okay—now she knew.

That night was rehearsal for the Founders' Day Parade, and the van from Seven Springs arrived while Alison was still at the kitchen sink, cleaning her hands with some product called Go-Jo, which Mr. Beachy had sold her, telling her that your ordinary bath soap couldn't handle real dirt. "Not a *man's* dirt," he'd said without thinking, then quickly added, "In a manner of speaking." She'd smiled and bought two tubs of the hand cleaner. And he was right: The stuff worked. The grease and brake fluid were up to her elbows, and she had just lathered up like a surgeon when the dancers walked in, bringing with them their smells of White Shoulders and cedar chests and aftershave. Mr. Rossi found her quickly, before, she guessed, someone else engaged him in regular conversation. All week long, he'd been talking about the Founders' Day Parade, and tonight he was decked out in his denim vest with the silver buttons, his face red and shining. He nodded, said "Hello," and then got stuck.

"Arthur, you look like a million bucks," she told him.

"And you as well, Miss Alison."

She smiled. She was wearing her very worst clothes, the ones she usually wore in the garage: a pair of jeans patched with pieces of red bandanna, and a T-shirt she'd bought at Goodwill, which said across the front SCHULTZ FERTILIZERS MAKE IT HAPPEN. There was a picture of a squirrel in an apron, holding a flowery watering can and tending a small mound of grass. The squirrel now wore a beard of grease.

"So, what do you know about Go-Jo hand cleaner?" she asked him.

"Well, it's a soap, essentially. . . ." He hesitated, never quite trusting that she actually wanted to hear him spout trivia.

"Tell me more," she said.

"I think most people know that soaps in general date back to about 1000 B.C."

"The Egyptians?"

"You might expect that, but it was the Romans, in fact. In the midst of some animal sacrifice, fat boiled off the unfortunate animal, mixed with potash from the fire, and found its way into the Tiber River. Women there, washing clothes, found that these strange gobs made the job go a bit more expeditiously. Voilà."

"That was easy," she said. She rinsed off, dried on the dish towel.

"Indeed it was." He looked at her, blushing, a vending machine waiting for its next quarter. Too bad the single women in the group all found him at best tolerable. He really was a sweet man, and brilliant, in his narrow way. Sarah tooted her whistle to signal the start of dance lessons. Mr. Kesler gave a loud sigh to signal his annoyance at having been reduced to pushing the button on the boom box, which they were using to make sure it would work during the parade. They did a walk-through of some new twisty arm move that Sarah called "the bread box" (where did she get these names?), and then they all took to the floor, the Harmons wearing matching Hawaiian shirts, Lila Montgomery, in her penny loafers and jeans, dancing with Mrs. Skidmore, who had already downed the first of her usual two beers. Mr. Rossi stood by, watching, almost leaning toward the dance floor in his eagerness to get out there, tapping his toes and snapping his fingers like some hipster member of the Rat Pack. The poor man. Alison wiped her face with the dish towel, then tapped Mr. Rossi on the shoulder.

"If you don't mind a little dirt and grease, let's go."

He looked at her, puzzled, until she took his hand and pulled him onto the floor. She felt a little shock wave of hesitation through the room, especially from Sarah; for two years now, Alison had watched these lessons, and not once had she danced. Too clumsy, she always told them. That was true, and even more so now with her dancing grown rusty, but so what? Mr. Rossi took her hands in his big doughy paws and began rocking back and forth. She followed his lead, the gravity of his impressive bulk looming over her, and he handled her as though he believed her arms were thin sticks that might snap off in his grip. She felt the floorboards flex under their movements, Mr. Rossi getting into it now, lifting her arm to turn her, the speakers of the boom box squeezing out a tinny "Caldonia" by Louis Jordan. It was a fast one, and Alison kept missing steps, landing once or twice on Mr. Rossi's wide feet. "I'm so sorry," she said, in that close-up way peculiar to dancing, but he seemed too happy to notice, smiling as though he couldn't help himself, his face shining with effort. She'd forgotten how much fun this was. Marty had never been much of one for dancing on those infrequent occasions when they went out. He was like so many guys, waiting for the slow songs and then feigning dancing with an extended hug and that tottering Frankenstein side-to-side movement that men seem to prefer. Mr. Rossi surrendered himself to motion, spinning her quickly now, so that her own dancing was reduced to mostly hanging on. On each spin the shark's tooth she wore on its silver chain kept flying up and tangling in her hair, until she paused long enough to take it off and toss it onto the coffee table, and he grabbed her up again, spinning her twice, finding her hand somehow behind his back as he turned, her face locked into a smile that mirrored his own as they both forgot now to watch their feet, her hair swinging out in splayed curls that whipped her cheeks. So good it felt, all of it, the music and the motion and the timing a kind of liquid ribbon spooling through her bones. Then the song ended. The Harmons, standing next to her and Mr. Rossi, smiled and clapped for them. She hugged Mr. Rossi, and he patted her shoulder.

"You're so good," she said. "Really, you are."

"One is only as good as one's partner," he said, slipping back into his awkward formality. His face looked baked, scarlet. Alison was out of breath, her muscles warm and loose. He kissed her hand and gave a little bow.


During the first break Sarah pushed out of the swinging kitchen door so hard, she almost hit Mrs. Skidmore. Bill followed, both of their faces darkened with whatever argument they'd just had inside. Sarah got herself a Dixie cup and made a show of popping it down on the table, filling it with chardonnay, and taking a long gulp.

"Hey, Tyra," she said, "about time for your smoke break, is it not?"

Tyra said that anytime was time for a smoke break. Since she'd been off the oxygen tank, she seemed to be celebrating with cigarettes. She and Sarah headed out onto the back porch, passing the shiny pack between them. Alison followed Bill through the swinging door back into the kitchen.

"What was that all about?" she asked.

Bill shrugged. His face looked haggard, his eyes dark-circled. All those late nights putting food on the house. "I told her I was taking a little break."

"From the pregnancy . . . project?"

"No, no. Lord, no. From work."

"You're quitting your *job*?"

"Nah, not quitting." He reached in his shirt to finger a necklace, one Alison had never noticed before. Not like her simple shark's tooth, but some kind of talisman on a leather cord. God knows what strange rituals Sarah had been putting up with in bed all these months. "I've got three weeks' sick leave saved up. Three weeks I can focus on the project, as you call it."

He worried the necklace, not looking at her. Probably steeling himself for another round of common sense. Bill was forty-two now and had always been prone to sickness, so of course Sarah was angry. Alison felt bad for him, trying to hold out hope in the face of what everyone else regarded as stupidity. Maybe hope *always* looked stupid, like the people lined up last week at DISCOUNT RAGE, buying up Powerball lottery tickets even though the evening news kept telling them they had a better chance of being struck by lightning while being stung by bees. Or the people from Seven Springs, a handful of years away from dying, but still trying to learn to dance. Or Mrs. Harmon, who in addition to dance had recently started piano lessons. Or the town itself, building a lake and waiting for tourists. Or Marty, with his projects, his Yellow Pages business plan, his perpetual-motion machine.

Or her.

Of course, that must be how *she* looked, pouring money and months into a basket-case Corvette—not brave or dauntless or spirited, just stupid. Stupid to Max, stupid to Sarah, to Ernie, to Mr. Beachy (who, like some TV drug dealer, supplied her habit), to all of Wiley Ford. But what amazed her was how *lavish* that stupidity felt, the best kind of self-indulgence. It felt big, expansive. Like Noah hammering away in the desert, Napoléon finding his way off Elba Island, Edward VII chucking the throne for some divorcée from Pennsylvania. Pessimism seemed easy, if you thought about it, a thin black string you could tug with your little finger, drawing down some heavy curtain. The optimists had it hard, thrumming along on hope, enduring the world's sad stares. All those times she used to berate Marty, was *that* what he'd felt, a kind of buried exhilaration? She looked at Bill, his tired eyes. Naturally he wanted to ditch his job; he was having the time of his life.

"Hey, laugh all you want," Bill said, mistaking her smile. "My mind is made up."

"We're both so stupid," she said.

He shook his head. "Afraid I don't follow."

"Nothing. It was a compliment."

He smiled, only because she was. "You're losing me, Al. What's your point?"

Just then, the music started up again, and she heard Mr. Rossi calling her name.

"My point is," she said, "you better just take half of that sick leave. Save the rest for when the baby comes."

Late, late that night, something woke her up. She lay in bed, listening for the muffled arguments of Bill and Sarah, or for the distant noise of the men in the lake, but heard nothing. When she got up and parted the curtains, she saw the Seven Springs van rolling to a silent stop on the gravel, the headlights out. Though she saw only his gray shadow, she knew immediately that the figure exiting the driver's door was Mr. Kesler. Poor man, he really *was* sick, maybe Alzheimer's or an early senility. As she pulled on her sweatshirt and shorts and considered phoning Max, Mr. Kesler began moving not toward the front door of the house but toward the garage door.

Alison cupped her hands to the window to watch as he walked along the side of the garage and cupped his own hands to the narrow window, looking in. It made her think of being a kid and going with her father to Swauger's Barbershop, seeing herself reflected in those opposing mirrors, an infinity of pale green light. Mr. Kesler

turned and stood in the driveway with his hands on his hips, looking up at the house. She instinctively pulled back. Was he looking
for Max? Her? The riders for his van? She thought of those stories
on the nightly news every so often, elderly people wandering off
alone. He opened the passenger door of the van where he kept his
records, closed the door, then walked around the back of the van,
carrying his wooden box. Instead of making his way to the house,
he turned and headed toward the lake, across the dewy lawn, picking his way slowly over the stands of weeds and cattails, then stepping down the steep bank into the mud. Alison turned quickly and
padded downstairs in her bare feet, avoiding the squeaky stairs so
as not to wake Sarah. Her brain went into panic mode, sifting half a
dozen thoughts before she reached the bottom stair tread. Maybe he
was throwing his records into the lake, his confusion twisting to
insult the decision to use the boom box for the Founders' Day
Parade. Or maybe he was looking for his car, finally believing his
own lies. Or, God forbid, he might be throwing *himself* into the lake.

By the time she made it to the edge of the mud, he was halfway
out, trudging along with faltering steps, sometimes uttering a curse
word. She stepped in after him, aware of her bare feet in the muck,
half-expecting a nail or glass shard to pierce her foot.

"Mr. *Kesler*," she said in that whispery shout people use in movie
theaters. *"Gordon!"*

He paused briefly, listening for what he must have thought he
heard, then resumed walking. Alison rolled her eyes. "Gordon!" she
said, louder this time. He stopped in his tracks but didn't turn to
her until she called him again, then waited until she caught up
with him.

"Mr. Kesler, are you okay?" She fought to catch her breath. "What
are you doing out here? The dance—"

His appearance stopped her. He wore a black knitted watchman's
cap, a black sweater, and dark pants, instead of his usual jumpsuit,
and some kind of black makeup—grease, or that stuff football players wear—around his eyes. He looked like Alice Cooper commit-
ting burglary.

"What night is this?" he said. "Where is everybody?"

"Oh, for godsake, Gordon. I might be naïve but I'm not a moron."

He looked at her for a long space of time, his eyes like crude drawings of eight balls. "Well, then, I won't insult your obvious intelligence."

"You probably already are, but go ahead. Explain yourself."

He drew a long breath, drumming his fingers on his lips. "No doubt you're familiar with the Japanese concept of losing face? Suffice it to say, I'm about to lose mine."

"Well, the way your face looks right now, it wouldn't be a huge loss."

He smiled. The box he clutched on his hip was not his wooden record box, but a plain cardboard one that had once held Jack Daniel's. "If you remember, we discussed how that car has sunk into the mud. I believe you said it could be twenty feet under by now."

"No, actually I never said any such thing."

He pointed at her. "Yes, right you are. I believe your prediction was eight to ten feet. In any case, as I told you then, with all the buildup and everyone looking to me as their big hero, I hate to let everyone down."

"Not your fault if that poor car got lost in the mud, is it? How could anyone blame you?" She was letting him dangle and spin a bit. Easy to see how Max found this so enticing. And he was right: She *had* missed the point of The Boy Who Cried Wolf.

"We always blame those who let us down, Alison, even if it's not their fault. The town expects to find a car down there, take pictures, the whole nine yards."

"Well, maybe they just will. You said yourself, and the paper agrees, it's probably in that deep middle part. Soon as Max drains that, I bet it'll be sitting right there. All polished up. In fact, I bet the engine is still running."

He licked his lips nervously. "Now you're pulling my leg."

"Yeah? How's it feel?"

He looked at her as though he were genuinely puzzled. He shifted the box, then set it down.

"Gordon," she said, "I heard about the Lou Gehrig baseball you bought for your son."

He shook his head, smiling. "Wouldn't believe what I went through to track that one down. Paid out the hummer, too. Then some collector tries highway robbery—"

"Listen, Max and I are kinda-sorta dating, Gordon. He's told me lots of things."

"Sure, sure. Beautiful woman like yourself. He'd be a fool not to be dating you, if you give him the chance. Yessir."

She laughed. "You're amazing. Truly. You should start your own religion or something."

"Well, there's money in it. So what if I did?" This sudden anger struck her as odd, as though he really *were* starting his own religion and she'd stumbled across his plans. But he was probably just like nearly every other man she'd ever known—backed into a corner, they get defensive to the point of idiocy. She recalled an argument with Marty where, to make some now-forgotten point, he'd taken his only two good dress shirts and cut the sleeves off.

Alison tapped the whiskey box with her muddied toe. "What's in the box? Sunday collections?"

He gave a long, heavy sigh, rubbing his eyes with thumb and finger, accidentally swiping the greasepaint into sad-clown makeup. He pulled off his cap, his silver hair dented in a ring.

"You're a mess, Gordon."

"Alison, there isn't any car in the lake. Never was. Before you stands a prevaricator."

She started to tell him this was old news by now, then stopped herself. After all, he was, in his way, coming clean. And he did. He told her all of it, how he'd made up the story, brought it to life by sheer force of will, retelling it over and over until the story stood up under its own power and began to walk around, took up residence in Wiley Ford. He spoke evenly, without much emotion, a man confessing an affair he's grown weary of.

"You know, if you told everyone what you just told me, you'd have that monkey off your back. Just look at politicians, everybody's a big fan of public apology."

"Public humiliation, you mean," he said. "Media attention instead of stocks in the town square."

"The *Press-Republican* isn't exactly 'media attention.' I mean, last week they ran a front-page story about the new Harvest Queen. Turns out, she gets her driver's license next year."

He half-laughed, stuffed the watch cap into his pocket. "Yeah, but still." His mouth searched for words. "I just can't, Alison."

"And this Alzheimer's thing isn't going to fly, and you know it."

"Had *you* going, missy."

"Yeah, but I'm easy. And even if they did buy it, it would just give them a reason to say more terrible things about you, figuring you won't even have enough mind to notice."

His face turned grim. "Hadn't thought of that."

"Besides, say you live another twenty-five years. Long time to maintain an act."

"Cursed with long life. All right then, plan B."

The wind kicked up just then, chilling her bare legs, her feet cold in the mud. The round eye of water at the lake's center purled in quiet folds. All the men were gone, their lamps extinguished. The moon gave everything the blue-white tint of skim milk. Mr. Kesler bent and opened the flaps of the box, revealing a jumble of car parts.

Alison knelt in the mud. Old car parts, most of them rusted, pulled from some junkyard. Half of a knurled steering wheel, a speedometer, a cracked mirror, a taillight lens, and, beneath a few odds and ends, three heavy hubcaps stamped CHRYSLER in their centers, stacked like dinner plates.

"You ever watched a magician, Alison?" Mr. Kesler asked, speaking now in hushed tones. "A little wiggle under the tablecloth is all he needs to make us believe the rabbit is there, just before it vanishes."

She nodded. "And a few busted parts in the mud is going to make people believe in the car underneath it."

"Smart girl." He picked up the speedometer and tossed it out into the middle of the water. The splash was quiet, a sudden ripple, then gone.

"Of course," he said, "there's the problem of you. You've got the keys to the castle, so to speak." He tossed in the rearview mirror, the taillight.

"Yep. I guess this is the part of the movie where you rub me out, to keep me quiet."

He smiled. "The Wiley Ford Mafia. Bingo games and church raffles are our usual rackets." He flung the broken steering wheel, and she watched it tumble end over end, a wounded game bird splashing down. "Unless, of course, you're one of us."

"Gordon, don't you ever get tired of this?"

"Tired of talking to beautiful women? Who would ever admit to that?"

"Okay, let's cut the bullshit. I mean it. Don't you think about your son? You know, the one who grew up with a compulsive liar for a father?"

He tossed a piece of chrome trim into the lake. "The big teary father-son scene, that's what you'd like to see, huh? Martin and Lewis, reunited. Not gonna happen. Ask him. He means to bring me down like I'm one of his silos. Let me tell you, Alison, I'm an old man, and this is the county of my birth. That car is all I have."

"You *don't* have it. That's the point."

"The point is, I do." He held up one of the wide chrome hubcaps and sailed it toward the water. It skipped once, like a bright stone, and disappeared. He looked back at her, and there were tears on his face. A con, she thought. More lies.

"Are you going to help him?" he said. "Bring me down, I mean?" He choked on his words. Bravo, she thought. Still, it was not an easy thing to watch an old man cry, performance or not. The last time had been Marty's father, at the funeral. Her hands were shaking.

"Mr. Kesler . . ."

He took another hubcap from the box. "Or maybe it's like I said before. You're one of us." He offered her the hubcap, the last one, his box empty.

She watched her fingers curl around it. A fraud, a polished lie offered up before eight thousand people. Or maybe he wasn't so much a liar, The Boy Who Cried Wolf, as he was just another stupid optimist, preserving a fantasy, sacrificing junkyard parts to his own invented ghosts. The hubcap felt chilled, absorbing cold from the night, and the hard edge of it bit into her finger as she curled it back like a Frisbee and flung hard, Mr. Kesler smiling at her now, his tears vanished. She watched as it flew, catching and throwing back the moonlight, like some scratchy tabloid photo of a UFO. And that's exactly what it was, this impulse to help him lie, to help him further deceive his son—some hard object thrown from her, flying through the dark, obscure and unidentified.

—from the *Haynes Automotive Repair Manual:*
*Chevrolet Corvette, 1968 thru 1982*

Whenever wiring looms, harnesses, or connectors are separated, it is a good idea to identify the two halves with numbered pieces of masking tape so that they can be easily reconnected.

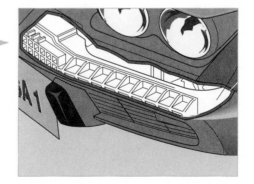

# 8

They left for Morgantown after Alison had spent the morning with Mr. Beachy, learning about engine hoists and stands. Bill had taken her wheels down to Smitty's and had new tires mounted, so that now the Corvette could roll, its tires no longer mush. Together, they had pushed it a bit, just enough to shove it past its ruts. The small movement of the car had thrilled her—two inches seemed as good as a thousand miles. After her morning at AAAA, looking over all the catalog parts she couldn't afford, Max had met her for breakfast at the Red Bird, and then they drove over, holding hands in the truck, listening to Placido Domingo and Theresa Stratas, the high notes making the speakers buzz. The demolition job Max had lined up was a twelve-story building, which had once been the Hotel Morgantown.

"I guess they didn't rack their brains thinking up names for the place, huh?" Alison said as they parked across the street.

"It's to the point," Max said. "You have to admire that."

The sign for the hotel was still in place, once-fancy gilt lettering on a dark green wooden board, all of it now peeling and flaked. For the past ten years, it had been used as a "flophouse," as Max called it, some kind of shelter for indigent men. The front door handles were laced with chains and a padlock, and Max unlocked them with a key he carried on a cardboard tag. The street around the hotel looked as indigent as the men who had once lived here: scattered nests of paper scraps trapped by chain-link fencing, brown bottles smashed in the gutters, the sidewalk broken and buckled, sprouting weeds, a rusted washing machine in the alley between buildings. The brick facade loomed above them, striated with pigeon droppings. Brass doors opened onto columns of dust and the odor of urine, the red carpets rolled up and leaning slumped in the corner. An outline of dirt remained where the front desk had been. Plaster had trickled down from the ceiling into neat little piles, as though some child had scooped them up.

"You know what?" Alison said. "Every impulse I have tells me to give this place a good cleaning before you tear it down." The idea made her think of Lem and Pammy, who by now had likely finished her house, all of it new, painted, and empty.

"It's really an amazing old building, if you can overlook all the squalor."

"Squalor. That's a word you don't hear every day."

Max walked around the narrow lobby. "Yeah, I got it from the 'Word Power' section of *Reader's Digest*. My father subscribes."

"Every old person I know subscribes. It's like you start running out of time, you want to read everything in condensed form."

"Well, I read it all the time now. Learning new words every day."

"What on earth for?"

He shrugged as he snapped the key off its paper tag and slid it onto his own key ring. "To keep up with you, I guess. You're a smart woman."

She stopped and looked at him. One of Marty's constant worries had been that she would grow bored with him as she became more enamored of her colleagues in the history department. He told her once he was getting smaller and smaller from where she was, an ant on the ground. Early in their marriage, talk of going back for her doctorate had sent him into the basement for weeks.

"And you're a smart man. One of the smartest I've ever met."

"Well, thanks. That's very beneficent of you."

She smiled. "I know men ready themselves for dates, same as women," she said. "But you never hear of anyone *cramming* for a date."

"Yeah, but you're impressed, aren't you? Admit it—you venerate my recent linguistic proficiency."

"Of course. You know what they say about the size of a man's vocabulary."

He clicked his tongue. "Such indecorous licentiousness."

"Okay. Stop that now, and I might stay."

"All right, all right. Come on. I'll give you a tour."

She followed, stifling a yawn, every wash of sleepiness reminding her of the night before, out until the wee hours, helping Mr. Kesler put one over on the town, on his own son, who was right this second tugging her along into the quiet of an old hotel, this man who might possibly love her. She'd felt charitable last night, helping out a sad old man, the way she'd helped a sad young one—Bill— perpetuate his own dumb hopes. They were slowly forming a club, a secret society of losers who put their belief in belief, instead of in the ordinary world of sex and loss and hurt, like everyone else. She thought about how Mr. Kesler had nearly cried, or had cried. She could see him now, his salty tears gathering the makeup into tiny black pearls, but that was a lie, too, wasn't it? Hadn't she noticed him *not* crying, despite all his upset and worry? Moments, like history, slowly harden into mistruth and fabrications. A severed ear. Henry Ford and his soybean suit. Mr. Kesler and his tearful agony. He'd begged her, was how the story went in her mind, and against that she held up the freshness of the memory, which told her he'd merely offered, merely held out the last hubcap and made her complicit in his lies. She's taken it, taken on his years-long burden of bullshit, of lying to an only son. Only later, with the passing of time, could she tell herself he'd begged her, and she *would*, she knew. The way she'd lied to herself about Marty until his basemented presence called her on it. She felt awful, as though she'd slept with someone else, as if she'd betrayed Max already, while they were still so new.

The line of open doors down the hall spread alternating rectangles of light on the floor. Brass numbers hung loose from the wooden doors or were missing altogether, the rooms no more than boxes, minus their furniture, which had been sold at auction. The third room they passed had its walls and ceiling entirely covered in aluminum foil, its former occupant, according to Max, fearful of Russian radio signals entering his brain and controlling his actions. Here and there were old cigar butts and bottle caps, a piece of toast, a broken yardstick, gum stuck to the wall. Another room was covered in *Playboy* centerfolds, another with careful pencil drawings of fish and birds, another with ancient peeling wallpaper patterned with roses. It all felt like some museum display, an exhibit on natural habitats. At the end of the hall, someone had left behind a milk crate with a type-writer atop it, all its keys jammed.

"The men who lived here—what happened to them when the place was sold?" Alison asked.

Max shrugged, picked up an old Chinese take-out menu from the floor, then dropped it again. "I don't know. What happens to anybody? They died, they moved, they went to jails or hospitals. They just went away."

The gray-yellow light of the building, the corners of shadow, weighed on her, a lead vest that hindered her breathing. How right he was, and how sad that he was right. Everyone just went away, eventually, gathered back up into that filmy nothing that had brought them here in the first place. She'd envied Marty and his easy faith, that he'd believed in a better place, that he'd believed in *some* place, any place. They would argue about the church, about religion, but those arguments never lasted long; he would clam up and retreat to the basement as she pelted him with the Crusades, the Inquisition, Pope Benedict IX. She told him once that *that* was her fear, that people who died just got lost in the nothingness, a black emptiness crowded with the dead. She'd tried to make a joke of it, saying that she worried death was no more than a big shop-ping mall, minus lights, and that we ended up as lost children, wan-dering, scared, looking for a grown-up. Marty smiled, told her he believed much the same, only the lights came on and every store was a toy store, giving everything away for free, forever. How she'd envied that.

She drew close to Max as he led her downstairs, telling her she had to see this. They walked into an emptied kitchen, the walls where the fans had been still darkened with grease, and then through wide doors that opened onto the hotel ballroom—an expanse of warped parquet floor, wires hanging from the stamped-tin ceiling where a chandelier had once hung. Their footsteps echoed woodenly, dust spilling upward into the parabolas of light from the high arched windows across the side wall. At the front of the room was a low stage, antiquated speakers still fastened in the corners.

"Some place, huh?" Max said.

"Wouldn't Sarah love this? For her classes? I wish we could move it out to the lake."

Max nodded. "Dad told me there used to be five hundred people in here on a Saturday night, sweating it out in evening clothes, full orchestra up there, everyone loading up on champagne cocktails."

"Your father doesn't strike me as the champagne cocktail type." She pictured him from the night before, elderly heavy-metal burglar, pathetic and devious.

"Well, he was only here once. On his honeymoon."

"You've got to be kidding me." She looked at him. "Or . . . maybe he's kidding you?"

"Not this time. I've seen those slides all my life. Pretty much the way he described it. Back then, drive for an hour and that's your honeymoon. Two nights they spent here."

She watched as he moved around the room, his neck cords tight as he looked up at the ceiling.

"Max, I don't see how you can tear this place down."

He smirked. "Oh, come on, Alison. I already have a Hotel Morgantown ashtray, I don't need another souvenir of my parents' marriage. Especially one that takes up half a city block. And it's coming down whether I do it or not."

"You have a job to do, Herr Kesler?"

"That's mean."

"I know. I'm sorry. Still . . ."

"Look, I love old buildings. This one had its day, and now it's structurally not all that sound. Besides, my parent's marriage was a lousy one, even if they had a couple of happy nights here. You shouldn't romanticize everything."

True enough, she did that. She thought about all the picture books she'd read as a kid, the way *things* always wanted something. Trees that craved friends, raindrops that cried because they hadn't landed on buttercups, rocking chairs that only wanted someone to sit in them. The idea had its appeal, that somehow the whole world needed us, every bit of plastic, every bit of wood.

"We ought to dance in this place. Someone should dance here one last time," she said.

He looked at her.

"Well, you said don't romanticize *every*thing. I can romanticize some things, can't I? I can romanticize you."

He told her to wait there, then disappeared back through the kitchen. While he was gone, Alison sat on the small stage and imagined young Mr. Kesler there with his new wife, dashing and awkward in his wedding suit, the two of them slightly drunk, anticipating their bed upstairs. She saw him laughing, his teeth shining, his face spilling over with all the possibility and hope that had pulled him into marriage in the first place, that pulls anyone into marriage.

Just then, Max returned with the dusty boom box from the back of his truck. He carried it to the middle of the floor, set it down, and raised the antenna.

"Batteries are old, so don't expect much," he said. He clicked it on to the noisy buzz of static and blipped the dial past nothing, a random voice or two, sports reports, until he found the only signal strong enough to reach them, from the campus radio station a few blocks south. They were featuring, it turned out, a retrospective on ZZ Top, loud, pounding songs, guitars and heavy drums. A nervous-sounding student DJ, rattling his notes.

"Oh, for godsake," Max said. He hit the off button.

"No, no." Alison started laughing. "Leave it on."

Max turned it back on. Over the churn of guitar and bass, the singer growled about his fast car, about women's bodies, about liquor and love. In the faltering light, Alison walked over and took Max's fingers and pulled him up and to her, her body like origami, full of edges, folding into him. She led him, turning him in an easy circle until he drew up her hands and began a clumsy waltz, a grade-school box step, circling around the radio, each pass between it and the window breaking the signal and producing a quick wash of static before the music pulled itself back in. The static was a light-house beam, tracking their passes, until they stopped and he kissed her, his beard lightly abrading her chin, his tongue tracing over her lips. The band sang a song devoted to beer, but by now she wasn't much listening, hearing only the static of her own pulse in her ears, the soft exhalations of breath at her ear, and they sank together down into the dark of the floor, where the angled light, sliding up the opposite wall, no longer reached.

They pitched their sleeping bags on the stage and slept there instead of in any of the cramped rooms, the air in those rooms close with the gloom of the men who had lived in them. Toward morning, rain started up, an opaque and chilly downpour that signaled an early autumn. The rain produced a thin echo that dragged her up out of a deep, unmoving sleep, the sound like applause in some far-off room. Alison reached across and rubbed his back, let her fingers mesh with the skin drawn in furrows over his rib cage, and slid closer, taking him into her hand. They made love a second, slower time, quietly, the palms of their hands black with dust from the stage floor. After, they realized they'd forgotten food and so made a breakfast from what Max could find in the truck: a bottle of water, a box of vanilla wafers, and the paper sack of stale pistachios. They sat cross-legged, eating qui-etly, listening to the downpour, while she thought about the night before, his hands and his body, trying not to compare him to Marty.

The rest of the morning was spent working in the basement, Ali-son holding a flashlight while Max ran his drill off the generator, drilling holes into the brick columns that stood in rows. She shone the light around, finding blank spots where the water heater and furnace had been, old wooden chutes for coal and laundry, dis-carded signs advertising the dining room on the top floor. From one of the wooden beams hung what looked like some child's first-grade art project, a mobile made from a coat hanger, yarn, and flashing pieces of aluminum foil. She thought again of two nights before, of tossing the hubcap into the lake. Maybe the whole plan was so dumb, it wouldn't make any difference. The men fishing the lake would find the stuff and throw it away; no one would ever know about it. She looked over at Max as he leaned to wipe his face with his T-shirt. What if she just told him? What would be the big deal? He might just laugh it off, though he hadn't been laughing the other night when his father showed up in the driveway, hadn't laughed at any of Gordon's lies or his efforts to protect those lies. If only Max could see his father the way she did: a desperate old man, digging his nails in, clinging to air. But she supposed you could never see your father or mother, your husband or wife or lover as anyone other than someone wielding your own bestowed trust, levering your faith against your love, one direction or the other. And if she did tell him, and the plan worked, she knew what might happen: Max would call his father on this lie, too, his eyewitness there at his side, holding his hand, making love to him in old hotels.

Max clicked off the drill, pushed his goggles up. "I feel like a coal miner down here. Let's go find some sunlight."

"I'm starving."

"Sunlight and food, then."

The small corner market down the street was open, and they bought microwave burritos and nachos, sodas, and a bag of M&M's, which they took back to the hotel, up the twelve flights of stairs, up an iron ladder, and out onto the graveled roof. Industrial gray boxes were situated here and there, air conditioners, maybe, or fans. This was a football Saturday in Morgantown, and off in the distance they heard the cheers rise up out of the quiet. Just as they were about to sit with their food, they noticed a man sitting in the corner of the rooftop, legs stretched out before him. He raised his arm and gave them a friendly wave, and Alison felt a stir of fear ripple through her.

"What the hell . . ."

"It's okay," Max said. "That guy's been hanging around since the first day I went through this place. Just nod a lot; he's fine."

They walked over, passing the cardboard trays of food. "Hey, Tom," Max yelled. "What's up, dude?"

"Yo, hey. Maxwell!" Tom said.

"Maxwell?" Alison whispered.

"He's one of those nickname guys. You'll have one soon enough."

Tom looked to be in his late fifties, with close-cropped white hair under a Batman baseball cap, a deep tan, and a black elastic band holding his big square glasses in place. He wore flower-print beach shorts and a POW/MIA T-shirt. He looked like one of those damaged Vietnam vets always featured on TV news magazines.

"My buddy Maxwell," he said. "And you brought your lady friend along to hold the flashlight."

"That's pretty astute, Tom," Alison said, strangely happy to hear herself described as someone's "lady friend."

"Hell, I'm about half-psychic, you know."

"Half?"

"This is Alison Durst," Max said.

"Ali*son*," he said loudly, pronouncing the second syllable like "sewn."

"Tom used to live here," Max said. He lit a cigarette and offered the pack to Tom, who took two. "Very top floor."

"Were you in the war or something?" she asked, pointing at his shirt.

"Yeah, the war of the sexes. I was a POW for a while. Now I'm missing in action." He laughed at his joke, revealing large front teeth. She imagined he must wear the shirt just so he could repeat the joke.

"Where do you live now?"

"Ah, you know. There's always a pal, always a couch. Pals and couches." He nodded.

Alison took another nacho and offered Tom the tray. He took one, popped it into his mouth, and patted his stomach, smiling. Under his leg he had a stack of paper, playbills and flyers that looked like they'd been torn from telephone poles. One of them, resting in the V of his legs, had been folded into a paper airplane. Alison wondered just how screwed up this guy was, sitting up here. He saw her looking at the plane.

"I used to fly," he said.

Tom held the plane up, his fingers lightly quivering. "I had an old Piper Comanche. When the money for that ran out, I did RC planes for a while, and when that money ran out, I made plastic models. Hellcats, Mustangs, Japanese Zeros. And when *that* money ran out, here I am." He tossed the plane so it hit the knee of her jeans.

"And when that money runs out?"

He laughed, readjusting his cap. "This one is free, Ali*sewn*. All free."

"My father used to do RC planes," she told him.

He nodded. "That's cool."

"Tom worked as a flight mechanic for Piedmont Airlines," Max said.

Tom shook his head. "Then they got bought out, like everyone else. Fired the old guys and the new guys. Kept the middle."

"So how do you earn a living now?" She tried to say this without concern in her voice.

He bent a corner of the plane. "Oh, I have a small pension, and I play the horses over in Charlestown."

"I thought that was how you went about losing money, not making it." She offered him the last nacho, and he took it.

"Not if you're good or careful. I'm good and careful. The Wizard of Odds." He smiled, chewing.

"Alison is a mechanic, too," Max said. "Cars, though, not planes."

"Oh, I am not."

"Oh yeah?" Tom said. "What are you mechanicizing?"

Her face warmed. "I have a 1976 Corvette. I'm just fooling around with it. I don't really know what I'm doing."

"God Almighty, 1976," Tom said. "Our peanut farmer takes office, Chairman Mao heads for that great collective in the sky, the *Viking* hits Mars and fails to reveal any little green men. Oh, and the Bicentennial, all that off-the-rack patriotism."

"Is your last name Rossi?" Alison asked.

"No, ma'am. Bittner. Seventy-six was a watershed for me. My daughter was born."

"What's her name?"

"Susan Marie Bittner. I still like it. I called her 'Soupy.'"

"What's she doing now?" Alison wondered how she could let her father live this way.

"God knows," Tom said.

"That's too bad, Tom," Max said.

"No, it's a good thing." He folded the creases of the airplane, sharpening them with his thumbnail. "If He didn't know, then I'd be worried."

"Go ahead and fly it," Alison said. "I want to see."

"Are you in deep soul love with your lady friend?" he asked Max. "With Alisewn?" He put the final fold in the plane and held it up to check its evenness.

"Well," Max said, cutting his eyes at her. "Could be. It's too early to tell, probably."

Alison smiled at him. Could be.

"Could be, my skinny white ass," Tom said. "If you're in love with someone, you know before you know. You know before you're born. *A priori,* my friend."

"Then maybe it hasn't sunk in quite yet," Max said.

This answer seemed to satisfy Tom. He turned and knelt at the ledge of the roof, gently tossed the pink plane over. It sailed evenly, circling around on updrafts, out over the rooftops as it slowly spiraled down. By the time she took her eyes away, he'd already folded two more, and he handed one to her, one to Max.

"Hold up for me," he said, starting another. They held their planes and waited. Max kept looking at her, holding her glance, conjuring up the telepathy that lovemaking induced, that secret shadow play of intimacy. "Just a final filigree and we're good to go," Tom said, licking his fingers to straighten the creases. Alison looked back at Max, who was watching Tom. Deep soul love, she thought, imagining, for the first time in two years, another kind of life for herself. One of blown-up silos and redneck opera cruising and pistachios and old men on rooftops, but still—a life.

Finally, Tom finished and counted three, and they tossed their planes over into the breeze, a blue one, a yellow one, a black-and-white one. The planes swooped and spun, lifting and then turning, circling. Tom clapped his hands and shouted, "Dogfight! Dogfight!" as the planes looped into the hazy dusk that hung over the city, as another cheer went up from Mountaineer Stadium.

They left Tom napping in his corner of the roof, going back down to finish up what work was left for now: drilling holes, checking the lean of the building with a plumb line, and loading sand, chicken wire, plastic sandwich bags, and rags into the basement, where it would all wait until Max's order of dynamite came through. Max explained that this job would not be like another silo in another abandoned field. The police would be there that day, to cordon off five blocks surrounding the building. The mayor had already arranged for a photo op of himself pushing the button to set off the charges, which meant that someone from the *Dominion Post* would be on hand, along with TV cameras from local news and a crowd of onlookers.

"Man, you're like a rock star," Alison said, settling herself in the truck, noticing for the first time how weary her bones were from all the stair climbing and lifting.

"You think?" Max looked up at the building one last time, probably running through his mental checklist. Her own checklists, her long categories of dates and names, had gotten lost somewhere over the last two days, pushed from her mind by thoughts of work and sex and deep soul love.

"Sure, all you need is some babe in a spangly dress on your arm."

He laughed. "Do you have a spangly dress?"

"Not hardly."

"This'll have to do, then." He hooked his finger in the watch pocket of her denim overalls and pulled her to him, kissing her deeply, both of them giving off musty attic odors. Sometimes some of Sarah's dancers, with a new romance of their own, or new medication, a recent joint replacement, would repeat the old cliché, saying they felt like teenagers again. Alison always resisted the impulse to ask what that meant: Screaming tantrums? Back-stabbing gossip? Bad poetry filling diary pages? Pimples? But now, she had to admit, she knew what they meant. Here she was, parked in a truck, making out, gently sucking Max's tongue, her hand on his thigh, about to head home while opera music swirled around them in the noisy truck. It all felt so good.

Later that night, in the dark, they lay on her bed with a quilt thrown loosely over them, wind gently shaking the window screen. It seemed strange that for so long she'd thought of that wind as a breeze off the lake, had described it that way a dozen times, only now the lake was mostly gone, but the breeze remained. Max's breathing was slow and even, though his eyes were liquid and shining in the dark, looking up toward the shift of light on the ceiling. She leaned up on her elbow and told him a story about the time when she was seven years old and her Aunt Jeannie gave her a Chatty Cathy doll for her birthday.

"I didn't even like dolls and never had. I mumbled a thank-you, took it out of the box, and pulled the string. It said something dumb, 'I want a cookie,' or something like that. Then Sarah tried it, and it said, 'Please brush my hair.' I thought it was the lamest toy on the planet."

Max smiled, still looking up at the ceiling. "So, what happened?"

"I put it—her—on a shelf, then started looking at the box she came in. Probably playing with the box instead of the doll. Anyhow, the box said, 'Chatty Cathy, the Talking Doll' or whatever, and then I read, on the side, 'Says eleven different phrases.' I mean, good Lord, I just about had a heart attack."

Max turned his head toward her. "Sorry to be dense. I don't get it."

"I thought she only said eleven things *total.* Ever. In her whole life. We'd already used up two of them without even really listening. I mean, *wasted* them, you know?"

He laughed. "You didn't like her anyway."

She gave him a small shove. "Now you *are* being dense. It's like having eleven wishes. You don't want to blow any."

"So what did you do?"

"I went Secret Service on everybody. 'Don't touch the doll!' 'Get away from the doll!' She stayed on the shelf, and I kept trying to figure out what would be an appropriately weighty occasion for another string-pull. I imagined spacing them out over my entire life."

"When did you finally figure it out?" He gathered her wiry hair in his fingertips.

"Well, you know Sarah never passes up an opportunity to explain some incidence of stupidity. So she did, finally."

"And what happened to Chatty Cathy?"

"Garage sale, probably. Salvation Army, the island of misfit toys. Who knows."

He was smiling but sleepy, his eyelids weighted. "Somehow," she said, "the last two years have felt like that. Like Chatty Cathy."

He looked at her. "You mean you feel like her? On a shelf?"

"Not exactly that. And not me, really. More like . . . I don't know. The time."

"I'm not sure how you mean."

"Like, even if she *did* only have eleven things to say, you have to pull the string anyway. If that makes sense. I don't know."

She left it at that and fell asleep happy, slipping down into her pillow, under the crook of his arm, beginning that slow tumble into dreams, which, despite her quiet happiness, came in as dreams will: dark, insistent, and bottomless.

If several components or circuits fail at one time, chances
are the problem is a fuse or ground connection, because
several circuits are often routed through the same ground
connection.

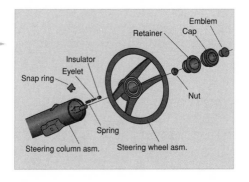

# 9

Two days later, Max figured out the electrical problem was not the battery or the mice, but just bad grounds, dirty connections in the fuse box or at the starter, or anywhere, really.

"Well, how do we fix that?" Alison asked.

"You need a special tool," Max said, staring into the engine bay. "Probably very expensive, too."

"More good news. Mr. Beachy can build a new wing and name it after me."

"Wait here," he told her. "I think Sarah has the tool you need."

"Sarah? Her idea of a tool is a coffee cup."

He wiped his hands on his jeans. "Just wait."

He disappeared into the house and came back in five minutes, carrying a pencil. He offered it to her, holding it on outstretched hands.

"What? I write a letter and ask for real help?"

"No, you use the eraser to clean the electrical connections. Just erase all the gunk."

She took the pencil, feeling dumb, doubtful, as if he'd just handed her a spoon to remove the wheels. Sure enough, though, when she tried the first connector at the fuse box, the dirt erased easily, turning the black to bright copper. She did this for all the connectors she could find, back to the battery behind the driver's seat, while Max sprayed oil into the cylinders through the spark plug holes.

"I thought oil went in the thing on top," Alison said.

"Usually, yeah. But your cylinders are probably a little rusty, and you might not have oil pressure first time you start it up."

"But if they're rusted and I try to start the engine, I'll break a ring, right?"

He smiled. "You're getting pretty good at this. And you could break a ring, but we'll deal with that if it happens. Let's just get it running first."

She *was* getting good at this. More and more, she knew exactly what she was looking at when she bent under the hood, knew what was wrong and how to fix it. She would visit AAAA Auto Parts and listen to Mr. Beachy explain things she already understood, wanting to absorb not so much his knowledge now as his quiet patience. She'd come to love the new rubber and clean oil smell of the place, the worn wooden counter, the fringe of fan belts, the cartoonish religious tracts. Someday, the Corvette would be done and she would no longer have any excuse to walk in there and lean on the counter next to the gum machine. Someday, that counter wouldn't even exist, nor Mr. Beachy with his patient explanations. He, his store, would go the way of the Hotel Morgantown, of those tuxedoed bands in the ballroom and the indigent men who came later, of Marty and her old, empty house. Ashes to ashes must be the world's oldest economy, and amazing, really, in its scope. *Every* damn thing found its end, and as you got a little older, you could mourn a wooden counter almost as easily as you could a dead husband. But thinking that way was probably just sentimentality, a Hallmark card to your wonderful self and your wonderful existence. Everyone seemed to believe that change was good—she'd seen the idea expressed on bumper stickers—but why? Change was just the world gearing up to get along fine without you. So maybe that's why she'd thrown that hubcap into the lake, just to let Mr. Kesler keep his own damaged past for a while, lies and all. She knew from her marriage that the worst kind of history was one built on lies, because when it finally crumbled away, all you had left were doubts and regret, half-ghosts of everything you did wrong. When the Hotel Morgantown was no more, Max had told her, the local officials planned a historical marker to note where it had once stood. But there were no markers for imaginary hotels, no forged baseballs in the Hall of Fame, no plaques to failed marriages. Lies crumbled like dust in the wake of moving forward, and even the dust was a lie, and crumbled into nothing.

She finished erasing the last of the crud from the connections under the hood, then handed the pencil back to Max.

"I ruined your special tool," she said. "I'll save up and buy you another."

"Come here. I want to show you something." He popped open the driver's door and invited her to sit. She sat in it for the first time since the night she'd claimed the car as hers, and stuck the key in the ignition.

"Don't try to start it," Max said. "Just turn it one click."

"Here goes nothing."

"Wait," Max told her.

"Okay, now you're teasing me."

He stepped and pulled the creaky garage door closed, shutting them into near dark. She turned the key, and the dashboard lit up yellow and green and white, one turn signal flashing. It seemed miraculous, that little glow of life, a tiny blip on its heart monitor, an eyelid flutter in the midst of the car's long coma.

"Holy *shit,*" she said, smiling up at him. She clapped her hands twice on the steering wheel. "Can't we start it?"

"Give that oil time to do its work, loosen it up a bit in there. You'll need new gas, too."

"Still, this is pretty incredible."

"That ain't nothin'," he said. "Pull that."

She pulled the switch, and the headlights, hidden in the nose of the car, slid upward on a steady, low hum. One set of bulbs was burned out, the other shining against the back of the garage door.

"Just a couple bulbs," Max said. "Easy fix."

She nodded as she clicked on the stereo, which also worked, though nothing would tune in, only a whitewash of buzz.

"Damn, I was hoping for a little ZZ Top," he said.

She kissed his hand, leaning against her window frame. "We need to get a box of pencils. Forget all that stuff I bought. Let's just erase every problem this thing has."

He stroked her cheek with his thumb. "Yeah," he said. "I wish."

That night, Alison sat on the porch with Sarah, drinking a beer, gently pushing the glider with her toe. The dancers would arrive in an hour, more practice for the Founders' Day show. Sarah was unhappy about their progress. This was, she said, the dumbest class she'd ever taught. Dumb as toadstools.

"Think you're being just a little hard on them?" Alison asked.

Sarah stopped the swaying of the glider. "You think I have a little reasonable cause to be mad?" She pointed to Bill, whom they'd been watching off and on for the last twenty minutes. He'd used his telephone spikes to climb into the bare upper branches of the trees around the yard, where he was hanging small metal garden pails full of sage and lighting fires in them, the pungent smoke falling in tatters over the yard and house. He'd carried them up on a rope attached to his work belt, and the remaining pails swung down behind him like temple bells.

"So get mad at him, not them."

She shook her head, her teeth gritted. "I'm so pissed, it spills over. Nuclear anger. I'll have to bury it in concrete for a thousand years when this is all over with."

"He means well, I guess is what I'm supposed to say."

Bill pulled another pail from the rope and looped the handle over a branch.

"Yeah, right. So did . . ." Sarah puffed out her cheeks. "Who am I trying to think of?"

Alison shrugged. "General Custer?"

"There you go. He meant well, too. Meaning well is bull, and we both know it."

Bill held the long-handled barbecue lighter down inside the pail of sage until the smoke began drifting up. He coughed. Alison didn't know what else to say. Sarah finished her beer and set the bottle on the porch. "I'm getting out of all this."

Alison looked at her. "What do you mean?"

"What do you think I mean? I'm leaving him. I can't stand this anymore."

"Sarah . . ."

"Well, to clarify, he'll be the one to leave."

Alison picked at the bottle label with her thumbnail. "He asked you just to give him until his sick leave is up, right? Then he'll quit?"

"That was the plan."

"Well, did you agree to that?"

"Yes, I sort of agreed to that. But wouldn't you think he'd stop *now*, knowing how I feel?"

Alison finished her own beer, and renewed her efforts with the glider. "Bill follows the rules. You know that. He's going to bust his butt to get you magically pregnant, for however many weeks, then when time's up, he'll quit. I know it."

Sarah was watching her husband, her look far off and clouded. Just then, he dropped one of the small pails he had hooked to his belt, the pail banging through the trees branches, spilling its contents. Sarah's breath caught, her hand jumping up to cover her mouth. "Please be careful," she said, too quietly for him to hear.

"At least give him his sick leave and then see what he does," Alison said.

Sarah nodded, wiping her eyes with her thumb. "And if it continues, I'm not kidding."

"I know."

"He's gone."

"I know."

Bill got the last pail lit and sat in the Y of a tree branch, just watching, the smoke rising into pale arms and settling out around him.

That night at the dance practice, everyone kept asking Alison where her "young man" was, falling into that kind of collective wide-eyed encouragement people usually save for slow children or the desperately shy. She didn't mind. Didn't mind that Sarah kept referring to

Max as Yosemite Sam (she'd seen the tattoo, apparently), didn't mind that Mr. Kesler kept giving her secret looks, as if they were both trench coat spies in some old movie. Twice she went out to the garage to turn the key in the ignition and to listen to the buzz of the radio, watch the headlights rise up Lazarus-like from the peeling hood of the Vette. Inside, she drank wine and ate the cheese and crackers and danced and danced with Mr. Rossi, who kept explaining to her how one day the Mississippi River would change course and head straight for the Gulf, leaving New Orleans sitting on the banks of a stinky sewage ditch, and how the OSS had once launched a plan to put estrogen in Hitler's food and turn him into a woman. She just took everything in, thinking about Max, who had gone back to Morgantown to make some measurements of the hotel. It was the most fun she'd had in a long time. Even Bill had given up his alchemy for the night and demonstrated several new moves with Sarah, showing off, dancing her into sweatiness.

Her mood carried into the next morning, when she awoke alone in her bed, the first real bite of autumn chill carried in the air. Max had stayed over in Morgantown, sleeping in the ballroom again, calling her after midnight on his cell phone. His voice echoed in the big room, where she imagined their handprints, fossils, still dotting the dusty stage, their sounds of lovemaking seeping into all that old wood and plaster. He told her that he and Tom had drunk quart bottles of Rolling Rock on the roof, then flown paper airplanes for half an hour, writing little notes on them and sending them off. One of the notes had been to her, telling her he missed her. She'd told him about Mr. Rossi, and Hitler's potential breasts, and how much she wanted him back in Wiley Ford.

As she got out of bed, there was some commotion outside, and through the window she recognized Tanner Miltenberger pulling up on his motorcycle with the battered sidecar, where he kept his scuba equipment and recovered golf balls. Following him in her big living room–size Cadillac was Frieda Landry, wearing her wide hat and pearls, and some photographer draped in cameras, wearing a fisherman's vest.

Word spread, as it will, through the town like a flu, and soon enough Mr. Kesler was there on the banks of the lake, some of the brooding boys from the vo-tech school, a few neighbors from around the lake. Mrs. Skidmore arrived with Tyra Wallace, the two of them smoking cigarettes and drinking big cups of coffee from 7-Eleven. Tanner Miltenberger looked over his small audience, the first he'd likely ever had for a dive, and smiled, his teeth half-missing and brown. He sat in the grass and tugged on his wet suit, zippering it up the back. Alison stood off to one side, her hands in her pockets, taking it all in until Mr. Kesler sidled up beside her, his powder blue jumpsuit rumpled, smelling of old sweat.

"If this doesn't fly, our little ruse," he said quietly, "thanks for trying anyway."

"Why wouldn't it fly?" She drew back a little at the word *ruse,* but that's exactly what it was.

"They're expecting to find a *car* down there, Alison, not a few scattered parts."

"But parts equal car—wasn't that the plan?" She found herself speaking in low whispers, her mouth near his ear, drawn into the intimacy of lying.

"This lake has an eight-foot drop-down stream, and they'll never be able to drain that. I mean, drain the lake, the stream is still there, okay? With me?" She nodded. "The *plan* was to say the car was somewhere on the bottom of the stream, and the parts back that up. I wasn't planning on any goddamn diver going down and searching the whole thing. I mean, this is Wiley Ford; we don't have divers."

"So what?"

"So, it's a magic trick, remember? It's the parts you can see and the bottom you can't. *That* equals car. You send Tanner Miltenberger backstage, tripping over all the wires and mirrors, it ruins everything."

This made sense to her. Even with the parts, the question remained: Where was the car? Mr. Kesler stood beside her, cracking his knuckles while Tanner Miltenberger fought with his flippers.

"It's like Nessie," she said. "The Loch Ness monster. If they could drain that lake, no more story."

He nodded. "You got it, missy. Told you you were smart. Yessir, not knowing preserves our faith. If they ever found Christ's bones, Christianity would turn into Amway. The New Testament becomes last year's almanac."

"I guess I have a lot to learn about duplicity, Gordon. Here I thought you hired Tanner Miltenberger to corroborate."

"No, ma'am. My loving son hired him. This puts me in check, right? Tightens the screws? We'll see."

The idea almost scared her, that Max might be doing this, making a chess game of his father's humiliation. And what scared her was not that he would do it, but that she had no idea if he might be thinking of such a thing. That you could never, ever really know another person, put on your own flippers and touch their dark and murky bottom. Long friendship didn't do it, nor marriage, nor sisterhood. A magic trick was right: You'd think you understood someone, had your eyes on the very last truth of them, and when you reached out your hand, that truth became nothing, the solid bottom melted into silt.

"He told you he hired Tanner Miltenberger for the express purpose of *not* finding your car?"

"Don't be naïve, Alison. No, of course, he said Mr. Miltenberger was checking out the dam, something, something. Gobbledygook."

Just then, Tanner managed the second of his flippers, then stood up, starting for the mud. He flapped out into it, tipped and awkward, while everyone stood around the banks, watching him walk down the steep pitch of the lake bottom, past the stone buildings of Colaville, past the wide arch of the bridge, under which the stream still flowed, widening out near the dam. He paused for a second to peer inside the door of one of the buildings, the one that had once been the company store. The whole thing looked so strange, a frogman down in a crater, taking a walk through a ghost town, window-shopping. When he reached the point where the arm of the stream widened out, he strode on in, vanishing in slow increments.

While they waited, there was not much to say, and talk fell to the snap of cold weather, the prospects for the high school basketball team this winter. Some of the vo-tech boys stepped inside the garage, checking out the Vette. Mrs. Skidmore told a story about a man named Winston Ackerman, who was reputed to have stayed in his house when the Corp of Engineers flooded Colaville, refusing to leave. Frieda made notes while Mrs. Skidmore explained how Winston had argued his position with a shotgun, had tacked down his rocking chair to the front porch with angle irons, then bound himself to the chair with a logging chain. He didn't want his face floating up for all those developers and town fathers to laugh at, Mrs. Skidmore said. He was staying put. When the waters began to rise, the last anyone saw of Winston Ackerman was him sitting chained to his rocker, shotgun across his lap, a cat cradled in his arm, a plate of sausage and beans on a table beside him.

"Oh, for godsakes," Gordon said. "That rot will be in tomorrow's paper, I'm sure."

"You're just jealous," Alison said.

"I suppose next week we'll have Winston Ackerman sightings. 'The Rocker Man of Wiley Ford.' Banging his logging chain against his bean plate." Gordon nervously polished his glasses with a handkerchief, huffing on them repeatedly, frowning at the results. Alison kept her eyes on the fading ripple where Tanner Miltenberger had disappeared. She imagined an entire city for him down there, instead of the one or two ruins left standing, imagined the water flooding over again, imagined the car as real and him climbing in the door, starting the engine, taking a slow tour of Colaville, waving at the bony remains of Winston Ackerman and his cat. She shook the idea away and focused on the pool of water where Tanner had disappeared, the muddy banks tapering down. Love, death, lies—they could all be so big when they were hidden, so cavernous in the dark of imagining them, and then so small and shallow when the dark drained away.

When Tanner Miltenberger came up dripping out of the water, arms held aloft as though he were being taken hostage, he held in his hands two of the hubcaps they'd tossed in. Alison watched, and felt Gordon lean in against her shoulder. "His and hers," he said. The next morning, sure enough, there were photos of Tanner Miltenberger in his wet suit and mask, carrying the two hubcaps. He looked like some space-movie alien, big shiny eyes revolving at the ends of black tentacles. The article confirmed the name *Chrysler* stamped on the side of the hubcaps, and Tanner's assertion that there were more parts down there, which he would've gone in for again, except for his bad back. Frieda Landry spent a long time describing the hubcaps, writing, "The vagaries of weather and time have done little to dull the coruscating shimmer that must have caught the inquisitorial eye of our own young Gordon Kesler." There was no mention of the condition of the dam, and the question of where the rest of the car might be never came up—not in the article, and not at Mr. Beachy's store, not in any of the gossip around town, nor in the Red Bird Cafe, where Alison sat, waiting for Max to make it back from Morgantown, to join her for lunch, to witness the quiet triumph of his father's prevailing lie.

Late that afternoon, they sat on the front porch of the house, dipping carburetor parts into a bowl of kerosene and cleaning them with old toothbrushes. She and Max worked in silence, laying the parts out on newspaper to dry. As they worked, the Founders' Day week of celebration officially began with the boom of a cannon from the high school track, signaling the start of the annual Founders' Run. Twice around the quarter-mile track, then out into the town, down past the dry cleaner's and the Honeybun Bakery, ending back at the track. All of the runners were in costume, the men wearing tutus and long blond wigs, the women in fireman coats and greasepaint mustaches, some of them carrying tennis rackets or giant cigars or poodles along the way. No one, not even Mrs. Skidmore or Frieda Landry, could remember how or why this particular tradition had gotten started, and Alison was glad for that. It was her favorite kind of history, the history with no past, like those celebrities who are famous and recognizable, but no one can recall exactly why.

Max had been held up in Morgantown and had missed that morning's paper and Frieda Landry's article, missed the cycle of gossip that had carried with it the car parts and Tanner Miltenberger. Once, when they first took to the front porch, he'd started to open the paper and read it, but she had grabbed it away from him and quickly spread it out on the porch floor for their dirty parts. How silly was this, hiding a paper from him? And for what? A fifty-year-old lie and some junkyard scraps? Alison picked up another carburetor jet and scraped it with the toothbrush, watching Max the whole time. The thought hit her again that he really couldn't care this much, that she'd somehow gotten caught up in Mr. Kesler's own paranoia, and that when Max did find out, he would laugh for five seconds and that would be the end of it. It was such a little thing, nothing.

"Be fourteen," Max said as he looked up at her.

"Pardon me?"

"Be fourteen," he said again, smiling.

"What are you talking about?"

"Oh, seven," he said.

"Let me guess," Alison said, "*Reader's Digest* is teaching you encryption."

"Bingo," he said. "I mean, no, not that."

By now she was smiling, too. "Are you drunk?"

"Not yet. I'm just asking you out. I want to go to the church hall tonight, play a little bingo."

"You do? I thought you hated all the small-town crap."

"Not bingo. My mother and I used to go all the time. I rock at bingo." He scrubbed a part, then wiped his fingers.

"I didn't know it was possible to rock at bingo."

He smiled. "Well, then, you've got a few things to learn."

St. Patrick's hall was crowded with banners and people, the former because of Founders' Day events and the latter because of the special one-thousand-dollar bonus game. Several people from the dance class were there, and it was strange to see them outside of Sarah's living room, strange to see them eating hot dogs and enjoying a regular life. Folding tables stretched the length of the hall, leaving little room for the coffee drinkers huddled around the concession area. Smokers were herded into a loft area upstairs, where the bingo caller sat in a corner with his microphone and ball machine, announcing numbers and lighting them up on a big scoreboard—like God, dealing out the evening's fate. Alison sat beside Max, the two of them manning five cards between them, covering them with the little cardboard disks as the numbers were called. The games moved with what felt like blistering speed, and there were endless variations—four corners, round-robin, fifty-fifty. Some of the ladies (as most of the players were) around and across from them managed a dozen or more cards, forsaking the cardboard disks and using fat Hi-Liters to mark their numbers. The smells of hot dogs and pizza and cigarettes became the warm odor of anticipation as the numbers echoed and flashed, culminating every ten minutes or so in the familiar shouts and the little buzz of excitement surrounding the winner. Every so often, the action would taper off into a lull, the game would halt, and God (actually, Benny Pappas from Joe and Benny's Pizza) would make announcements of anniversaries, or sick people to be remembered in prayer, or the next dance at the fire hall. Sometimes he would pick on individual people in the crowd (in this way, Alison thought, he *was* kind of like God), singling them out for teasing about their new car or new hairstyle or aftershave.

The person directly across from them, a woman with penciled-in eyebrows and the smoothest skin Alison had ever seen, took advantage of the lull to rearrange the good-luck shrine she had set up around her place, a complex heap of teddy bears, Beanie Babies, rosary beads, and photos of her grandchildren. Alison leaned back in her folding chair, holding Max's hand. Lila Montgomery waved from across the hall. Tyra Wallace made her way down from the smokers' loft to hug them both, and Max bought them Cokes and hot dogs. Benny Pappas announced that Crystal and Jeremy Engle's baby was doing better and would be home soon from the hospital and that Denton Jamison had left his headlights on in the parking lot.

"And speaking of cars," Benny said, his voice a muffled echo, "I suspect our local law-enforcement friends best have their ticket books at the ready when a certain hotshot Corvette is soon speeding through town."

Alison reflexively laughed with the rest before realizing he was talking about *her* Corvette. Every player from the two tables around them had turned to look, smiling. Max squeezed her hand under the table.

"You're just hoping I'll take you for a ride," she shouted up to Benny, and everyone laughed again.

"Oh, I think that seat will be occupied," Benny said in his most leering voice. It was Max's turn to blush. As new as she and Max were, she realized, their story had already been set down in the mind of the town, already written and familiar. The lonely young widow marries the handsome munitions expert. Frieda Landry could have written it. Alison remembered how she'd anticipated missing the car, missing AAAA and Mr. Beachy, knowing that change took everything away. But really, what did she know? Did she know more than an entire town, more than the years that had given them a religion built on repetition, a God who let someone win every game? She saw herself then for how she'd been these past twenty-three months, viewing the town as beneath her for all its provinciality, a town that had lost hundreds to wars and a few more each week to the ordinary ways of dying—she'd thought she knew loss better, knew it more, took it to her empty bed each night. But loss had pulled her out of her life, while the town kept moving on, kept imagining its own existence, its own life—like some fairy-tale creature, dreaming itself into being. It was a town built on quiet belief—that the tourists would show up, that Gordon's car was down there somewhere, that her Corvette would soon draw speeding tickets. Not a bad way to live a life—write your stories out of what you imagine, and imagine out of whatever past sustains your future. If you missed one or two, if the tourists didn't show, then you'd played enough cards to win the next one, or the next. Her failure with Marty had been a failure of this same kind of imagination, their unwillingness to foresee a future of happiness, and in that unwillingness the further unwillingness to carve out a space in which that happiness might occur. Already, in the eyes of the town, she and Max were speeding through town in a shiny Corvette, wedding rings on their fingers, their children filling the elementary school and trying out for peewee football. She could imagine a worse future. Could, but—for now—didn't.

They jumped back into another round of bingo, and Max even won twenty-five dollars on one of the quickie games. They kissed, and Benny Pappas, missing nothing, embarrassed them all over again. Just as they settled in with their cards for a new game, there was a small flurry of commotion by the front door.

"Hold the phone and stop the presses," Benny nearly shouted through the mike. "Here's the man of the hour."

"Who?" Max said. They both looked back in time to see Gordon—once again, the late Mr. Kesler—walking through the entrance, carrying a paper Food Lion sack and dressed not in his usual jumpsuit but in a plaid sport coat and orange shirt, a porkpie hat on his head. He looked like he was there to sell everyone a used car.

"For those of you who didn't read this morning's paper," Benny announced, "be sure and talk to Gordon tonight and ask him what's what."

"What is what?" Max said, turning to Alison. She felt her face warming, her eyes burning.

"A little of Gordon's past, and, I might add, our very own past, came out of that lake yesterday," Benny said. "A part that's soon, I understand—am I right on this, Tilda?—to find its way into the Mineral County museum."

As if it were scripted, Gordon reached into the paper sack and withdrew one of the chromed hubcaps, waving it above his head and beaming, the hubcap shining under the lights. Some of the people there applauded, while Gordon collected backslaps and handshakes.

"I don't get it," Max whispered. "What is that?"

The woman with the penciled-in eyebrows leaned across the table. "Congratulations," she said to Max.

"It's a car part," Alison said.

"Not your Corvette . . ." He looked genuinely confused, and in that second Alison knew that Mr. Kesler had lied to her about Max hiring Tanner Miltenberger, about wanting to "tighten the screws."

"No, not my Vette." She could hardly breathe. "Uncle Crawford's Chrysler."

Max looked back at his father, still collecting congratulations while Benny announced the last game of the night, while the hubcap made its way like a collection plate up and down the long tables.

"Not possible," Max said. "He's lying. That thing didn't come out of the lake."

"Well, yes, he's lying, but also yes, it came out of the lake." The warmth and smoke smell and noise settled over her, pressing her down, sticking her shirt to her back. She felt the hot dog and Coke churning her stomach.

"Alison, there's no Chrysler *down* there, just an old, old lie." He looked, for half a second, as if he doubted this assertion, as if, like the rest of the town, he wanted to be pulled into believing.

She leaned in to whisper. "The parts are down there because he put them down there. He threw them in so people could find them."

Above them, Benny called out, "I-forty-three," and the players marked their cards.

"How do you know about this?" Max said.

She looked at him. It's such a small thing, she wanted to say. Just an old man's story, just let it be.

"He told me," she said. Her own lie.

"B-twenty-three," Benny called. Clouds from the smokers up in the loft spun in slow wisps around the arc lights.

"Why?" Max said. Across his shoulder, she saw Gordon heading in their direction, smiling, carrying his hubcap in both hands like a salver.

"No, he didn't tell me." She shook her head. "Max, this whole thing . . . it's just so *mindless*. I mean, what's the point?"

"He told you and he didn't tell you? Which is it, Alison?"

Gordon slowly made his way down the aisle toward them, stopping now and then to show the hubcap to someone else. Benny called, "G-nineteen," and flashed it on the board.

"I helped him," she said as evenly as she could. "He had a whole box of parts and I helped him throw them in."

He drew back to look at her. "Why? Why would you do that?"

"I don't know." She shook her head again. "It was a whim; I thought I was helping."

Max's face had grown tight and hard, his round glasses reflecting the arc lights.

"Tell them," he said. "Tell everyone—her—" He pointed to the woman with the Beanie Babies and teddy bears. "Tell her right now what you just told me." His voice grew louder.

"Max, please . . ."

"Tell her it's a lie." A muscle throbbed in his jaw.

"Why does it matter?" she said. She reached out, expecting him to draw back. Instead, he took her hand and held it flat on his palm to examine it, her hand some found object, a vaguely interesting rock. He set her hand back on her leg.

"If you don't understand that," he said, "then you don't understand a thing about me."

He stood up to leave just as Gordon reached them with the hubcap.

"Your old man made the paper yet again, son," Gordon said. He offered the hubcap, and Max took it. From where she sat, Alison saw his face reflected in the chrome, curved and distorted, a portable fun-house mirror. The name CHRYSLER, stamped in red, cut across the middle of his rounded face.

"That's really nice, Dad," he said. What else could he say? The whole town thought it was nice, too, the nicest thing that had happened to them in a long time.

"You see that?" Max held the hubcap out to her, she saw herself reflected in it, the entire room behind her held in that curve of polished steel. "What do you have to say about that?"

She could say to everyone here—stand up, as in class, and lecture—that somehow a myth could look like only a cheap lie to someone, while it held great truth for someone else, like those optical illusions where the drawing is both a skull and a beautiful lady. She could tell Max to let it go and stop torturing himself with the past, tell Gordon the same thing, ask for a show of hands, *how many here had shitty fathers?,* ask God in his corner how it was that a single betrayal could be so small and weigh so much, could be held in nothing more than a junkyard scrap that in turn could hold the whole town in its shiny face. But God had just called the winning number again, and a small whirlwind of celebration stirred near the back, while the rest tossed their used cards in quiet defeat. It was the last game of the night. Alison said nothing as Max turned and walked out. Gordon strode into the mingling crowd with his hubcap. Benny Pappas shut down the scoreboard and drew a canvas cover over the ball machine, putting away his deification for the night. Back to earth, back to making pizzas, back to being human again.

**—from the *Haynes Automotive Repair Manual:***
**Chevrolet Corvette, 1968 thru 1982**

Regardless of how enthusiastic you may be about getting on with the job at hand, take the time to ensure that your safety is not jeopardized. A moment's lack of attention can result in a mishap. The possibility of an accident will always exist with any restoration project, and it would be impossible to compile a comprehensive list of all dangers involved in any such undertaking.

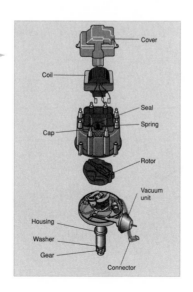

# 10

Days passed with no word from Max, days in which she kept calling his cell phone, imagining it ringing out in that big empty ballroom, echoing its beeping little tune. Mr. Kesler had been all over town making appearances, had been asked to cut the ribbon at the opening of Flow Motor's new service center, posed for pictures at the Mineral County museum, and had spoken to a group of Cub Scouts as part of the Founders' Day festivities—he and his hubcap, as if they were Hollywood's brightest new couple. Finally, she gave up on Max's phone, went to the Red Bird and loaded up on coffee, and headed to Mr. Beachy's to prepare for a long night of work. She noticed on the way that DISCOUNT RAGE had fixed the burned-out neon tubes only to have others go bad, so that the sign now read DISCO BEVERAGE.

She laid out for Mr. Beachy everything she had done on the car, everything she thought she had left to do, at least to get it running. The day before, a new credit card had arrived in the mail, and she'd called the number to activate it. For now, she wouldn't think about how deeply in debt she was.

"I want the car to run," she told Mr. Beachy. "I want to get the thing moving as soon as possible, and drive it the hell out of here. Excuse my language."

He waved away her apology, began thumbing through the thick catalogs. "I'm not too keen on that lake of fire business. Just a story for scaring kids, as far as I'm concerned." He leaned across the counter and showed her all the belts and hoses she would need, plus new spark plugs and spark plug wires, oil filter, air filter, points, and condenser.

"This is shade-tree stuff," he told her. "You could do this in your sleep, Alison."

"That's more or less the plan."

He boxed all the parts and rang up her purchase. While they waited for the new credit card to be approved, he dropped a few tracts into the box. "New ones," he said. "Thought about you when I got them in."

She pulled them out and looked at them. The first one showed a smiling cartoon wife with her kids, ascending into heaven on a cloud-draped escalator, moving toward the beams of light above them, while back on the ground her husband wept over his family's wrecked car. Inside were more cartoons, illustrating a predictable story about Fred and his family finally attending church and praying together after putting it off for many years, saving their souls just a day before the terrible wreck. On the last page, the father was smiling over their graves while a cartoon balloon from his mouth said, "I know that they are with the Lord now, and someday I will be, too!" The tract was titled "BE NOT AFRAID."

"Is this how you picture it?" Alison asked. Mr. Beachy looked up from stapling her receipt to the box, startled. She'd never really talked about the tracts before.

"You told me once it was hard for you to believe," she said, "so I just wonder about this." She showed him the cartoon. "It just seems too easy." She thought of Marty, imagining the afterlife as a mall full of toy stores.

"Well, maybe that's the message, that it *is* easy. More so than we think."

"But escalators? Sunlight? You really want to spend eternity in an atrium lobby?"

He took the tract and held it at arm's length to read it. "We just can't picture it, so we make it up best we can. No artist could imagine it."

"And you really believe this? That we should all be not afraid?"

He thought about this. "Faith is a steep and rocky path, but for the most part, yes, ma'am, I do believe that."

The thought came to her then that had Marty lived, had he never had any accident that day in Lem's backyard, he would have turned out much like Mr. Beachy. A quiet faith filling up a quiet life. Would he have ever convinced her, won her over to thinking this way? She couldn't say; she was only the man on the ground, standing beside the broken car. The family got clouds and heavenly escalators, while he got only religious tracts and wreckage and his own failed imagination. It didn't seem fair. But even if she had never believed with him, knowing Mr. Beachy had shown her something even deeper, maybe—she could have loved Marty. Over time, his child-ishness worn down to a simple sweetness, his years of faith and work adding up to a kind of lived life, old age plowing into him a little deeper, she could have. Mr. Beachy cleared his throat.

"Until you need to do an overhaul," he said, "you've just about spent your last dollar in here. Take her down to the transmission shop once she's rolling, and then Dave Fisher is your man for body and frame work."

"But I can still come here and talk about theology and brake pads, right?"

"Oh, you have to, Alison. And I want a ride in that car when it's done."

She leaned across and kissed his cheek. "You got it."


Wednesday morning's mail brought an envelope from Lem, Polaroid photos of her finished house, all the rooms freshly car-peted and painted, the floors polished. A short note from Pammy told her everything was done, and done right, the way Marty would've wanted it. She showed the photos to Sarah.

"Man, they did a good job," Sarah said. "Looks new."

"But the pictures are . . . weird, you know?" Alison said. "They're like ransom photos. 'If you ever want to see this house alive again—' "

"—then go live in it?" Sarah said.

Alison didn't answer, just thumbed through the stack again. It didn't look new at all, really. In fact, it looked ten years old, like the first year they lived there, all of the stuff right back where it had been, the hooks in the corner draped with Marty's field coat and ball caps.

"They forgot the velvet ropes," Alison said.

"What do you mean?"

"A security guard."

*"What?"*

Alison shook her head. "Nothing."

Sarah was quiet a minute, leaning on the sink, watching her. "You won't go back there, ever, will you? I mean, we should all just chuck that idea."

Alison looked at the harsh photo of her old bedroom, the clock radio glowing and blurred on the nightstand. When she tried to put herself in the photos, sitting on the couch reading, or at the stove cooking, it seemed fake, like one of those cardboard "pose-your-own-photo" cutouts of ex-presidents on the streets of D.C.

"I can't."

"Then sell it. It's never looked better. Use the money for a new place."

"I can't do *that,* either, Sarah. I can't just unload it after all the work they put in."

"Well, what's your big idea, then?"

She shrugged. "I don't have one. I can't go home and I can't stay here. You know what I'm like? A drunk at closing time. Except one thing . . ."

Sarah smiled. "What?"

"I'm not drunk."

That afternoon, Bill began painting all the trim on the house lavender, and planted two holly bushes in the front yard. She didn't even bother asking anymore. His efforts were no different from hers or anyone else's, everyone just spinning their own little hamster wheel, thinking their wheel was the most important one in the whole world. She skipped the final dress rehearsal for the parade, and spent her evening in the garage, installing all the new parts Mr. Beachy had sold her. He was right: She didn't really even need her manual very much for this stuff. It took time, was all, a few bruised knuckles. Near midnight, she was under the car, draining oil, and heard the dancers leaving, heard their excited talk of the parade, heard the van pull away and Sarah close the front door. As she filled the crankcase with new oil, she could hear other sounds, the men fishing the drop-down stream and its small bulge of remaining lake, Bill nailing something else to the house and, from the sound of it, to the trees out front. He had only a few days left on his sick leave. Another drunk at closing time.

At one in the morning, she gapped and installed the spark plugs, changed the wires, checked and set the points, checked the static timing, and closed the hood. She was done with the engine, for now at least, assuming she didn't have to pull it for something major. Next would be bodywork, all that expensive disaster Max kept talking about the first time he'd seen the car. But for now, the car could stop and it could go. She sat in the driver's seat, slid the key into the ignition, and turned it. Nothing. She popped open the battery access, twisted the connections and tightened them, then tried again. The engine turned over, filling her garage with fumes, not quite starting. Something, a trick Mr. Beachy had taught her . . . what was it? She tried the key again, winding it out until the turning slowed, her battery draining. What was that trick? She pictured someone smoking . . . a lighter . . . *lighter fluid*. She got out, finished the coffee in her thermos, and made her way into the dark house. After a quick, quiet rummage through drawers of dead batteries and corn-on-the-cob holders and clothespins, she found the familiar skinny yellow can. Back in the garage, she popped the hood, removed the air filter, and squirted some of the fluid down into the throat of the carburetor. How much? The last thing she needed was a fire, some middle-of-the-night catastrophe. She erred on the side of just a little bit, then sat back in the driver's seat.

On the first turn, the engine kicked over with a throaty *floom* that rattled the walls of the garage, and sat idling. It ran. The damn thing was *running*. She leaned back, fingers shaking lightly on the steering wheel, and just listened. The idle was not quite even, missing now and again. Probably the timing was off, but not too bad. And loud, the exhaust rusted through. She jumped out long enough to replace the air cleaner and latch the hood, to check the house for lights to make sure she hadn't awakened anyone. The *sound* of it, of her car. Like that coma patient she'd always imagined it, suddenly sitting up in bed and asking for steak and potatoes, asking who won the World Series, inviting her out for a walk. *Out.* She could take the car out. But no, that would be dumb. Her brakes hadn't been bled yet, still had to be pumped just to get any pressure, and no one yet knew how bad the chassis was, if the car was even structurally sound, as Max liked to say. If only Max could be here. So much of the work had been his anyway. She closed the door and flicked on her headlights, watched them slide up, one set still burned out, then levered the gearshift into first, released the brake, let the clutch out. The Vette rolled evenly out onto the gravel drive.

*Where to?* She said this aloud to the passenger seat, as if the self that watched her were along for the ride, then turned and looked back at the empty space where the car had sat for so long, and in answer to her own question shrugged and started down the driveway, tires crunching on the gravel, the engine rough but not awful, shocks squeaking. Finally, she made the paved road and the car settled out as she picked up a little speed. Then she tried to brake and braking was not good, the pedal needing three hard pumps before she got any pressure. But once it pressured up, the new brakes held. She'd stopped in the middle of the road, her one headlight mispointed off to the weedy side of the road, the dashboard glowing. She clicked on the radio, and the oldies station gave her Steppenwolf singing "Magic Carpet Ride," which seemed almost appropriate, except that magic carpets didn't rattle and scrape along the pavement. As she started up again, she tilted her head back and looked through the open top at the map of stars pasted to the wide sky, noticing then how really cold it was, too cold for an open car and no coat, but who cared? She said it out loud, giving her voice to the wind, speaking again to her imagined self: *Who cares?* She worked through the gears, then, as Midlothian Road straightened out, she downshifted into third and punched it hard, the car fast enough to press her back into her seat. Midlothian made a gentle rise as she shifted to fourth, the speedometer showing eighty-five now, a long stretch of blacktop before her, the wind a noisy, lunatic thing that lived somewhere above the car, and it felt so good, driving this way, arms sprouting goose bumps, hair tangled out behind her, the car fighting her only slightly, pulling right, the engine buried and rumbling under that long silver hood. She took it to ninety, howled at the night, heard small bugs popping off the windshield as the needle edged up a little more. Then she thought about her brakes, her mushy brakes, and eased off, backing down to the speed limit as the car hit the edge of town.

She drove through the square, under the DISCO BEVERAGE sign, past the window of the Red Bird, where Mr. Davidow stood in the faint light of closing time, closing out his register. She drove past the dry cleaner's, past a pair of teenage boys sitting on the Greyhound bench, both of whom whistled at her. Past the Honeybun Bakery, Joe and Benny's pizza, and the building, now closed, that had once been the YWCA. She left town and came in toward the lake from the other side, all the way around Loop Road, past Sarah's driveway, then off again, another turn around the lake, then another. She thought of Lem and Marty's plan for a perpetual-motion machine, magnets mounted on turntables or some such thing, their plans just vague enough to believe in. She had the car going, so what now? And with barely another thought, she turned hard off Loop Road, back onto Midlothian, out onto I-68, heading toward Morgantown.

Half an hour into the trip, she realized how stupid this was, in the same way all impulses are stupid: She hadn't thought through all that could go wrong. The car could break down, or break in *half,* according to Max; she had no registration, no license plate, a burned-out headlight. It was 4:00 A.M., she hadn't slept, and she was wearing a T-shirt and jeans and clogs, freezing in the middle-of-the-night chill. She kept to the speed limit, as though it had been dictated to her by God, and tried to relax, dialing in a talk show on the radio, whistling and patting the steering wheel, as if nervousness would be the first thing the cops noticed. Her car ran. Every so often, she reminded herself of the fact. It ran pretty well, too, with only that little blip in the exhaust—the timing, it had to be—and the tendency to pull right, and the squeaks. The brakes weren't much of a worry on a highway trip.

Near Finzel, she passed God's Lighthouse of Redemption, a big tacky church with a nautical theme, a lighthouse in place of a steeple, its revolving green light shining out over the cow pastures and Christmas-tree farms. Their roadside signboard read GOD IS A PORT IN EVERY STORM, and she imagined the preacher wearing a blue blazer with gold buttons, white slacks, and a little white captain's hat, the ushers in yellow slickers, tossing out life preservers during the altar call, the walls of the church decorated with nets and cork, like a seafood restaurant. She drove past, smiling. A little farther down, a dead deer lay twisted at the side of the road, its mouth still wet-looking, and farther still, a trucker had pulled off and was peeing at the side of the road, lit up by his own taillights. The moon rolled along overhead as the talk show faded out and some old doo-wop song faded in. Something under the car dropped down enough to scrape the pavement, but she kept going, past a lawn chair sitting in the median, a case of empties in the middle of the road, the bright suddenness of truck stops at the tops of the off-ramps. Finally, she pulled off into one and left the Vette idling, afraid that if she turned it off, it wouldn't start again. The windows inside were fogged over with the steam off the coffeemakers, and a radio hidden somewhere at the back of the counter played country songs. Two bleary-eyed men in plaid shirts and caps sat at one of the booths in back, eating plates of eggs and drinking Cokes, both of them looking at a crossword puzzle.

Alison bought coffee and a package of little powdered doughnuts, and, on impulse, a pack of cigarettes, even though she had not smoked since grad school.

"You headed east or west?" the man behind the counter asked

her. He had the thickest black hair she'd ever seen, and a shirt pocket stuffed with tire gauges. She told him she was headed to Morgantown.

"You're kind of late for Morgantown," he said, which struck her as an odd thing to say. Did they close Morgantown at night? Then again, maybe she *was* late, maybe Max had finished his work there, moved on, was sleeping in some other hotel, some other town.

Back in the car, she found the same country station that the man had on in the store. Some song about tears and raindrops. She never understood why this music—so effusively sad and woeful, so maudlin about love and heartbreak—had been embraced by truckers and redneck boys and workingmen. Maybe they needed an antidote to all that male stoicism. Or it was code, sent out to the women in the world: *Listen to us, we're just as sad and broken as you are.* She drove, keeping her speed down, smoking in shallow drags and flicking her ashes through the T-top.

She took the airport exit into Morgantown, then tried to remember—right or left? The last thing she needed was to get lost in town in the middle of the night. Morgantown didn't have all the problems of a big city, but it did have its share of bad stuff, even gang violence, though she always imagined the gangs in West Virginia as just minor-league farm teams for real gangs. Finally, the terrain started to look familiar, and she made her way downtown, rode in her rumbling, scraping car up and down the grid of streets until suddenly, almost without realizing it, she was in front of the Hotel Morgantown. It was 5:30, the first edge of slate-colored morning just beginning to peel back along the horizon. By now, she was shaking with highway cold and nerves, her teeth chattering. She turned off the Vette, then quickly restarted it, just to be sure. The engine ticked in the quiet cold. Off somewhere in the distance was some grinding, mechanical sound, like a giant fan turning. Music echoed from somewhere, and a dog barked a few times, then stopped. The wind gusted, paper cups and leaves moving up the lighted sidewalks as if they had someplace to be.

The doors of the hotel were chained shut, and, now that she

thought to look for it, Max's truck was nowhere around. She rattled the doors a few times, knocked, peered inside. Where could he be? She walked around the back, where the tall windows opened up on the ballroom, and stood on a trash can to look in. Empty. She knocked on the window a few more times before giving up. On the way back around front, she noticed the door to the kitchen, behind the trash cans, had been propped open slightly with a soda can. She recognized the kitchen from last time, the stove with its shadow of grease, the fans above it missing.

"Max?" She walked through the ballroom, trying not to let her clogs echo so loudly. "Are you here?" Somewhere in the building, water dripped. She found their vanilla wafer box still on the stage, and some of Max's det-cord spools sitting by the basement door.

Upstairs, the carpet rolls had been removed, and here and there holes had been drilled into the walls. She called his name on all the floors, knowing he wasn't there, but reluctant to leave. Though the Corvette had gotten her here, it seemed somehow impossible that it could take her back. At the end of the top floor, she climbed the iron ladder and opened the door out onto the roof. Dawn had arrived, finally, the sky a lumpy pinkish gray. There was a dampness to the air and hints of low fog, as though it had just rained. She walked around on the gravel, looking over the edge, even though it made her dizzy. From here, the Vette looked pretty bad, the silver paint peeled and blotchy, a dull gray underneath. Maybe it would be like a house—paint would make it look new. But silver wasn't quite right; something about the silver and maroon together was just too tacky, a bridal suite in Las Vegas. She could replace the entire interior, but she liked maroon. Black paint would look good. Black and maroon. She squinted at the car, trying to imagine it with brand new paint. Then she spit over the side and watched it fall, wondering what the attraction was—almost every male she'd ever known was a big fan of spitting over the sides of things. Probably half of the Colorado River was spit.

"Ali*sewn*!" she suddenly heard, and jumped so her knee banged the low wall around the ledge. When she turned around, it took her a second to find Tom, who sat in the opposite corner from last time, knees to his chest, bundled under a blanket.

"Damn it, Tom," she said, "you about sent me over the side."

"Aaah," he said, almost a gargling sound, "you don't want to do that." He slurred his words, and she noticed then the scattered pile of quart beer bottles beside him on the gravel. She walked over to him and squatted down.

"Are you okay, Tom?"

"Me? Yeah, I'm just a little sick. Upset stomach . . . an undigested bit of beef, a blot of mustard, a crumb of cheese, a fragment of an underdone potato. You know . . . the usual."

She pointed. "Four quarts of Bud."

He smiled. "The reference eludes me. However, I'm in bang-up shape. Never better." Beneath his blanket, a collection of paper airplanes lay crushed and wrinkled.

"Are you sure?"

"I'm sure."

"Have you seen Max?"

He looked at her, squinting, his lips cracked. "Since you're his lady and I most decidedly am not, I ought to be asking *you* that, shouldn't I? Trouble, I take it?"

"Yes, trouble. He's not here?"

"He was yesterday, drilling most of the day. Brought me a sandwich and we broke bread around noon. That was the last."

"Well, thanks anyway, Tom."

"Is he not treating you well?"

"He's fine . . ." She hesitated. "Maybe you should ask how I'm treating him."

Tom pulled his blanket higher around his neck, the wind stirring the airplanes in tight circles around him. "I have a hard time pegging you for any meanness."

"I lied to him, Tom."

He clicked his tongue, coughed. "They say all politics are personal, right? Well, the inverse is also true. Just say you're sorry and try to mean it. Everyone lies."

She smiled. "You're pretty cynical for a man who plays with paper airplanes."

His laugh drew him into a hacking fit, his face reddening. "God love you, Ali*sewn*. I'd keep you even if you did lie." He held up two of the wrinkled planes, his yellow fingers shaking. "Have at it," he said.

She took the green one, and he took the white, and they tossed them again on the count of three, watched them limp and loop their way to the ground.

"Tom," she said, still looking with him over the ledge, "where I live, they flooded a town to make a lake, and when they did, one man refused to leave."

"Harry Truman," Tom said.

Her mind jumped to the atom bomb and the Marshall Plan. "What are you talking about?"

"Harry Truman is the dude's name who did the same thing when Mount Saint Helens blew. Refused to leave. I guess that twenty-five feet of scalding ash kept him warm for the winter."

"Our guy was named Winston Ackerman. He chained himself to his front porch."

"A flair for the dramatic. I wonder if those guys form a club in the afterlife. Dumb Asses Anonymous or something." He shook his head, his eyes still following one of the planes, which was lifted on updrafts over and over.

Alison looked down at him, the top of his head covered with thinning brown hair and faint scars. "Listen," she said. "I hope you don't have any plans for joining that club."

"Me?"

"Yeah, you. When this building comes down, you'd better have someplace else to be."

"Friends and couches. Don't worry over me, Alisewn."

She nodded and patted him on the shoulder. "Hey, if you see Max, tell him I'm looking for him."

"He'll be around. Why don't you leave a note?" Tom produced a chewed-up Bic pen from his windbreaker and offered her the back of one of his stolen flyers. She scrawled a quick note, telling Max she would be in her garage or at the Founders' Day Parade, that she wanted to see him, that she was sorry. Tom folded the note and stuck it in his pocket, where, she imagined, it might stay forever.

She was pulled over by the state police only a hundred yards or so from her exit. It was not yet rush hour, the sun just an idea of orange low on the horizon, the policeman's eyes puffy with fatigue. She had not slept at all, and felt jangly and frayed. While the cop ran her license through his computer, she sat in the chill and smoked another cigarette before deciding it was a bad idea and chucking the entire pack out the window into the ditch. Dumb. Now he would write her up for littering. She had smoked at grad-school parties when she and Marty first started going out, and though he didn't like it, he said nothing until after they were married. He had used on her the argument that her body was God's temple, a justification that struck her as so old-fashioned and quaint that she'd been moved to hear him use it. Now that she'd made the connection, it struck her as exactly the kind of reasoning Mr. Beachy would use. What a thing, to have married a man who thought her body was a temple, a place of worship, who wanted only to love it and see no damage done to it. And what had she done? Mocked his argument, asked him why it was okay to stuff God's temple with Vienna sausages and pork rinds. She was clever and funny, that she was, but if she was also touched and moved, what would it have hurt to have shown him that as well? She imagined him sitting right beside her, right now, in the passenger seat, the way all those TV psychics insist the dead stake us out, sitting in his floppy work boots, his leather watchband smelling of sweat, his hair trimmed too far above his ears. "I'm sorry," she whispered, and if she could find any faith in anything, have any of the belief that had come so easily to him and to Mr. Beachy, then she wanted only ten seconds' worth, enough to believe that he heard her.

The cop, it turned out, loved Corvettes, and so he let her off with

only a written warning. She told him to go get some sleep, and he
smiled and patted the car.


She napped for a couple of hours, her sleep fitful and interrupted
by the shouts and noises of Sarah assembling everyone for the
parade, the screen door banging with the arrival of the Seven
Springs crowd, rehearsal music from the boom box and the shuffle
of all those pairs of feet. Finally she gave up, got up, and showered,
the drive to Morgantown coming back to her now like some elaborate dream, the conversation with Tom seeming days or weeks ago,
instead of just a few hours. She let the warm water wash over her,
trying to forget Max's presence in this same shower with her just
days ago. Time kept slipping out from under her, a fun-house floor
beneath her unsteady feet. Her sleepy brain played tricks on her,
and twice she shut the water off, thinking that someone was calling
her name. When she closed her eyes, she got a picture of Harry
Truman, the ex-president, holding aloft his DEWEY DEFEATS TRUMAN
newspaper while piles of scalding ash fell down around him.

She took her coffee out onto the front porch and suddenly saw,
as if it had been that way all along, that the dam was gone. Yellow
bulldozers moved over and around the empty space where the dam
had been, a child's mouth with a tooth knocked out. The lake was
almost totally dry now, except for the drop-down stream, which—
though it was a wide, slow-moving creek—looked insignificant at
the bottom of that big lake bed, skirting around the dam through a
big trench gouged out by a backhoe. She stood a moment, watching
the bulldozers crawl around, wondering what was going on. What
happened to Max? To blowing it up?

In the morning's mail was another packet of photos from Lem.
They no longer even looked real to her, they looked like photos of
someone's dollhouse, paper floors and balsa-wood stairs. She didn't
know how to read the fact that Lem was sending the photos. Maybe
he was just proud of his work or hoping to tempt her back into her
nice new house. Maybe he was just being a good friend. But it also

really did feel like he was sending ransom photos, with the same kind of threat behind them: Pay up. And she *did* owe him, in fact. Had never, since Marty's death, paid enough sorrow or sympathy, enough guilt or suffering. And who better to pay it to than Lem, who had lost the one person he most loved in the world? Now he'd built a shrine, and she was absent even as penitent. She stuck the photos away in the kitchen drawer.

Mr. Rossi, all decked out in his silver-buttoned vest, his hair slicked back, moved around the edges of the living room while Sarah shouted out a string of reminders and some of the others practiced their moves. He paced back and forth, rubbing his hands together, bouncing on his toes. Last year, he'd been nervous, too (he was one of only three repeat students), saying he didn't like an audience and never had. She stood with him now, patted his big shoulder, and told him he would be fine, the best one out there. He smiled down at her.

"You're a charitable soul, Miss Alison," he said.

"They should make you keynote speaker. I bet you know more about this town than anyone."

"Well, I know a good bit. Did you know Wiley Ford once elected a pony as mayor of the town? Had to go to state court to overturn it."

She smiled. "See what I mean?"

"But they don't want to hear about that down at the shrine hall. They want to hear about all the captains of industry who hail from their fair burg. As if any existed."

"Dates and occasions," Alison said. "Believe me, it's the same in teaching. Everybody learns the little rhyme about Columbus. No one cares that he had blond hair and was known for gambling."

Mr. Rossi nodded. "Last spring, after I won the tournament at Charleston, I was asked to speak at the elementary school. I mentioned in passing that an elephant weighs less than the tongue of a blue whale, and the next day I got a phone call, someone wanting to know why I was spreading indecency through our schools. Indecency!" By now, his face was red, as if he really had been spreading indecency.

"We're two of a kind, Arthur," Alison said.

"That we are."

A few minutes later, as Bill and Sarah were herding everyone out-side to the van, the phone rang. Sarah told Alison to let the machine get it. After the beep, Alison heard Max's voice saying something about the note from Tom, about missing her by fifteen minutes. She picked up.

"You're there," he said.

"Barely. The parade is in half an hour."

"Alison, listen," he said, then fell silent.

"To anything in particular?" she said, smiling, almost crying with relief at hearing his voice.

"All this crap with my father, it just makes me nuts. It always has."

"Yeah, I know. And I don't understand it."

"Is he there now?"

"He's in the van, waiting with the rest."

"Waiting for you?"

She looked out the window, saw Sarah's car roll forward in the drive a few feet. "Yeah, for me. Want me to wave them on?" She felt her rib cage rising up with her breathing.

"No, I'll meet you there, at the parade. Just give me forty-five minutes or so, okay? I have some things to say to you, but not on the phone."


Nothing about the parades ever changed—Founders' Day, Hal-loween, Arbor Day, all of them featured the same attractions: fire trucks and police cars and the county's lone EMS vehicle, all with lights flashing; a quartet of VFW men in their woolen uniforms, marching with white wooden rifles; several antique cars ferrying beauty queens and the mayor; pickup trucks sponsored by Joe and Benny's and the Red Bird, filled with groups of children from the Catholic school, boys with their clip-on ties and girls in their plaid jumpers; a single car from the ham radio club; a few motorcycle rid-ers in leathers (Tanner Miltenberger was among this group); the Falcons marching band, baton twirlers leading the way; and a group of stragglers waving little plastic American flags. Some of the details changed: New politicians would be elected to ride in the cars; last year's Harvest Queen had moved on to the state college to major in PE; a local business had failed in the last year, or newly opened. But for the most part, one parade looked pretty much like any other, with half the town turning out to watch the other half march down Main Street.

Alison helped Sarah get her dancers ready, gave Mr. Rossi a kiss on the cheek for luck, then found her place along the sidewalk, in front of the Red Bird. Mr. Beachy sidled up beside her, and she thought of that night when they had sat in the diner and had coffee, and she wondered now if they could sit in there again and she could tell him how much he reminded her of her late husband, or of what her late husband might have turned out to be, if he'd been allowed to turn out at all. Probably the idea would sound nothing but morbid coming out of her mouth, and he would be embarrassed on top of it. She commented instead about the parade, which had finally got going after a slow start. The town's four police cruisers rolled along, flashing and honking, followed by the EMS vehicle. Mr. Beachy leaned toward her and said that now was the perfect time to commit a crime on the east side of town. She laughed. Up and down the gently sloping sidewalks, teenagers from Pizza Express sold slices out of insulated bags. Duncan's Bar had a small area where patrons could drink beer outside, cordoned off with frayed rope and traffic cones. Rolling slowly behind the last fire truck was an old T-Bird the color of mint toothpaste, a Model T hot rod, and a convertible Mustang. All three carried teenage beauty queens in tiaras and spangly prom dresses, waving their gloved hands at the crowds.

"Looks like the year for Fords," Mr. Beachy said. "Come next year, you'll be out there."

"I'll be Miss Farm Bureau?"

"Your *car*," he shouted above the noise. "In the parade."

The hay truck Sarah used for her dancers appeared at the top of the street, waiting its turn to join the parade, the dancers sitting awkwardly on the boards. Alison checked her watch, waiting for Max to arrive, standing on her toes to see above the crowd, looking for that almost metallic shine of his hair. Mr. Beachy bought a slice of pizza for each of them. The farm queens rolled on past, giving way to the feathered hats of the marching bands, the gut-shake of the bass drums and bright flash of the trombones in the sunlight, the fat kids and the short ones making the best of their ill-fitting uniforms, the baton twirlers happily showing off, ignoring the occasional drop. It was such a moment, a snapshot of an early September afternoon when a small town took the time to regard itself with nostalgia and love, such a perfect moment then that Alison, just a day later, would hold it in memory and turn it over like some relic, wondering at how an afternoon could be so innocent, caught up in a moment so fine, never knowing that the next could be so terrible.

Test the brakes at various speeds with both light and heavy pedal pressure. The vehicle should stop evenly without pulling to one side or the other.

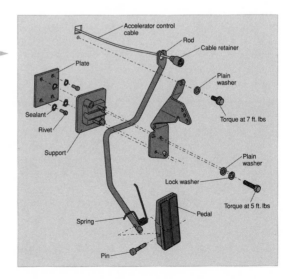

# 11

The waiting area of the ICU at Sacred Heart Hospital looked like any other—vinyl furniture, a table full of Legos, magazines scattered across end tables, a potted plant, a soundless TV mounted on the wall. Like someone's rec room, Alison thought, cheerful and mundane, trying to fool us into thinking that we're home and comfortable, that everything will be okay. It would be more honest if they made it look like a dark alley, or if they made it rain. She tried to explain this to Sarah, but fatigue played havoc with her words.

"You aren't making any sense," Sarah said.

"I know. I don't even know why I said it."

"But I know how you mean," Bill said.

"Does anyone mind, please, just shutting up for now?" Sarah said. She wadded a tissue in her hands. "Ali, go home and sleep."

Except for her quick nap that morning, she actually hadn't slept since the night before she drove to Morgantown. Already, this day— the one that had started out so brightly at the parade—was edging into dusk, the fluorescent lights up and down the hall taking on weight as the light through the windows dimmed. Lack of sleep became a buzzing, popping thing centered somewhere behind her eyes, which felt scalded and dry. Lila Montgomery and Mrs. Skidmore had stayed until dinnertime, and then got a ride back to Seven Springs, promising to return soon.

Along the wall, a woman sat knitting, bands of green and white spilling out of her lap and onto the floor, while her little boy played under one of the tables. He kept stacking Legos and knocking them down, methodical as a production line. His face was smeared with something dark—grape juice, it looked like—his hair spiky and dirty blond, quivering as he muttered to himself. Someday, he might be famous, Alison thought. He could be president, or could pitch a no-hitter in the World Series, or could kill twenty people, and in her mind he would always be the Lego boy with juice on his face, even though she would never be able to connect who he was now to what he might become. That's what always seemed wrong about history, that you could never link the president to the boy he'd once been, except in the most general terms. The time he sat under the table knocking down Legos would never make the biographies, because that moment wasn't important, and yet at the same time it was vitally important because as the grape juice dried and the Legos made another tumble, Mr. Rossi was down the hall, unconscious, hooked to machines. Someone should write *that* down, how much hung on every moment, but you could never do that, could never get in even a tenth, a hundredth, a millionth of it, because *everything* happened in that moment. If you devoted your entire career to the history of the human race during one minute, from 4:00 until 4:01 on some Wednesday afternoon, your efforts would be folly, because you would never exhaust your subject, never get to the bottom of anything. You could pare it down the way Ernie did, reduce it to a time line, and say, *Here is what happened,* knowing it was nothing like what had happened. Or you could do what she'd done and pick and choose, land on whatever flashy bits of history appealed to you and hoard them away—bring them to your students, instruct a whole generation of Mr. Rossis ready to take on the world through trivia games. She decided then that when he woke up, she would tell him this, how his own throwaway knowledge was as important as any other.

When he woke up.

She saw it all again and again, a tape loop through her brain. The flatbed at the top of Main Street had eased along, just barely moving, brakes squealing as it drew to a stop, the Try to Remember Dancers' banner strung along the side, wind slapping it against the truck, the banner decorated with music notes and spangly stars and the outline of a champagne bottle spilling bubbles. The high school band, well ahead of them, stopped playing and marched in formation, and Mr. Kesler propped the boom box in the truck window from his place in the driver's seat and pushed the button to start the music. Alison pulled Mr. Beachy to a better spot, for a better look. In the street were the crushed remains of the Jolly Ranchers that had been trampled by the band and the discarded crusts of pizza slices. Threads of steam rose from a manhole cover, and the music came out scratchy and distorted, "Sing, Sing, Sing" by Benny Goodman, a fast one, and just three couples, all that would fit on the flatbed, got up to dance—the Harmons, Bill and Sarah, and Mr. Rossi and Lila Montgomery. They moved in quick loops and shuffles that bounced the truck on its shocks, Lila gorgeous in a slinky little pleated dress, Mr. Rossi in his silver-buttoned vest, and the Harmons, as always, in matching pastel shirts and white pants. They all looked better than they had at the Arbor Day Parade, smoother, more practiced. Sarah was gorgeous, and really so good, she and Bill both. It was easy to forget that, and Alison thought that they never seemed more happily married than when they were dancing. Mr. Rossi spun Lila, cupped her tiny waist in his wide hands, his big red face smiling and sweating. As he stamped his foot on the floor and gave a loud *whoop,* Mr. Rossi flung Lila out from himself and spun around to mirror her, then crumpled over the side of the truck. He didn't teeter at the edge or wave his arms or try to catch himself; he just went over, frozen one second on the bed of the truck and the next tumbling backwards to the road, his head making a hollow sound on the pavement, his glasses clattering off his face, the steam from the manhole rising up from between his ankles.

The marching band crowded onto the sidewalk, holding their instruments overhead while the EMS vehicle backed up the hill to where Mr. Rossi lay sprawled. The back doors fell open, the workers still clutching their bags of Jolly Ranchers to toss out the window, the wheels of the stretcher dropping out from beneath it. Down at the west end of the street, the front of the parade was still going on, unaware of what had happened. Alison ran around the circle of people who crowded near Mr. Rossi, trying to see him, trying to find Mr. Beachy, listening for Sarah's panicked wails, which kept rising above the other voices, and watching, still, for Max. When finally they had Mr. Rossi on a board and loaded, a heavy brace around his neck, the ambulance had made its way silently downhill, parting the parade as it went.

The day of Marty's accident, she had spent several hours in a waiting room similar to this one, though she was waiting for nothing: He'd been pronounced dead in Lem's yard, the swing set strung with yellow tape. Just as she thought of this, the silver doors swung open and Dr. Tabor made his second trip out to where they all sat, shuffling down the hall with paper slippers over his shoes. He was pale and wispy-haired, with a young, almost doughy face. He spoke in a low, tired voice, employing the language of doctors in hospitals; the only parts Alison really heard were "head trauma" and "stroke," and "cerebral hemorrhage." FDR had died of a cerebral hemorrhage, his last words a complaint to his aides about his "tremendous headache."

"Wait, I'm confused," Sarah said. "Did a stroke cause him to fall, or did he just fall and have the hemorrhage?"

"Well, who can say?" Dr. Tabor said. He pulled his glasses off the top of his head and looked at the lenses. "Something caused the bleeding. The trauma, if he just fell. Or maybe a stroke caused the fall. Hard to say unless someone saw him exhibiting stroke symptoms."

Sarah turned to Alison. "You were watching, did you see him exhibiting stroke symptoms?"

Alison shoved her hands in her jeans to stop them from shaking. "I don't know. What are they?"

The doctor scratched his chin. "Dizziness, confusion, loss of balance . . ."

"Well, yeah, he lost his balance. He fell off the truck."

"Yes," the doctor said, "but sometimes a loss of balance is just that. Did he seem disoriented?"

"He was dancing, twirling around," Alison said. "How are you supposed to tell?"

He shrugged. "I suppose you can't. Anyway, let's concern ourselves more with his prognosis."

"Which is?" Sarah said. Bill stood beside her, rubbing her back. Where the hell was Max?

The doctor gave a half shrug. "Hard to say. We're draining fluid; then we'll see where we are, cognitively speaking. Questions?"

"Can we see him?" Alison asked.

"Soon enough. Anything else?" He started patting his pockets then, searching for something. Not finding it, he gave up, turned, and disappeared through the stainless-steel doors.

"I *wish* we could get a doctor that's maybe older than fifteen," Sarah said. "Did you see the little Snoopys all over his scrubs? What are those, his pajamas?"

"He's fine," Bill said. "He seems to know his stuff." For all his belief in the mystical, Bill had always seemed to have an equal faith in doctors.

"Mr. Rossi will love this, when I tell him about it," Alison said.

Sarah looked at her. "Love what?"

"All that business about whether he fell first or got sick first or did the sickness make him fall, and no one knows. Don't you see?" The two of them stared at her. She opened her hands before her, as if revealing the obvious. "He's a trivia question now. Only he knows the answer. It's perfect."

"Bill," Sarah said, "please take her home and get her some sleep."


She did sleep, fitfully, through the night, and awoke to the slant of light that used to bring the flashes of lake to her walls, but now only fell flat in a dense, pale spill. Downstairs she found most of the dancers sitting in the living room, drinking coffee and eating the Oreos that Bill had put out. They looked like nervous children, their mouths dusted black with crumbs. Mrs. Skidmore was smoking, telling a story from thirty years ago about a diving donkey at the county fair and how he'd been rescued by local animal-rights people.

"Hippie types, you know," Mrs. Skidmore said, and drank her beer. Alison thought of Max and his Natural Causes Ranch. "Good people, though," she said.

"Can somebody tell me what the latest is?" Alison asked. They turned as a group to look at her.

"They put that donkey out on Charlie Magusson's old farm, out where Taco Bell is now," Mrs. Skidmore said, annoyed to have her story interrupted.

Bill stepped over beside Alison. "Sarah and Lila are at the hospital," he said, whispering.

"And?"

"But the donkey knew just one thing in this life, and couldn't be happy unless he got to dive," Mrs. Skidmore said, smoke coming out with her words. "Brayed day and night."

"No real change," Bill said. "He's in and out. They drained the bleeding."

Alison winced. Over and over she saw his slow fall off the truck, his head, the pavement.

"Charlie built him a ramp, all the way up to the barn loft," Mrs. Skidmore continued. "And down below he bought a backyard pool and filled it up. I can still remember that thing. Had sea horses painted all over it. Anyway, that donkey—name was Einstein, they *said*—would dive all day, like he worked on some assembly line."

"Sarah is all torn up over this," Bill said. "She thinks it's her fault."

"Well, it's easy to feel that way," Alison told him. "She'll get past it. And he'll be fine."

"Charlie got to the point where he couldn't do nothing all day but stand out there with a hose and refill the pool. And that winter, he had to heat water for it in buckets, and haul it out from the house. His whole *job* became Einstein the Wonder Donkey."

"He should have charged some type of admission," Mr. Harmon said.

"He tried that, made a few dollars, and that's when the animal-rights types jumped all over *him*. Okay for Einstein to dive as a hobby, I guess. Just don't put him to work. Plus, you could stand at the fence and watch for free anyway. People got sick of it. Clomp, clomp, splash. Clomp, clomp, splash. All damn day."

Though Alison was only half-listening to the story, Bill was drawn into it, missing the last thing Alison said to him, edging over toward

Mrs. Skidmore. In his way, Bill had lots in common with Einstein the Wonder Donkey—perseverance, if nothing else.

"So what happened?" Bill asked.

"Eventually, Charlie, good-hearted as he was, got sick of it, too. Einstein would not stop for anything, except to rest a few hours at night." Mrs. Skidmore finished her beer and rattled the pull-top tab inside the can. "Finally, one Saturday night, Charlie just drained all the water from the pool, left it standing there, and that Sunday morning was the end of it. Clomp, clomp, thud, and that was all she wrote."

Mr. Rossi leaned back against the pillows, a tube taped to his mouth, his face bruised yellow and purple. The thing that always struck Alison were the little bits of normalcy that clung to people when they became patients—Mr. Rossi's glasses perched on his face and taped to the bandages on his head, the turquoise ring he always wore, still on his finger. Reminders of the ordinariness they'd swerved away from to be here. When she sat at the end of his bed, he didn't stir much, just moaned a little in his sleep, the machines doing their beeping, hissing work beside him. He was in a private room, his window overlooking strip-mining equipment up the side of a hill, the windowsill adorned with flowers sent by the dance group. As far as anyone had been able to determine, he had no family. Sarah had made calls anywhere she could think of, and Bill had called a few people he knew at the Shriner's club. Dead ends, over and over. No one, it seemed, belonged to him. She sat for a while, watching him sleep.

Later that night, while she was underneath the Vette looking for holes in the exhaust, she heard Max knocking at the door frame, calling her name. She slid out from under the car, the taste of rust in her mouth.

"I guess you heard," she said.

He nodded. "My father told me. And I'm sorry. The city engineers came by, worried I'm about to drop my hotel in the middle of the street."

"Your father. I haven't seen him since it happened." She stood up, dusted off her jeans. Max gave her a quick hug and a kiss.

"The whole thing is competition for everyone's attention." He shrugged. "So he's pissed. He's not page one anymore."

She looked at him. "He told you that?"

"He doesn't have to. It's just reasonable. I know his MO."

Alison snapped off her trouble light and closed the hood. "Maybe he's upset about all of this."

Max snorted. "Maybe he's going to sprout wings and ascend to heaven, too." His face looked pinched, sour.

"You know, he was *in* that truck when it happened, playing the music. And he and Mr. Rossi are friends. I see them talking at the dances."

"Friends?" He couldn't have looked more surprised if she'd told him they were lovers.

"Yes, of a sort. Sinkholes, I think, was the topic of conversation." It was the only one she could remember, and "friends" actually was a stretch, but maybe Mr. Kesler was the closest Mr. Rossi had to one, besides her.

"Sinkholes and how cars disappear into them, no doubt."

She shook her head. "Again with the car. You know, you *really* ought to let go of it. The story is older than you are."

"It's not the car, I told you that." He flipped through her Haynes manual, then closed it and looked at her, eyes obscured by his glasses.

"If it's not the car, then you can drop the whole thing, right? Forget about it? Smile when he mentions it?"

"Yeah, of course. *You* helped him. You're complicit in all of this now, so sure, let's drop the whole thing. Let the liars lie, right?"

Her face warmed. "What are you, a Boy Scout? You never told one lie in your life? Never did one dishonest thing? Your father tells these bullshit stories, and no one but you cares. Get over it."

Max swiped his arm and smacked the shop manual, scattering it and a few box wrenches into the dirt. "You don't know what it's *like,* Alison." He raised his hands, as if surrendering the idea of hitting anything else.

She took a step back from him. "No, I don't. So tell me what it's like."

Max picked the manual up, dusted the cover along the thigh of his jeans, and put it back on the bench. He sighed. "We used to have this workshop out in the backyard that Dad used as his office. Just a desk, typewriter, a radio. That was it. Almost every night, as soon as it was dark, he would tell my mother he had to work in the office, hang around in there for twenty minutes, and then just take off. Be gone half the night. His car was always parked down the block, and he'd leave a light and the radio on in the office. He'd wear this god-damn aftershave when he left, slick his hair down with water."

Alison sat on the hood of the Corvette. "She must have known."

"She would ask me, and my job was to back him up. To corrob-orate." Max picked up the box wrenches and arranged them on the bench. "I'd tell her I *just* saw him standing by the window, or that he was really busy with work, whatever. I couldn't even look at her. He paid me five bucks every week. My only chore."

Alison shook her head. "And she never went out to *check*?"

Max frowned. "My mother was deathly afraid of snakes. I mean, this almost mythic, biblical fear, you know? So of course he told her the backyard was overrun with copperhead nests. Told her they'd come out at night and fill the yard. I told her the same thing. She would send me out sometimes if she had to ask him something, and I would make this big show of putting on my work boots. Then I'd make up an answer to whatever question she had. Sometimes, after I'd gone to bed, I would hear her leaning out the back door, calling his name over and over, calling out to that stupid empty office."

For a second, she imagined him lying in bed and hearing that, feeling the way she'd felt those nights in her own room, staring at the ceiling. "You said he drove her away."

"One Fourth of July—I was thirteen—I just had enough. She wanted him to come inside and watch fireworks on TV with her, and I thought, God, he can't even do *that*. I ran out into the yard in bare feet, and she was shouting about the snakes, and I pushed open the door of the office and told her all of it, yelling across the yard that he wasn't there, that he was never there. She waited up for him that night, sitting on the porch crying, while up and down the block kids kept lighting sparklers and firecrackers. Two days later, she moved back with her mother. That was that."

"And he blamed you."

"Of course. Nothing has been his fault in sixty-eight years. Not one thing."

Alison watched him light another cigarette, his fingers unsteady. "So what happened after all of that?"

Max shrugged and blew smoke from the side of his mouth. "I lived with him and he kept up his bullshit. In fact, it got worse after that. He told people she'd thrown him over for someone else. Made everyone feel sorry for him. Told me I had to live with him because she didn't want me. My mother never got over it. She lived eighteen more years, and she just never did."

"I'm sorry. I am." Alison hesitated. "I don't think you've gotten over it, either. And you have to, at some point. You just do." She could remember Sarah saying almost those exact words a year ago.

"No, you don't have to," Max said. He took off his glasses and wiped them on his T-shirt, the cigarette pinched in the corner of his mouth. "Why should she? Why should I? Someone ruins your life, you just forgive that, just drop it?"

"Because . . ." She shook her head. "You told me I don't know what it's like. That's the wrong verb, Max. I don't know what it *was* like. Was."

He drew hard on his cigarette. "No. Something is over because it happened yesterday? I don't think so."

Alison's stomach tightened and she fought to keep her voice calm. "Right now, there is a man, a friend of mine, in the hospital with blood seeping into his brain, but you're upset because your father told you lies twenty years ago. The past is the past, Max."

"No, you lied to me. The same lie. The very same one, and you just picked up an end of it and carried it along. And you are not the past. You're right now, you're today."

She had no answer for him. "I don't want to do this. Not now." She crossed her arms, hugging herself. She wanted to get in the car and drive, take it up to ninety, the way she had the night before, take it even higher, as high as the speedometer went.

He rubbed his mouth. "Me either. I don't. I think we have something here, you and me. I mean, don't we?"

She nodded.

"But I can't *stand* it if you lie to me," he said. "*Anything* else but that. You have to understand that." His face twisted with worry, his eyes moving over her face, then moving away.

"I do understand," she said.

He put out his cigarette. "All I'm asking is that you make amends."

The word stopped her. It sounded like another word from *Reader's Digest,* one that no one really used anymore. "Amends," she said. "I'm *dating* you, Max. I didn't join AA."

He looked at her.

"Okay," she said. "I'll make amends. But can I tomorrow? Right now I'm so tired, I ache."

He nodded and stepped over to her. He slid his arms around her, and she let him. "I'm sorry about your friend," he whispered. "He'll be fine. I promise."

The next day Mr. Rossi was awake, his eyes rimmed purple, the tube taped to his mouth. Paralysis had claimed his left side, the doctor explained—for how long, no one knew. Sarah and Alison sat in chairs on opposite sides of him, the flowers from the dancers now joined by some from his Baltimore trivia contest group. None still from family, and finally they had realized the inevitable: He had no family. On his side table sat a pad and marker he used to communicate, along with the wadded-up sheets of past conversations with nurses or visitors. Frieda Landry had mentioned his accident in her "Out-n-About" column that morning, mentioning his trivia prizes and calling him "a local celebrity." When Alison read the column aloud to him, he gave them both a slow thumbs-up.

"How about that, Arthur? Pretty soon, you'll be dating starlets."

He motioned for the pad and pen. Alison had to hold it for him, propping it on his stomach as he wrote with his right hand.

FAMOUS FOR TRIV. OR FOR KISSING PAVEMENT??

Alison showed his scrawl to Sarah, and they both laughed.

He smiled behind the tubing, motioned to her, and wrote again.

1ST PRIEST OF CAT. CHURCH DIED FALLING FR. BELL TOWER

Alison read it over. "Here?" He nodded, and Alison showed the writing to Sarah.

"Well," Alison said, "that's what you get for opening a cat church. Now, a *dog* church might have worked." As usual, feeling nervous, she began making dumb jokes. Mr. Rossi motioned for the pad again.

NO LAUGH PLS . . . HURTS!

She patted his hand. Sarah seemed even more awkward than Alison, nervous, trying not to cry. Finally she gave up on talking and clicked the TV remote. The three of them sat for a while, watching some happy woman sell jewelry on the Home Shopping Channel. For some reason, none of the other channels worked. While they watched, she took his hand and every so often he would squeeze her fingers, as if to reassure himself she was still there. When Sarah clicked through, the other channels were working again. They settled finally on Mr. Rossi's choice, a show on PBS about chefs in Germany.

After a while, Sarah got up and said she was heading to the cafeteria. The Harmons would be there soon, to take their turn visiting. Sarah patted Mr. Rossi's foot, started to speak, but couldn't. He motioned for the pad.

HOT DOG + MILK SHAKE PLS

Sarah laughed. "Sorry, old man. All your food right now is pre-
pared by Chez Plastic Bag. No hot dogs for you."

He wrote again, Alison holding the pad.

DANCING IS <u>GOOD</u>. THANK U

Sarah cut her eyes at Alison, patted his foot again, and left
quickly. They sat in the glow of the TV, watching a man in a toque
beat eggs with a whisk. Mr. Rossi's breathing became slow and
steady, though when she looked over, he was not asleep. The chef
show ended, replaced by one about river otters. Mr. Rossi motioned
with his good hand for the pad and pen. While he wrote, Alison
studied his face. His silver hair, that usual ocean wave of pomp-
adour, had been either shaved away or hidden by bandages, his
big glasses smudgy with fingerprints, his left eyelid droopy and
half-shut. He finished writing.

I'M NOT GOOD

"No, you aren't," she said. "But you will be. Good as ever."

SCARY

"Yeah, I know," she said.

He went back to writing on the pad. Her arm grew sore and she
switched hands, standing with her back to him. What could he be
writing? She thought about Max last night, standing in her garage
and asking her to "make amends." Such an old-fashioned idea,
almost antique, something God might have asked for in Deuteron-
omy. What exactly did he mean?

Mr. Rossi put down the marker long enough to flip the page and
continue. He'd been writing for five minutes now. She had a sudden
image of him writing an entire book while she stood there with cob-

webs hanging over her. But then she worried, what if he is writing some kind of confession, a love letter he wanted her to deliver, a tirade directed at the family they'd been unable to find? What was she supposed to do?

He finished finally, tore the sheet off, folded it as well as he could and clumsily tucked it into her jeans pocket. When she started to take it out, he made motions for her not to. Then she understood that he wanted her to look later, after she'd left the hospital. Maybe it was a love letter to *her*.

Sarah came back and they made their good-byes to him, promising to return the next day, reminding him that the Harmons would be along later. Sarah let out a huge sigh as they moved through the sliding front doors and out into the sunlight. Alison looked around. The day looked almost too bright. Sun glinted off the windshields of the cars. Across the way, kids played in the school yard, tossing a yellow ball over a net. Everything looked baked, whitewashed. Alison kept putting her hand over the folded-up letter in her jean's pocket, but she didn't want to look just yet, not now, with Sarah here. Later would be better, alone in her room.

"Your old college should offer a course in what to say to people in hospitals," Sarah said.

"Yeah, but who would teach it?" As they walked to the car, Alison realized she'd forgotten to ask him the one thing she'd meant to: whether he'd felt sick and fallen, or just fallen by accident. He was *still* the only one who knew the answer, and probably he preferred it that way.


Alison changed into her grease-stained clothes and spent the afternoon under the car, trying to figure out where the scraping sound was coming from, stopping long enough to hear updates from Sarah after she'd talked to Dr. Tabor or the Harmons. She crawled underneath with her trouble light, just looking, frustrated. The whole thing seemed impossible to figure out: The sound was there only when the car was moving, and she could look for it only when the car was still.

She shook everything, tightened a few rusty bolts. She banged on a few parts with the back of a wrench, and finally she gave up.

Later that night, after Sarah and Bill were asleep, she took the Vette out again. No one yet even knew that it was running, let alone that she was driving it. She felt like Mr. Rossi, hoarding her secret knowledge, though if Max had bothered to ask last night, she would have told him, taken him for a drive. It no longer worried her that the car had no tags or registration; somehow, at 2:00 A.M. in West Virginia, it felt as if the law didn't really apply. The road she'd found on the opposite side of the lake into town was long and straight, with only that soft rise toward the end, and she drove it up and back, turning around in the town square to drive it again. Once, before she ran out of road, the speedometer needle tipped up toward 100 and she felt her heart flipping wildly behind her ribs, felt her breathing resume when she slowed. She loved the car, but worried about it, too. Probably just her imagination, but on curves, the car felt loose somehow, as though it might twist free of itself. Mr. Beachy told her in the store once that rust could get so bad that cars had broken in two when their owners tried to jack them up. She thought about the interior, too. It would look pretty shabby once the outside had new paint. One of her catalogs advertised kits that let you replace the entire interior—the seat covers, carpet, door panels, and dash—make it all new, even change its color if you wanted. But the kits were expensive, and she had no clue how to install any of the stuff. On top of that, she'd have to farm out all the bodywork, or else learn to weld, and she had no intention of ever getting anywhere near a welder. She would be here years, not months, trying to finish the car, in way over her head. The idea filled her with dread, as did the idea of teaching again, of moving back to her museum house. But neither did she want to linger on—now that she'd driven the car, she wanted it finished, behind her.

Flushed and windblown, she eased quietly down the driveway and backed into the garage. It was near three o'clock in the morning. One of the headlight doors got stuck in the up position when she clicked the switch off, refusing to glide back down into the nose of the car. Tired as she was, she slid under the bumper for the second time that day and clicked on her trouble light. Nothing looked wrong. She jiggled the wires a few times, disconnected and then reconnected the vacuum hose. It was the side with the good beams, so she just left it. She could fix it later. The silence she noticed in her garage so late was the missing voices of the men who used to fish the lake, their laughs and shouts. They'd gone home now, given up. When she closed her eyes, she could still hear the echo of them, of all the life carried in those voices. She clicked off the trouble light, and when her eyes closed this time, they stayed closed, and she felt herself falling into those imagined voices, sinking into sleep.

She awoke to the slam of the storm door, awoke stiff and sore, damp and chilled, her hand still curled around the trouble light. Outside, in ashen light, the moon still up, she found Bill, his tool belt strapped around his waist, standing in the front yard just looking around, drinking coffee.

She smiled walking up to him, shivering a little. "So what's the plan now, throw coffee on the house?"

He seemed a little startled, even though he'd just watched her walk up. "Nah. The plan is go to work."

"Work?" She just then noticed his gray phone company shirt, the pocket protector full of small tools. "What about—"

"Time's up. Game is over and I lose." He blinked quickly and drank from his cup.

"Bill . . . it wasn't like it was a competition. You didn't *lose.*"

"I *did* lose. Can you get it all done, can you make a life before time runs out? That's the game. Have everything in place before it all starts to quit or die or get old."

Or *rust,* she thought. "Bill, you have a life. A nice home. Sarah loves you."

He nodded, tight-lipped. "All true."

"You did everything you could. I'm sorry."

"Yeah. Me, too." He pitched the rest of his coffee into the grass, got into his truck, and drove away.

**—from the *Haynes Automotive Repair Manual: Chevrolet Corvette, 1968 thru 1982***

Mechanically, power diminished over the years with the advent of emission controls and the use of smaller V8 engines, but even so, the performance and ride still provide an unequaled driving experience.

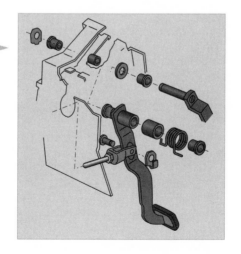

# 12

The day brought little change in Mr. Rossi. Alison visited in late morning, talking to "the child," Sarah's name for Dr. Tabor, which everyone else had begun using. He didn't help himself much, either, wearing the Snoopy scrubs, a Three Stooges tie. He told them there was swelling in Mr. Rossi's brain, that they planned another MRI for the afternoon. He was sleeping, almost in a light coma. Most of Seven Springs Village had gone into full emergency mode, reserved for sicknesses and deaths—which meant, for the most part, the preparing of food. Pies, cakes, and casseroles, having no other place to go, ended up at Sarah's house. The only person Alison hadn't seen since all of this started was Mr. Kesler. Maybe Max was right about him; maybe he was off pouting because the accident had stolen the attention away from his car story. Hard to believe that anyone could be that petty. She didn't want to believe it. The decorations for Founders' Day had been taken down from the storefronts and telephone poles, and the town looked stripped somehow, exposed and embarrassed about what had happened. The sign for DISCOUNT BEVERAGE was out completely while workers stood on ladders trying to repair it, and enough autumn air had settled in now that the big windows of the Red Bird were filmy with moisture dripping down. At home, she and Sarah sat at the kitchen table and ate leftover casserole heated in the microwave.

"I saw Bill off to work this morning," Alison said.

Sarah nodded. "Good, because I didn't. I slept in. This hospital crap wears me out."

"He was upset."

"We had a deal, Ali. Time was up. Besides, food all over the house? Fire? I didn't sign up to be married to the village witch doctor."

Alison stood and began clearing dishes. "I know. I just feel bad for him."

Sarah still sat, staring at the spot where her plate had been, and then she began crying, her face unchanged, tears dotting the place mat. "For maybe a day and a half, I believed him. I mean, I had *faith,* you know? This is gonna work, for whatever crazy reason." She shook her head. "So, I was wrong, Bill's back at work, and faith is bullshit. I just don't want my hopes lifted up anymore. I want them left alone." Alison rubbed her sister's shoulders for a moment, then finished the dishes and left the kitchen. There was nothing to say, beyond the kind of pep talk she'd given Bill, and that would never fly with Sarah.

That night, the three of them sat in the living room watching the local news on TV, Bill with his company shirt untucked and boots unlaced, tilted back in the recliner, Sarah doing her usual trick of reading a magazine and watching TV at the same time, and Alison half-watching, thinking about Mr. Rossi, Max, her car, about the order of the British monarchs, Mr. Kesler, and Bill's failed magic—thinking all of it and none of it, vaguely aware of the man on the TV screen, who was saying something about gun control and violence in our schools. Fall was settling on West Virginia, and Sarah kept the front and back doors open in the evenings, a passageway for the outside smells of cool air, the last grass cuttings of the year, the creosote from the exposed lake bed. Earlier, Sarah said, some people from Maryland had parked at the edge of her drive and walked down to take pictures of Colaville, the tilted buildings and broken-backed stone bridge. Finally—dried, emptied, and seventy years too late—the lake had attracted its promise of tourists.

An infomercial for some kind of outdoor grill came on, some has-been celebrity nearly orgasmic in his excitement over the invention. Sarah and Bill headed silently up to bed, and Alison sat watching the screen. When she was a kid and turned off the TV in the dark after her parents headed to bed, there would still be that little blue dot in the middle of the screen, and she would sit watching it. The show after the show, she thought of it. The show all shrunk down and reduced to the size of molecules, all the actors and their sitcom problems squeezed down to a little pea of light.

She went out to the garage, got in the Vette, and drove off, going out to the lake road, then onto other roads she'd never been down before, into little towns much like Wiley Ford, a handful of churches and bars, a VFW hall and fire hall, a liquor store. Dried fields of corn divided one town from another, or junkyards piled with dead cars, or long, low industrial complexes. She passed a business called the Lift King, then one called Jenny's Machine Tools, houses and pole barns and trailers all mixed in together, laced with gravel roads and barbed-wire fences. A pile of leaves smoldered in the dark, someone's controlled burn from earlier in the day, a glowing red eye in the middle of the yard. The Vette's open top drew in the smell of the burning, and other smells, of skunk and cold air and Chinese food cooking. Around tight corners the car produced a new sound, the scrape of metal on metal from somewhere under the front right wheel well. She'd brought one of Bill's old WVU sweatshirts with her, and she steered with her knees long enough to pull it on against the chill. She loved these late-night drives, and it made her sad to think of winter coming on, when the roads might be too slick with snow or ice to drive them. But by then, the car would be done, all sleek and black. Black for sure, she decided just then, to blend it in with the night and the asphalt, to make it part of them. She would have the car registered and tagged and insured, everything legal, but somehow that made her sad, too, like the coming of winter. Part of what she loved about these nighttime drives was that no one knew she took them; *no* one, not even the cops, not even her sister. It was as if she went out of existence for a few hours, as if she'd been abducted. Only she was abducting herself, taking herself away, accountable only to Alison.

The gas gauge swept over toward E, and so she turned the Vette around and headed back. The house was dark, and the missing noise of the bulldozers pushing the new dam into place was noticeable at night by its absence. Already, Bill had told her, the dam was just about done, an earth dam a simple thing, really—just stones and logs pushed up together, around a core of clay, the way a kid would make a dam. With the dam complete, the lake would start filling again, the town reburied, possibly for the last time. She imagined all the ghosts of Colaville resigned to it, watching the progression through broken windows, grateful for their weeks in the open air.

When she got up to the front door, she was startled to see someone sitting on the front steps, not Bill this time, but Sarah, her cigarette a glowing button in the shadows. Alison felt suddenly busted, a sixteen-year-old sneaking in the house.

"Hey, you scared me. I was just taking the car down the road to check something—"

"The child called," Sarah said, her voice flattened at the edges. "Mr. Rossi died while we were in there watching the fucking infomercial." She drank from the wineglass perched beside her.

Alison stood there, the words washing over her, finding their way in through tiny paths of understanding. The orange button moved to Sarah's mouth, then away again. "How?" was all Alison could manage.

"Seizure, another stroke, they think, if the first one was a stroke to begin with. Basically, his brain died, is how the child explained it."

A ragged, breathy noise escaped Alison's mouth, the minutes before, the rush of the car along the road, tugging at her, at *now,* wanting to pull her back in time, into their dark comfort. Her hands shook as she dragged them through her hair, as one fluttered down like a windblown scrap to settle on Sarah's head. "God," Alison said, a prayer, an accusation. So sweet, Mr. Rossi was, the sweetest man she'd ever known, and for half a second the thought angered her, as though his sweetness had been what killed him.

"We've got to go down there in the morning," Sarah said. "Somebody has to sign all their crap. Looks like the job falls to us."

Alison nodded. "Where's Bill?"

"Upstairs, sleeping. I let him sleep. He takes bad news so hard, I just . . . No reason to tell him until morning."

Alison nodded again. "It wasn't your fault, Sarah."

She looked up, ground out her cigarette against the sole of her shoe. "I remember about a year's worth of time when I had to tell *you* that, and you weren't even there when Marty got killed."

"Maybe that's *why* I thought it was my fault."

"You wanted to save him so you could keep saving him, right? Clean him up, teach him a thing or two?"

"In a way, yeah."

Sarah lit another cigarette, the lighter bringing her face into sharp relief, then allowing it back into the dark. She drank. "You and Bill are two of a kind. Only different. He's going to save me and the whole world."

"And the difference?"

"He thinks alien priestesses are going to land UFOs here and rescue everyone. He's just speeding the process along."

"And me?"

"You're the alien priestess."

Alison nearly smiled. "Well, I envy Bill. It'd be nice to believe that. But I'm not trying to save anybody anymore."

"Good, because you can't. You can't save a soul. Hey, I oughta tell Mr. Beachy that, he needs to know."

Alison nodded, not knowing what to say.

Sarah looked up at her. "You're supposed to be arguing with me. Bill is going to tell me twenty-five times in the morning that this was for the best."

"Well, no arguments from me. I agree with you. You can't save anyone. Not even yourself." Her eyes felt hot and full.

"Hey, Ali"—she was slurring her words—"that's not what I meant."

"Too bad, because you would've been so right. Look at me. Exhibit A on how not to save yourself."

"Please stop."

"I couldn't save Marty, couldn't even clean him up. Couldn't save Mr. Rossi and can't save me. I had thought to start with a car, you know. Tackle inanimate objects and work my way up."

"The car, the car." She poured her wine out in the grass, the way

Bill had with his coffee when the day began. "You are saving the car, Alison."

"The car is a piece of shit. It's falling apart. I've already put more into it than it's worth." They were Max's words, more or less, but true enough. The whole thing was folly. She worked the shark's tooth back and forth on its chain, then squeezed it, letting it cut into her palm. Sarah was crying now in her silent way. Alison turned and headed toward her garage, blood throbbing in her temples. She sat in the car in the dark, looking out through the garage door into the tunnel of paler light, out at the corner of the dried lake she could see from this angle. Soon the lake would fill again, the docks floating instead of limp against the banks, the light reflecting into her window. Mr. Rossi wouldn't be here to see it. She remembered with Marty, and even with her grandmother before that, the way time divides itself into before and after whatever terrible thing has happened. And it would keep dividing, would divide again, twice, when her parents died, again and again with whoever died after that—Max, or Sarah, or Lila, or Bill, or God knows who. Time just kept halving and halving and halving, like Zeno's Paradox, the arrow that never reaches its target. We are shot through time, aiming toward—what? Death? Understanding? That must be it, because we reach death all too soon, but understanding keeps falling, always, away and away. She turned the idea over in her mind, but it was only that, an idea, a floating scrap in the slow wash of grief. She laced her hands through the spokes of the steering wheel, cried quietly for Mr. Rossi, and slept.

In the full light of morning, she put on her one girl dress, had coffee with Sarah and Bill (who, as predicted, kept saying that Mr. Rossi's "passing" was for the best), and headed over into Ridgely to make arrangements with Tucker Funeral Home. The director, Vernon Tucker, greeted them in the parking lot, as though he'd been waiting there. He wore a too-short pale gray suit and a thickly knotted, oily-looking tie that reached only to about the middle of his belly.

He was friendly enough, though, donning the narrow glasses he wore on a cord around his neck to read their names and Mr. Rossi's name off a page in his notebook, taking care with pronunciation, his jacket puckered around his elbows. He drew them into his office, offered them a green vinyl couch as he sat behind his desk.

"Now, according to this, the deceased has no family per se, so you have been appointed to oversee the disposition. Am I correct in that?" He looked at them over his glasses. The shelf behind him held the photographs of all the peewee football teams he'd sponsored.

"Is that legal?" Sarah asked.

"Yes, that's correct," Alison said. Typical Sarah, looking for a loophole.

"Yes, ma'am," Vernon Tucker said, "the deceased did a pre-arrangement with us back in 1985, and recently amended it to add your names as executors."

"Would you mind calling him 'Mr. Rossi' instead of 'the deceased'?" Alison said. Something about the word made him sound like some species, as though death imparted only a generic title.

"Nineteen eighty-five?" Sarah said. "Talk about planning ahead."

"Yes, ma'am." Vernon shuffled his notes. "You can take advantage of the calendar and lock in your arrangements at today's prices, then sit back and laugh at inflation."

"I'm not sure inflation will be my first worry when I'm dead," Alison said. The whole place was starting to give her the creeps, not for its aura of death, but for its aura of used-car lot.

Mr. Tucker gave a gentle, practiced laugh. "Now then, the de— Mr. Rossi arranged for a cremation, no funeral service per se. He was a man of austere tastes."

"Did you know he was a champion trivia player?" Alison said. "He used to win tournaments all the time."

"How much is all this costing?" Sarah said.

"The prearrangement takes care of all costs," Mr. Tucker said. "That's its very reason for existence. However, there are a few sub-sidiaries for you to consider."

Sarah frowned. "Such as?"

"As for the cremation itself"—he lowered his voice—"you have a choice. Mr. Rossi paid for a direct cremation, which includes our standard container of either cardboard or particleboard, and refrigeration in lieu of embalming, all inclusive."

"Oh, God," Alison said. "You're putting him in a cardboard box?"

"For a small fee, you can select an alternative container, such as one made of composition materials."

"What is that?"

"It's just composition materials. Space age." He smiled, proud of the recent developments in the burning of bodies.

"It all turns to ash anyway," Sarah said. "What's the diff?"

Alison closed her eyes. It was helping, in a way, to be talking like this. Helping to distance her from the fact that he was, simply, gone.

Mr. Tucker leaned back in his squeaky leather chair and let his glasses rest on their tether. "Now, as for the disposition of the cremains—"

Alison looked up. "Cremains?"

"Yes, ma'am. The ashes themselves. You have a choice of urn design, or you can stay with the one picked out by the deceased."

"Well, he picked it," Sarah said. "Wanna stay with that?"

Alison was still stuck on the word *cremains*. It felt so horribly diminutive, given what it described. A word invented by advertisers, along the lines of *brunch,* or *telethon.* Sarah tugged her sleeve.

"Well . . . maybe. Let's see the one he picked out."

"Excellent idea," Mr. Tucker said. He left through a side door in his office and came back a few minutes later carrying a cheap plain brass box, like something meant to hold recipes.

Alison took it when he offered it, turned it in her hands. "This is it?"

"Our economy urn, yes."

"But it's not an urn, it's a box."

Sarah took it from her and worked the tiny latch.

"Urn is more its function, ma'am."

"I don't think so," Alison said. "An urn is *urn*-shaped, right? It looks more or less like a vase."

"An urn," Mr. Tucker said, irritation edging his voice, "is a container meant for holding the cremains of the deceased."

"If I put ashes in my sneaker, does that make my sneaker an urn?"

"Alison, it's okay. Calm down," Sarah said. Alison drew a deep breath and nodded. Why was she so upset over the stupid urn? It didn't mean anything; it wasn't Mr. Rossi. She remembered feeling the same way after Marty died, angry that the mundane world kept stamping along its way, angry that papers had to be signed, checks turned over, catalogs consulted. It turned death into—she didn't know what, exactly. But she could imagine that, someday, every funeral arrangement would be handled by Wal-Mart.

"We have more traditional urns," Mr. Tucker said, his own exterior smoothed back into place. "We have one with the *Last Supper* done in scrimshaw. Another with a beautiful painting of a trout fisherman in the river, if the deceased was one for that."

"We'll stick with this one," Sarah said. "It'll be fine."

That night, there was a dance lesson, but no one danced. They all sat around drinking coffee, remembering Mr. Rossi, making him better, more well liked than he really had been. We redeem the dead in this way, the way Alison had spent the early days after Marty's death watching their last Ocean City video over and over, remembering it as the time of their lives, instead of a trip she hadn't wanted to take and he had insisted on. The Harmons, Mrs. Skidmore, and Lila Montgomery seemed sad, but not too sad—this loss, Alison imagined, just another chip in the stone that had been chipped away at for so long now. They'd been through this many times before and would again. They drank their beer and coffee and tea, comforted Sarah and Bill, and sprinkled sweetness and laughing over the fresh memory of Mr. Rossi. What else was there to do? Near midnight, Alison slipped out the back into the bite of autumn cold and made her way to the garage. She had left a message for Max but was unsure at this point whether to expect to hear back from him or not. And still Mr. Kesler had not made any appearance, the others puzzled, too, over his disappearance. Maybe he and Max had simply ceased to exist, the whole Kesler bloodline absorbed back into the nothingness it had come from.

When the others had left and the house was dark, she started the Vette and drove. She went the way she had the night before, out along the unfamiliar roads, past the Lift King and Jenny's Machine Tools, looping through back roads with her one headlight showing the way, pushing the car up past ninety in the straightaways, the steering wheel quaking lightly in her hands at that speed, the engine throaty and rich. She followed the road out this time, ignoring the scrapes and squeaks of the car, until she came out to a road that did look familiar, right below the bridge into Cumberland. She took it, riding into the coppery glow of the arc lamps, through the empty streets of town, past the boys who had parked their own cars in a row at 7-Eleven, showing off for no one. She tried to pretend that she had caught herself off guard by ending up in her old neighborhood, at the top of Holland Street, but really, she'd been headed here all along. She clicked off the lights and coasted to a stop in front of her house, rolled down her window to look at it. The place looked good—new paint, mulch along the walk, the gutters tacked back into place. Lem and Pammy had done so much, had made the house shine.

The last picture in the last batch Lem had sent was of a new WEL-COME mat on the mud porch. That sweet man, trying to welcome her back to her own house. Those photos weren't ransom pictures so much as they were what Lem wanted to say to her and couldn't, what everyone had been saying to her for two years: *It's okay now, everything has been washed clean, your life is ready for you to inhabit once again.* She wished it could be so, wished that her old life could be spruced up and made ready to go, but the truth was that such a life just wasn't hers anymore and never would be. She noticed then the basement lights on, the narrow rectangle of yellow light, the windows along the foundation no bigger than loaves of bread. Marty, are you still down there? she wondered, remembering the night she'd seen him, as if he'd never gone. And she knew he was there, would always be there, that Lem and Pammy had done what they'd done to keep him there. But she could not be there. Not ever. The house was not hers anymore.

But she knew whose it was.

She had to drive for a bit to remember the way but finally found the row of trailers where Lem and Pammy had lived for as long as she'd known them. They were old-style house trailers, not like the new modulars, their wheels blocked with bricks and grown over with weeds where the mower didn't reach, their aluminum sides striped with aqua and pale pink, TV antennas propped on their roofs. Lem and Pammy's was the neatest of them all, with the small yard landscaped and trimmed, the dirt raked where the grass didn't grow, Lem's beat-up station wagon parked in the gravel beside the dark house. She found a scrap of paper and a pen in the glove compartment. Leaning on her thigh, she wrote as neatly as she could:

*Dear Lem and Pammy,*
*Here is what we're going to do. I want you to have the house, because in fixing it up so nicely you have claimed it, or earned it . . . something. Since I know Lem is already protesting before he even reads this, I won't give you the house but will sell it to you for $900, which is enough money to put a new interior in my car. I love you guys, and won't take no for an answer. I'll call the bank tomorrow to arrange everything.*
   *Love,*
   *Alison*

She folded the note in half and clicked open the storm door enough to slide it in between the two doors. Buster, their German shepherd, started scratching and whining, and as she climbed in and started the Vette, she saw a light go on in the front room. The car crunched along the gravel as she backed out, and as she slipped it into first gear, Lem's face, as big and white and blank as the moon, slid into the gap between the curtains and watched her leave.

The next day, more plans were made with Vernon Tucker, although Sarah said she was leaving Alison home this time. Mr. Rossi's pre-arrangement had short-circuited any kind of ceremony attached to his death at all. Alison could imagine him blushing from all the attention. But still it felt frustrating, the idea that he would be cremated, there would be no marker anywhere, and they would be handed that awful metal recipe box, as if it held all of him, the whole of his life. Already, Sarah had talked to Mr. Rossi's landlady, and most of his stuff would be sold at a tag sale, the proceeds to go to the Tri-State Trivial Gaming Association, of which he'd been a member for twelve years. Bill had taken half a day off from work to dish out casserole to the dancers, who still straggled by in ones or twos, seeming equally adrift without a funeral service to attend. Bill had been quiet since this whole thing had happened, had spent much of his time in his phone company uniform, as if doing penance for his earlier silliness. That's how it seemed anyway. He'd even given up his books on ancient gods and the Bermuda Triangle and Zen philosophy, trading them for evenings in front of the TV, absorbing the dull entertainment of sitcoms and football. He didn't mope or pout, never mentioned his ancient voodoo, never spoke of babies anymore. He smiled and helped with dinner and the dishes, did some work around the house, checked the progress of her Corvette—good old familiar Bill. But he wasn't quite familiar; something in him seemed broken, and, once broken, ignored.

Lisa at F&M Bank told her the transfer of the house would be no problem, that she would draw up the papers that afternoon (Alison thought, waiting on hold, that for years she'd entrusted all of her financial dealings to someone she knew only as "Lisa") and contact Lem and Pammy. So far, there'd been no word from either of them—maybe they had never gotten the note; maybe it had fallen into the mud or been blown away. She decided to give them the day and then call.

That afternoon into evening she spent under the Vette, trying to trace the whiff of gas she got when she walked into the garage lately. Either the tank had tiny pinholes of rust or something in the fuel pump was giving her problems. She had the radio on to take her mind off of Mr. Rossi, off the image of him forever falling off the edge of the truck, and how the others in that instant were still danc-ing even as he was falling, still twirling and smiling as his life on this earth was beginning its end. A man on the radio talked about para-noid government conspiracies, Pentagon cover-ups, black helicop-ters, and then cut away to a commercial for the Craftmatic adjustable bed. That seemed about right, seemed the best and worst of this world, the way the mundane kept shoving its nose into everything. Alison slid back on the shower curtain, her trouble light spilling shadows. The fuel tank looked fine once she'd wire brushed it, grown so oily over the years that rust never had a chance. She traced and felt along the fuel lines as well as she could, and they seemed okay, too. Must be the fuel pump; Mr. Beachy had said once he'd bet a dollar to a bag of doughnuts it would give her a problem someday. She missed him, missed leaning over the counter at AAAA. She missed Marty and Mr. Kesler and Lem and Pammy, and just as she thought to miss Max, as if she had conjured him up, he was there, calling her name with a question in his voice, knocking at the door of the garage.

"Alison?" he said again.

She slid out, the gas odor stinging her nose, and looked up at him. "Hi."

He shook his head, rubbed his scraggle of beard. "I'm really sorry about everything. I just got caught up."

"Caught up how? I needed you here."

"The Hotel Morgantown is turning into a monument to bureau-cracy. We've got three lawsuits already, and we haven't even blasted yet."

"Sorry to hear that." She sat up, leaned against the bumper of her car. "You heard about Mr. Rossi?"

"That's why I came over tonight. Part of why." He held out his hand and pulled her up into his grasp, hugging her tightly. She held on, face against his neck.

"He was a friend of mine," she said into that space. "Not just one of the dancers. I liked him." She began to cry, pressing her eyes against his shoulder.

"I know. He was a nice guy. I'm sorry, Alison. What can I do?"

She let the question dissipate, and clung to him, his hand stroking her hair. Her hand came up to hold his face, and then she kissed his mouth. "Do you want to take a ride with me?" she asked.

He took a step back, holding her hands, searching her face. He looked concerned. "You mean the Vette?"

"Yeah." She wiped her eyes with her shirttail. "It's the best. You just . . . I don't know . . . you disappear into it. I go almost every night now." *Please say yes,* she thought.

"I smell gas," he said. He looked at the car as if it intended to mug him.

"Fuel pump," she said.

"A leaky fuel pump could start a fire."

She looked away from him, sighed. "Well, it hasn't. And it's a short ride, and I'm not worried. If you are, stay here. You know, for someone who goes around blowing up things, you are an awfully cautious man."

"That's *why* I'm cautious."

She nodded. "I'm going. Stay or hop in."

He considered this. "This car isn't even registered. It doesn't have tags."

"I need *tags*?" She looked at him incredulously. "Have you ever just *done* something?"

He looked at her, saying nothing, and she got in the car, started the engine. He smiled at the sound, despite himself. Alison clicked on her one headlight and rolled past him, out of the garage and into the gravel.

In her rearview she saw him jog up behind the car and rap on the fender. She stopped and he got in.

"Where're we going?" he asked.

"Nowhere, that's the point."

"If you say so." He clicked his seat belt.

"Look what I found when I was cleaning up in here." She groped under her seat.

"Pistachios?"

"Almost." She brought up an eight-track tape, which she had found wedged under the passenger seat, the label wrinkled and distorted.

"Wow, a relic. Anybody good?"

"Well, it's Styx. Could be worse."

"Much worse. Plug it in."

She took the road that would bring them around the other side of the lake, driving slowly for Max, who kept his hand braced on the dash and seemed to expect, perhaps out of habit, an explosion. Usually, she liked the drive without any music, but now she needed something to fill the blankness growing between them.

She pulled over to the side of the road. "I meant to tell you, vandals got in here with bulldozers and tore your dam down, and then they got in again and built a new one."

"I saw. They're filling the lake already."

"So what happened?"

"I told them they ought to bulldoze it. That dynamiting would be dangerous."

"Why?"

"Well, truth be told, I wanted out of the job. The hotel is a much bigger fish."

She eased back onto the road. Tonight was warm, the last vestige of summer holding on. Insects kept flicking off the windshield as she drove. "Speaking of the hotel, how is Tom?" Styx started singing some song she remembered from junior high, one about Miss America.

"Tom? Oh, *Tom*. He's drunk almost every day. I guess that's how he is."

She found the road that ran past the Lift King and took the sharp right out onto it, the Vette making that scraping metallic sound again. Max winced and started to say something, but she shushed him. "I feel so bad for him. One day, he's going to be just like Mr. Rossi. He's going to die, and no one will even be there to claim his ashes."

"He has someone. He has an ex-wife or two and a daughter. He just fucked up with them; that's the story there."

She nodded. "So he deserves to die alone, right? Fuck up once and lose all sympathy, is that how it works?"

He turned in his seat and looked at her, touched her shoulder. "You're right. I react the same as you, I think, only instead of pity, I get pissed off. Old habit."

"Old, yes." She turned around in the road and headed back the other way, suddenly tired, suddenly not enjoying the drive. Max took her hand, and she let him, let him kiss the tips of her fingers, though if she could have chosen right then, he would have vanished from the car and let her finish the ride alone—no Max, no music, no low-grade argument. She parked in the garage and they kissed in the dark, the leather seats squeaking with their movements. His breathing deepened and he whispered her name as she leaned into him, leaned into how familiar he felt now, even though he was still so new. She slid awkwardly across the console of the Corvette and angled herself halfway back against him, her head on his chest. It wasn't him that felt so familiar, maybe, not Max Kesler, but just the warmth of another body, the vital beat of another heart. His arms came around her slowly, his mouth pressed to her hair, his thumb tracing the outer edge of her breast. She remembered the day in the hotel, on the stage, and how she'd imagined that day that she was a woman falling in love, telling herself stories about how good it could all be if she let it. But now, though nothing had

moved, things had shifted, and those stories seemed as sad as anything else that wasn't true when you really pinned it down. But still
she took his hand and pulled him out of the garage, across the yard
in the dark with the dew dampening their shoes, and took him quietly up the stairs, because those stories, like all stories, had their
power, and she might yet believe them again, might know them as
true in the middle of all that warmth and heart.

And sometime near dawn, Max breathing in the slow rhythm of
sleep, something worrying the edges of her memory woke her. In the
early light, she got out of bed and dug to the bottom of the hamper
for her good jeans, and in the pocket of them found the paper Mr.
Rossi had written for her, just days before, writing until she imagined he'd forgotten her standing there. She took the folded paper,
slipped on her flannel shirt, and stole quietly down the stairs into the
quiet clean of the kitchen, sat at the table, pressed the paper flat with
the heel of her hand, and stared for long minutes at his final words:

1. A human being once lived 19 days without food or water.
2. Because of the earth's rotation, an object can be thrown
   farther west.
3. Almost all the villains in the Bible have red hair.
4. Pearls melt in vinegar.
5. A fetus begins forming fingerprints at the age of six
   weeks.
6. Peanuts are used in the production of dynamite (tell
   your friend).
7. An Indian ascetic held his arm in the air for 45 years.
8. The Chinese character for "trouble" shows two women
   living under one roof (tell your sister).
9. Hummingbirds can't walk.
10.

She turned the paper over, but there was no number ten. Had he
meant to leave it off, or could he not remember ten things (she
doubted this), or had he maybe just gotten tired of writing? More

likely the latter—the word *walk* was so shaky she could barely make it out. But why . . . why this? He wanted her to tell Max about the dynamite, tell Sarah about the Chinese writing; maybe he just wanted her to *tell,* period. Tell about him after he was gone, talk about this odd relic he'd left her with, how much he'd known about everything and nothing, the strange way he had died. Then again, he was no Mr. Kesler, and had never really liked attention, so who knew *what* he'd wanted, what, if anything, he'd meant. It struck her then what a strange thing a life is—just a brief flash of noisy light, with mystery tacked on each end. She folded the paper and put it in her shirt pocket, then joined Max, pressing against him in the warm bed.

**DO** get someone to check on you periodically when you are working alone on a vehicle.

**DON'T** allow children or animals in or around the vehicle.

# 13

Max lay stretched out beneath the Corvette when he formally invited her to the hotel implosion. It was to be Saturday afternoon, and she would have the best seat in the house, four blocks south of the hotel itself, inside the barricades, standing next to the mayor and the lieutenant governor, with several photographers from the paper there, as well. He made it sound like an invitation to an inaugural ball. She shrugged, looking at the worn thighs of his jeans, at his legs sticking out from under the car, and told him she would be there. He kept clucking and making other noises of minor doom as he checked out the frame and suspension of the Vette for her. She looked back over her shoulder at the lake, which startled her with its filling up as it had with its draining. Almost every hour, it seemed a little more full, the small eye of water growing back toward the middle and expanding. Like a movie running in reverse—she half-expected to see the men return to their fishing by walking backward down the banks, their fishing lines unspooling through the air and onto the water as they turned the cranks of their reels the wrong way.

Max poked the bottom of the car with a screwdriver, which produced the same shower of falling rust as the first night, when the mice had dropped out of the car. She sat on the floor of the garage and rubbed his leg while he worked, still feeling the warmth and soreness of their lovemaking that morning. Maybe they'd been running the movie in reverse, too, getting back to where they'd been before she helped Mr. Kesler toss the car parts in the lake.

Max slid out and sat up beside her, the rust like paprika dotting his face. "That thing," he said, "is cancerous."

"Funny, that's what Bill calls rust, too."

He wiped his hands on his jeans. "The frame is shaped like a ladder, okay? You have about five rungs in the ladder."

"Crossbeams."

"Exactly. Well, three of your crossbeams are rusted through. Holes almost big enough for my fist." He showed her his hand.

"So, how do I fix it?"

"You don't. Or else you do a total frame-off."

She looked at him, brushed some of the rust from his face, and shook her head.

"That means," he said, "you take every part off the car. All of them, down to the frame, then you get a new frame or weld this one back up, and start all over."

She looked at the Vette as if waiting for it to explain how it had gotten this bad. "That would take years."

He nodded. "Yeah, most do."

"What if someone else does it?"

"You're talking maybe twenty thousand dollars. At least."

She drew a breath and let it go. Why did it seem like everything that existed was on some drunken headlong stumble into ruin? She clicked the trouble light off.

"I don't care," she said. "I'll drive it until it breaks. And it might not."

"No way. It's not safe to *move* the thing, Alison. And if you ever wreck, forget it. The car will break into four pieces, and you will, too, most likely."

"I'm not worried."

He rubbed her knuckles with his thumb. "Well, I am, okay?"

They sat for a while without much to say. She tried not to think about how many hours and dollars she'd already put into the car. Thousands of each, it seemed like. And for what? Cancer seemed about right, or maybe it was already dead, this car, and all she'd been doing was dressing it up in a suit, pinning a boutonniere to its pocket, rouging its face. She closed her eyes, thinking of Mr. Rossi, who was to be cremated that afternoon with no more ceremony than you'd burn a pile of leaves. Less, really. Mr. Tucker had told them to pick up his ashes at their convenience.

"I'll help," Max said, breaking into her thoughts.

"Help."

"With the car. A frame-off. We'll do the whole damn thing, okay? Make it brand-new."

She looked at him. "Really?"

"Really. Yes," he said, smiling at her like a kid.

"Okay, then." She imagined months and months in this garage with him, her car emerging newer than new, shining maroon and black. She imagined, or tried to, a slow falling into love. He took her hand then, the flakes of rust abrading her skin, and squeezed it.

"Thank you," she said, feeling nothing so much as a hollow kind of sadness, though she could not have said why.

Later, they sat on the front porch while Max explained the different phases involved in fully restoring the car. He talked on and on. Every bolt, he said. Every spring and washer. They would need to draw up a plan, a time line (she thought of Ernie, of another semester well under way); they would need to get busy before winter set in, or find a way to heat the garage. Then he switched gears, talking about the Hotel Morgantown, how fifty pounds of dynamite could bring down fifty thousand tons of building, how it would fall right inside its own footprint, how beautiful it would be to watch.

"What about Tom?" she said, interrupting.

"What about him?"

"Where will he go?" She had poured them each a beer, and they sat in the long afternoon light, watching the lake.

Max drank, shrugged. "Like he said, friends and couches."

She shook her head. "You know he doesn't have friends."

"Then, I don't know, a shelter or something."

She leaned back against Max. "Just make sure he's out of the building?"

"Tom is like a cat. He knows every little corner of that place. He hides in the walls. But the cops know him, and they'll be going through that thing with tweezers before we blow it."

"Tom cat."

"Yeah, that's him." Max slipped his arms around her, kissing the back of her neck so it tingled, and the day fell into darkness, slowly.


She awoke at the very first edges of light, Max lightly snoring, his mouth open. When she tried to imagine taking everything off the car, then putting it back, it seemed impossible. How could anybody even attempt such a thing? Like a jigsaw puzzle, in 3-D, with eighty thousand pieces, some of them broken and missing. It was enough of a worry to keep her from sleep, so she lay facing Max, resting in the narrow penumbra of his body warmth, looking at the Yosemite Sam tattoo on his bicep and tracing Sam's angry little face with her fingertip.

Later, they had the house to themselves, Bill having gone off to work in the early-morning dark, and Sarah stopping by Seven Springs on her way to the funeral home to pick up the ashes. Max told her that he was taking a day off, that he wanted to eat breakfast at the Red Bird and talk about their plans for the car, spend the day with her. He looked boyish in the mornings, his hair not long enough to be messed up, exactly, but kind of like velvet rubbed different ways. His eyes were puffy and narrow, his lips swollen from kissing. They drove downtown in the truck, the air chill enough now for jackets, for keeping the truck's heater on low, and they listened again to the tape of Pavarotti and Placido Domingo and Theresa Stratas, the slow build of the music somehow sadder under the flat gray sky of autumn. They held hands, and she thought that it felt almost like that first day, when she rode with him down that dirt road, only the windows were open then and her fingertips had slowly stained red as she gave up pistachio shells to the dirt and the wind and the late-summer heat. Now the windows were closed, the gearshift buzzed noisily between them, and there were no pistachios.

The Red Bird was nearly empty this late in the morning, and they took a table by the front window, looking out through the green filter at the square, at the trees full of browning leaves and squirrel nests. The walls above the counter were filled with the usual gray-ing photos of the food from the menu, dingy-looking plates of eggs and pancakes, washed-out hamburgers, like pictures from some dusty photo album. On the wall behind their table hung curling thank-yous from an elementary school group, full of dried paint drips and drawings of spiky suns, and, next to those, photos of all the Little League teams Mr. Davidow had ever sponsored, some of the kids by now probably the fathers of Little Leaguers themselves. The waitresses stood in the corner by the big flat grill, flirting with the ponytailed kid who did the cooking during the day. Alison rec-ognized several of the old men in their cardigan sweaters and bib overalls. They sat hunched over their plates, strung evenly as paper dolls down the length of the counter. The coffeemakers boiled their smells into the air, and the grill hissed when the kid with the pony-tail cleaned it, pouring water on the surface and scraping it with a spatula. The ceiling fan above the counter was missing a blade and spun, Alison thought, with a limp.

The night of lovemaking and excitement over the car had left her with a deep hunger, and the two of them ordered eggs and toast and extra bacon, coffee, oatmeal, glasses of milk, a plate of pancakes to share. Max asked for tomato slices with his eggs. After they'd eaten most of it and enough plates had been cleared away, he drew a piece of crumpled notebook paper out of his denim jacket. While Alison chewed the scraps of bacon, he spread the paper out before them and drew his time line for the car across the top. The first thing he listed was DISMANTLE BODY, with a little check-mark box drawn in beside it, and a target date, Christmas Day, then a sublist of tools and other things they would need to have, or rent, or buy. After that was PULL ENGINE and all the steps involved, with a New Year's Day deadline.

"You need one more item on there," she said, and took away his felt pen. Right after "New Year's" she wrote in KNOCK OVER LIQUOR STORE.

"After New Year's is good," she said. "They have lots of money."

He laughed. "Really, it won't be all that bad. I mean, it will, but we'll do the bulk of the work ourselves. Expenses will be pretty low, and we'll spread it out. What it will cost is time, but we have plenty of that, don't we? We aren't those guys just yet." He tilted his head at the old men lined up along the counter.

"Not quite," she said, and squeezed his hand under the table.

The front door whooshed open, stirring the rack of real estate circulars beside the door, and Frieda Landry walked in. She was without any of her big hats today, her hair frosted the color of pink lightbulbs. She wore another boxy wool suit, in blue this time, a silk scarf spilled over her shoulders and pinned into place with a brooch, a newspaper under her arm.

She waved at the waitresses and the cook, who began putting together her meal without her having ordered it. She sat at the table right next to Alison and Max and opened the newspaper to her own column, reading over what she must have written just the day before. Max didn't pay any attention to her. He was busy thumbing through one of the parts catalogs, bending down pages of parts that corresponded to their new time line. He was methodical; she had to give him that. Frieda Landry finished reading herself and turned the page, flipping back and forth between the comics and the obituaries. One of them made her laugh out loud, the back of her hand covering her mouth, her coffee spilling over into its saucer. When she looked up from the page, she caught Alison's eye and nodded, smiling at her, and then saw Max, who was chewing a corner of toast, scanning a page of pistons and connecting rods.

"Oh, Max. And Ms. Durst," Frieda said. "You are just the one I wanted to see." Alison didn't know which of them she meant. Frieda came over and joined them, carrying her coffee, settling herself in between them. She turned her chair toward Max, while he looked at Alison and gave a slight shrug.

"May I ask you a question or three?" Frieda said. Practiced, this little joke an old one.

"Sure," Max said. "I guess so." He still held Alison's hand under the table, and she felt him nervously working her fingers.

"Your father . . ." Frieda smiled and touched her neat hair, and

Alison thought, *please, please go away, please leave us alone.* "He's quite the something, isn't he?" Frieda said.

Max glanced at Alison. "That he is."

"I suppose you have grown up with hearing about the lake car all your life?" She withdrew her little leatherette spiral notebook and a thin gold pen.

Max gripped Alison's hand under the table, squeezing. Alison felt her heart expanding, thudding against her bones.

"All my life," Max said. "Since day one."

For some reason, Frieda wrote this down. "And have you heard there will be a special display at the county museum, all about the Kesler Chrysler? Right next to those mannequins dressed like miners, and all those pictures of Coalville. They kind of go along with each other."

Max pinched his lips together. "No, I hadn't heard that."

Frieda frowned at her notebook, apparently frustrated that she wasn't getting better quotes. "As his only son, you must be awfully proud of him. A local folk hero, really."

"Well," Max said, his fingers working, "since the story is so familiar to me, I don't have much to say about it. Alison here, though, she has some brand-new insights into the whole thing." He looked at her evenly, and her heart jumped up, her pulse noisy inside her ears.

"Insights?" Frieda said. "What sort of insights?"

Alison looked back across the table at him and barely shook her head. He squeezed her hand hard, squeezed her fingers together, held her gaze. *Amends.* The word circled back toward her from several nights before.

"She knows the truth about the Kesler Chrysler," Max said. "The real, honest truth. Think your readers might be interested in that?"

"Yes, of course," Frieda said. "Certainly." She scooted her chair toward Alison.

*Don't do this,* Alison thought. Max patted her hand now, the way you might encourage a child—*go ahead and just tell the truth,* and she wanted the truth just as badly as he did, wanted a truth that meant that her husband's memory had forgiven her enough that she could fall in love with a man, make a life out of moving forward. A life of restoration, of rebuilding. Every nut and bolt and washer.

"You . . ." She looked at Frieda, the pale blue of her eyes. "You mentioned 'folk hero,'" Alison said, "and that's an apt way to put it." Max rubbed her hand, patted it. He smiled. *Go on.* He wanted her to be his, to love him enough to dig him out of all those lies. "Like, say, Paul Bunyan is a folk hero. Or—"

Frieda smiled. "Or Johnny Appleseed."

"Well, actually Johnny Appleseed isn't the best example of the . . . of the type of mythmaking I'm talking about." She felt herself picking out words, stepping around meaning, self-conscious, the way she felt in class.

Frieda shook her head, writing. "What's wrong with Johnny Appleseed?"

"John Chapman actually lived," Alison said. "He actually did travel and spread seeds across the wilderness."

"Well"—Frieda gave a little bark of disgust—"I believe your father actually *lived,* did he not?" she said to Max. "Or was he just a spook all these years?"

He nodded and rubbed Alison's hand under the table. Patting her, stroking her. *You're doing fine.* "I think she means the claims he made, not the fact that he lived."

"Johnny Appleseed?"

"No," Alison said. "Gordon. Mr. Kesler." When she said it, his name felt all wrong in her mouth. She saw him the way he'd been that night at the lake, his eyes blackened, a happy bandit, stealing nothing more than another few weeks of attention. She wanted this to stop.

Frieda's face flushed deep pink, her faint instinct for story suddenly informing her, it seemed, that she was onto what amounted in Mineral County to a scoop.

"Aren't you a college professor?" she asked Alison.

"Well . . ." Yes and no was not a good answer, Alison knew.

"Yes," Max said, and laced his fingers with hers. "She is."

"And what you want to tell me about Gordon Kesler is that you have a reason for saying that he didn't do with that car everything he said he did?"

The question was so baffling in the way it was asked that Alison spent a moment trying to unravel it, Max looking at her, Frieda looking at her. But finally, the phrasing of the question didn't matter all that much. The truth, she told herself. That's what matters. He squeezed her hand.

"No," she said as Frieda scratched lines with her pen. "No, he didn't."

Everything goes away, eventually. This she knew above all else, lying in her room that night, hearing the TV click off, Sarah and Bill readying for bed. Everything disappears, the world a black blanket spread out then folded over and over by invisible hands, every person and object and era eventually vanishing under its folds. The house fell into silence, and Alison pulled her own blankets up over her head, as if trying out oblivion, as if by knowing it, she might avoid it. But that never happened, and someday the black blanket would enfold her, too. She fell asleep thinking this, dozed fitfully, awoke just after dawn with the hollow *plop* of the newspaper landing on the porch, and she knew then. Knew that Frieda Landry's article would be in the paper that morning, that after she'd left yesterday, she had driven straight to the office down on Main Street and submitted it, quick to get away with her first-ever scoop, quick to get away from Alison, who had, after all, deceived the entire town, or aided and abetted the deception. Only her crime was the more grievous, because she was an outsider, she knew, and not one of their own.

She awoke fully in her bed, alone, Max having gone back the day before, after their breakfast with Frieda Landry, and after they'd finished the time line and spent some time under the Vette, and taken a long walk around the lake. They hadn't said much and had touched only a little; she couldn't help thinking that now that he'd gotten what he wanted from her—enough truth to bring his father down—maybe all the rest was superfluous.

She stood and looked out through her curtains. The lake was up, only the roofs of the town showing, the stone bridge reduced to its backbone, the banks slowly receding. Colaville had gone away twice now, aging unseen. The lake had gone away and come back, but would go away for good someday. Max had gone away with a promise to return, Mr. Kesler in vanity or ego. Mr. Rossi had gone away as a trivia question and come back as a box of ashes, which Sarah, lacking a mantel, had placed on top of the entertainment unit. Come Saturday, the Hotel Morgantown would go away in a cloud of dust and explosion. The Corvette was going away slowly, in decay. Marty had gone away in the violence of an accident, and come back as an imagined ghost, preoccupied in her basement. Lem and Pammy had gone away in the dissolution of a friendship, Mr. Beachy in the dissolution of commerce, Bill's hopes of magic in the blank face of reality.

Enough light of a new day drew familiar sounds from the house, Bill and Sarah rushing about, making breakfast, the front door closing, the radio reciting the school lunch menus and the weather. A few minutes later, Sarah called her down.

"Have you seen this?" Sarah said, rattling the paper in her fist, then tossing it on the table. She looked fatigued and pale.

Alison sat at the kitchen table to put on her socks and shoes. Bill smiled and downed his coffee, then went out the door to work, probably sensing an argument unfolding. Alison looked over the Style page of the newspaper, but Frieda's column wasn't there. Instead, it was on the first page of the Region section, right beside the list of arrests for drunk driving: LOCAL PROFESSOR SETS RECORD STRAIGHT ON LAKE MYTH. One quote from Alison had been highlighted in bold print, "**Many such myths find permanence because people want to believe. Someone puts on a Bigfoot costume, and someone else takes his picture**." Had she really said that? She sounded so . . . finicky, pedantic. The whole time she'd spoken to Frieda, she'd tried to step around her own words, as though vagueness might lift her past what she was actually saying. The article described, in Frieda's usual thesaurus-driven style, the way that Mr. Kesler had invented the story ("an elaborate facade") and had planted the car parts ("a nocturnal transgression"). Frieda had not even bothered, Alison realized now, to implicate *her* in all of this, even though she had admitted to it yesterday. Better, probably, if your source was not one of the criminals. This version of events had been verified in interviews with Max Kesler, who had, the article noted, corroborated the professor's account. *Corroborated.* How he must have loved that word.

Alison folded the paper, sighed, and looked at her other sock still bunched up on the floor. What had she done? Now that the whole thing was in print, it looked awful. A blind-side attack on an old man, cheered on by his only son.

"How could you do this?" Sarah rattled the paper again.

"I don't know," Alison said. "Max was there . . . I thought I was telling the truth."

"Well, for godsake, Ali. If we plan to run around exposing people's lies, the *Press-Republican* is going to start looking like the *New York Times.*"

"It meant a lot to Max. . . ." She drank the coffee Sarah poured for her. "It's the *truth,* you know? You're supposed to think telling the truth is a good thing, right? Isn't this the message we got as children?"

Sarah frowned. "We also got the one about being polite. About not coming off like the Lone Genius of West Virginia riding in to educate the ignorant."

Although Sarah was one of the least qualified to lecture on politeness, Alison knew she was right. She sounded horrible in the article, dissecting the truth, trimming away the lies. Cold and methodical. The professor, in academic gown and mortarboard, big round owl glasses, using her pointer to indicate where the town's stupidity lay. And how had Max escaped almost all mention? He'd been sitting right there, nodding his head, turning the conversation toward Alison, yet his name only came up once, at the end of the article. The corroborator.

Alison shook her head. "I blew it. I'm sorry. Everyone is going to hate me."

Sarah put a clean bowl and a box of cereal on the table. "I won't hate you. But if you go to the paper with any of *my* lies, you're going to have a fight on your hands."

That afternoon she spent polishing the Corvette's seats with saddle soap, vacuuming the carpets with a spray-on cleaner, cleaning the glass and mirrors. It didn't look half-bad when she was done, only one small tear in the leather seats, which she fixed with rubber cement. She stood back, sweating, admiring her work, knowing it was only more dressing up, more rouge on the body of the car. The lake was full enough now to send the sun reflecting off it in all directions, to ripple across its surface when the wind blew. She'd heard nothing from Max all day, nothing about the article, or about the car, or about her. Nothing. On the wall of her garage was Mr. Rossi's last testament, as she'd come to think of it, his arcane list of nine theses tacked to the wall with nails she'd found on the bench. She'd read them over several times, his one disciple, and read them again now, absently, as she picked up the cordless phone and called the chain store body shop in Cumberland—the one she'd been warned away from for their shoddy work, the one Mr. Beachy called "El Cheapo's" (about the meanest thing she'd ever heard him say)— to find out that they could respray the car for about a hundred bucks. Not a real paint job, but from ten feet away, you probably couldn't tell the difference. Black, she told the man on the phone. The blackest black you have.

That night was the second dance class they'd had since Mr. Rossi had died, not because anyone really wanted to dance, Sarah said, but because they wanted someplace to go. Alison had just gotten done with showering and cleaning the grease from under her nails. They spoke in low whispers, as if they were at a funeral instead of just in the presence of Mr. Rossi's ashes, though as she listened from upstairs, she figured out that it was not his presence in the house that silenced them so, but hers. Her name drifted up the stairs with the clink of coffee spoons and saucers, and she sat on the top stair and listened, straining at the words the way she had as a kid when her parents were downstairs having some minor argument, or when Sarah was downstairs with a boy. She closed her eyes to hear better, afraid to go down and face them, afraid of the attention, and beneath the sound of the talking and the pouring of coffee and of Bill's quiet laugh and Mrs. Skidmore's loud one, there was another sound she almost recognized but couldn't quite. And then she did: careful footsteps on the carpet, like her own, late at night. She opened her eyes, and there stood Lila Montgomery, her jeans neatly pressed, her loafers flashing pennies.

"You can join the party, the sad party," Lila said. "We don't bite. Not at our age."

"Bite, stomp, kick. I'd better stay here."

"I was just on my way to the ladies', not hunting you down, Alison." Her hair looked perfect, like cotton candy.

Alison nodded. "But it's pretty bad, the whole thing. They must hate me."

Lila put her loafer on the next stair up and leaned on her knee. "Puzzlement, is the main deal. Everyone wants to know why you went to the paper. What the point was. Especially given our recent loss." She said this delicately, a practiced grief.

Alison sighed. "It's a long story. And in my own defense, the paper came to me, more or less. I wasn't thinking, exactly." She didn't bother mentioning that the paper had come to Max first.

"No, I believe you were thinking inexactly. Not considering ramifications. A town like this, about all we have is our old stories, after the plants close down and the mall opens up. Stories and old grudges."

"But you know it's not true. The car in the lake. The whole thing was a lie."

Lila rolled her eyes and smiled. "Of course it is. Not everybody knows that, but many do. You make so much of teaching history, then you ought to know how people are. You really think the first Thanksgiving went the way it's shown in all those grade-school pageants?"

She shook her head. "Another friend of mine says that everybody lies."

"Everybody chisels the truth into whatever they need it to be. We just needed a couple of stories attached to our lake, so it didn't seem so worthless. So stupid to have built it in the first place. All you did was come along and say, No, it was pretty stupid."

Alison nodded. Maybe her whole life would never be more than a series of quiet betrayals—Marty, Lem, Max, and now Mr. Kesler and all of Wiley Ford. She thought of the DOOMED TO REPEAT IT shirt Ernie bought for her that time; it seemed pretty accurate right now. "I'm sorry," she said. As much as she wanted to explain Max's involvement, that would just look worse, spreading the blame around.

"Don't be sorry to me. I'm not mad. But I will be if you don't let me find the bathroom."

Downstairs, Alison paused in the living room on the way to her garage, and it was worse than she imagined. Lila, of course, was the nicest of them all, as she was with everything. The rest sat around with their napkins and cookies and coffee cups, glancing up at her and then looking away, letting their eyes settle on the TV, where some smiling magician in a silk shirt was threatening to make the Statue of Liberty disappear. She gave a weak "Hi," and the others muttered the same back. Mrs. Skidmore added, "How are you, Professor?" Bill saved her, finally, offering her a cup of coffee to break the silence, but she declined. She wanted to say something to them, but what? Damn Max for doing this to her. Damn herself for going along. She wanted to tell them, Never mind, forget the article in the paper, forget the entire blip of the world that day, and everything that was in that article—and, by saying the words, put Mr. Kesler's Chrysler back where it belonged, in the deep mud of lake bottom and memory alike. But that was impossible, she knew, like folding a waking person back into the dream they wanted to keep having.

All that was visible of Colaville now was the very top edge of the bridge, that narrow backbone of gray and brown. The ends of the docks were floating again, though still too steeply to walk on, and the streetlamps that dotted driveways and backyards around the lake reflected where they always had, as though they had been waiting for the water to return. She stood looking out across the lake. What a mess everything was, a mess she saw no way of straightening out. Inside the garage, her Haynes manual lay spread open on the bench, the page edges filthy with grease, some of the pages by now pulling out of their binding. The book was open to the page on changing the headlights, which was her next job, especially if she planned to keep driving at night. Mr. Beachy had already told her never to replace one of anything that came in a set—brakes, lights, tires, spark plugs—replace them all. She had called him that afternoon to ask him to order the headlamps for her, and gotten pretty much the same reception she'd gotten just now in the living room, mitigated by his natural gentleness. He'd been cordial—that was about the best she could say—businesslike, for the first time in all their business together. Near the end of their conversation, she'd asked if he had any more tracts, told him she might swing by to pick one up.

"Well," he said, drawing the word out, "I'm sure they wouldn't interest you." *Snotty, eggheaded you* is what he meant. Before she could think of a response, he'd asked if there was anything else, told her that her order would be on Tuesday's truckload, and quietly hung up the phone. She looked now at the car, thinking only of those fist-sized rust holes in the frame, the car disintegrating.

The car. The damn car, her big plan. She looked at it as if challenging it to respond, to speak to her, defend itself, and then she raised her knee and kicked the front grille with the toe of her sneaker, snapping the plastic vents. She kicked again and heard the crack and watched the grille fold in on itself, then again so the pieces dropped away like teeth and fell to the dirt. Her pulse pounded in her ears, through her temples. The stupid fucking car, her religion, her salvation, her ticket out. She was done with it. She stomped the front bumper and cracked the fiberglass. Done with the car, done with Max. She stomped again, fiberglass shredding, her ankle throbbing. Done with marriage and teaching. She kicked the headlight, shattering it to bright bits that fell to the floor and into the folds of her sock. Done with everything else she had failed. She kicked the other headlight, catching her sneaker. She imagined kicking the car into pieces, the pieces into fragments, the fragments into bits, the bits into dust. She stopped. Breathing hard, sweating. Her whole leg throbbed now, her sneaker ripped. Outside, the dancers spoke and laughed a little as they left, and the lake water made tiny slapping sounds at the edges of the docks, a noise she hadn't realized was missing until she heard it again just now.

For a long stretch of time, she sat in the doorway of her garage, looking out at the lake. Already it was hard to remember exactly what it had looked like with the water gone. The bottom had been picked clean by scavengers, and whatever garbage they'd left behind had been gathered one afternoon by a troop of Girl Scouts. Now the lake would need a whole new history to amuse the ghosts of Colaville, new outboard motors dropped in, new fishing tackle, engagement rings, self-help books. She imagined the inhabitants of Colaville returning to their watery homes, wondering what had happened to all they'd accumulated, to all their trash, vandalism in reverse. And Mr. Kesler's Chrysler was no longer down there for them to admire; she and Max had seen to that. Maybe the ghosts of Colaville worried that they were next, their stories, and thus them, extinguished forever.

Finally, the dancers left, and one by one the lights in the house went off. Guided by no more than habit, Alison sat in the driver's seat of the Vette and fired it up, quietly tapped the accelerator a couple of times, and began to let the clutch out, rolling out onto the gravel. She pulled the headlight switch on the dash, and of course she had no lights. No lights and no frame. She rolled to the edge of the road, and the parking lights cast their mix of white-and-yellow light over the blacktop, wavery half circles, a man holding two lanterns before him. Enough light, she decided, if she went slow. There was never any traffic on those back roads anyway, and she could hardly be less legal than she already was, so she went.

Soon enough, she got used to it, straining her eyes to see ahead of her, the moon bright as a flashlight overhead, the tinted highway stripe disappearing under her. Before she knew it, Jenny's Machine Tools passed by in the narrow arc of orange light, the grass at the edge of the road the color of fire, whites of the speed limit signs glowing amber, her speed picking up. As she drove, her mind drifted back over the old familiar frustrations, trying to remember the names, in order, of the sixty-six British monarchs. Automatically, she thought of asking Mr. Rossi, but of course he had answered his last question, his last bit of knowledge now nailed to her garage wall. Not that he would've known that one anyway. It was too much of history, not enough of trivia. More likely, he would have known what the British monarchs ate for breakfast, what size shoes they wore, how many were left-handed. But that somehow seemed backward to her now—history was *more* about breakfast and shoes than lists and dates, the same way a town was about its lies, a person about his quirks and whims. Which mattered more in her memory now, the fact that Marty had been born in 1964 or the fact that he spoke to his radios when he worked on them? The cause and date of his death, or the way he liked to mug for the video camera, or the way he would eat a grilled hot dog but not a boiled one? She levered the gas, downshifted, and picked up speed. The British monarchs would just have to line up and march through history without her; she was done worrying the question.

As she crested the slight rise in the road, a fleshy ripple of brown and white streaked across her vision, held there by the yellow lights, her muscles bunching up inside her hands as she jerked the wheel hard right and her foot stomped stomped

stomped the brake pedal into the floor, into mush, until the brakes held and the car pivoted around itself, swimming across the road, tires chattering and squealing as the sweep of orange circled across the other lane of blacktop, the steering wheel pressing her chest as she was moving backward, shoved against the door, breathing rubber and gas, the gravel at the side of the road spitting against the underside, the car somehow missing the deer which had been close enough—she realized now, as the car drifted to a halt—that she could smell it, warm and sweaty. The Corvette sat sideways in the road, engine idling, back wheels in the weeds. Her hands shook uncontrollably.

She drove back along the road as slowly as she could, gripping the steering wheel, opening her eyes wide to press them against the dark. Her mind gave her images of hitting the deer, the car breaking apart, snapping at the crossbeams, the carcass of the deer tumbling bloodied and wet up the long hood and into her lap through the T-top, on her, that smell smothering her, sweat and feces. She slowed even more, and a car pulled in behind her, headlights bearing down. The police, probably. Someone had heard her noisy skid and reported it. She kept on, waiting for the jarring spill of blue light, but none came on the road around the lake, and none came as she slowed at Sarah's drive, though the car was behind her still, and none came as the car followed her into the drive, and now she thought about what to do, to honk the horn and wake Bill or to push out the door and make a run for it, and as she thought this the car behind her began flashing its headlights, and then stopped. The door swung open and in her rearview mirror, in the red of her taillights, she watched Mr. Kesler swing open the door of the Seven Springs van and hop down.

"Midnight rider," he said in greeting. "Wasn't that a song a few years back?"

She parked the car on the gravel and got out, hands still quivering, heart still churning. "I don't think Milton Tannenberger is going diving in a full lake, and I don't think car parts will do the trick this time."

"Yes, you've seen to that, huh?" He was wearing a tattered down vest over his usual zippered jumpsuit. "Put me in my place, once and for all, didn't you, Dr. Durst?"

"I'm not a doctor." She tugged her hair back then let it go, her hands nervous.

"You just play one in the paper," he said.

She walked down toward the garage, and he fell into step beside her. "I didn't mean to do that, exactly," she said.

"Another accidental newspaper interview." He laughed a little. "I understand you needed to clear your own conscience. But I thought confession usually involved self-confession, not somebody else's."

"It's one in the morning. Why are you out here?"

"Max told me it was the best time to find you without distraction, and I wanted to talk to you," he said, following her to the garage. Alison clicked on the light. They sat on the one stool and the stepladder at the workbench, as if a bartender might appear.

"Max told you?"

"Yes."

"When?"

He squinted at the ceiling. "Yesterday? Time runs together, more and more."

"Where is he?" She absently riffled the edges of her Haynes manual, her fingers still shaking a little.

"Working is about all I know. Is he not tending the home fires?"

She laughed a little. "We don't really have those just yet." She looked at him. "How come you're still talking to me?"

"No reason not to. Besides, I wanted to ask how much of your words in the paper came from my son. I'm guessing eighty percent." He unzipped his vest and laid it across the bench, pillowing his elbows.

She hesitated. "You know, I've been deciding all day whether to try and defend myself by sharing the blame. How'd you guess?"

"Well, your only enemy punches you in the back of the head, you don't have to look around very long to see who did it. And you aren't my enemy."

"That's a sad thing, having a son you can call an only enemy."

He nodded. "That might be an exaggeration." He took the pipe from his pocket and tapped it on the bench. "I probably have three or four enemies."

"All them as justified as Max?"

He raised his eyebrows. "Justified? I miss a couple of birthdays because I'm on the road, and he means to humiliate me in return. Not my definition of justified."

"And that's not the story I heard."

He tucked the pipe back into his pocket and looked at her, genuinely puzzled.

"I heard about a man sneaking out at night, parking his car down the road. A man who got his son to lie for him, to his own mother. Who stayed out half the night."

He blushed brightly enough that she could see his face darken, even in this weak light. "Well, I suppose most of that is so. Glenda didn't much care for me spending time in the bar, so a time or two, I did sneak away, and maybe I did ask him to cover my back."

"He said it was pretty much every night, not a time or two."

Gordon laughed. "You know how it is with kids," he said. "If it happens three times and you remember those three, it seems like it happened all your life."

"And you were just at a bar?"

He nodded. "Where'd he say I was, some church of Satan?"

She laughed. "Not quite that bad."

"He hates me," Gordon said, and as soon as he said it, he was crying, his eyes rimming silver in the dim light. He was lying, acting again, she knew. Just like the night at the lake, tears just another tool in his kit. Or maybe Max did have it wrong. Maybe he was like everyone else, and childhood wrongs grew bigger through the long lens of time passing. Who knew? There was, she saw, no way to know, no way to sort out the truth from the tangle of their past.

"So why the Lou Gehrig ball? All the stories? The car? Why all the bullshit and lies?"

He thought about this. "To polish things up a little. Give my beggarly world a little meaning. Say you're a man with a wife and a son,

a one-bedroom home, a ten-year-old car, and a job making cardboard boxes. Empty boxes, by the hundreds. That isn't much of a
life to hang your hat on."

"It is if the wife and son love their husband and father."

"That's the conventional wisdom. Love conquers all. Maybe so, if
love weren't so flawed to begin with. I'm no cynic, Alison; I love
love, but let me tell you, if you have a cardboard-box life and one
day you sit down and tell your son about the time you raced motor-
cycles, because right then there is a motorcycle race on TV, you *see*
the way he looks at you, like you're magic. You make him believe
you used to be in the circus, and one day you bring home a top hat
from Goodwill and tell him it was yours. You show your wife
medals from a war you didn't fight. You buy a mounted fish from a
tackle store up the road, and all your friends get a good story about
how you fought that bass for over an hour. You become something
in their eyes, then you become something period. That's the way it's
always been."

He was breathing a little hard, as if all that had taken effort,
which she imagined it had.

"She left you anyway."

He nodded. "Happens to the best of us."

"You know, you could've become something in their eyes with
the truth, too," she said.

"Yeah, but I guess I never saw the difference. Except now. Lies
collapse over time, don't they?"

She nodded. "They all do."

"Well, then, too bad for me. And too late. I'm an old man, and
couldn't go back even if I were a younger one."

She nodded. "I guess you heard Mr. Rossi died." She said this
with more edge in her voice than she intended.

He nodded, not looking at her.

"Where have you *been*?" she asked, leaning down to look at his
face. "Everyone was here, clustering around their grief, and where
were you?"

"Cut open and bleeding. Couldn't leave the house. I don't do all that well around death, never have. Arthur was the good one out of that whole bunch, the one I liked best. Or at all, really."

She smirked. "I barely saw you say two words to each other."

He jerked as if she'd yanked his clothing. "We understood each other. Never needed to say much. Someone your age and gender, you may not understand that. But we had our talks."

"Sinkholes."

"That was one." He nodded, looked at her. "He was good, and I miss him."

She studied his face, trying to see him all the ways Max saw him: liar, ruiner, con man. Maybe so, and maybe just now she was hearing the truest thing he'd ever said. It felt true, and *was* true, no matter who said it—Mr. Rossi was good, and he was missed.

"You know, if it's any consolation to you, about the article," she said, "the whole town hates me now."

He patted her arm. "And me. You're just the messenger."

"Yeah, but you're one of theirs. They have to forgive you. And according to Lila, some people already figured out there wasn't any car down there."

"That may well be." He reached under his glasses to rub his sleepy eyes. "But you know people want to hang on to their myths until they get exposed. You go along believing in Santa Claus, don't you? About age ten or so? You believe and you don't, hedging your bets. Then somebody in the schoolyard calls you on it, and what transpires? You denounce the whole business as baby stuff."

"Well, yeah—"

"And take a look at Saint Peter. Gives up his fishing business and a wife to follow Jesus down the road, then somebody calls him on it, and he turns tail, assails the whole thing. Three times, mind you. All you did was call the town on believing my crap, and they are ready with hammer and nails."

"Pretty fancy company you keep, Santa Claus and Jesus. And I don't think anyone is ready to crucify Santa for not being true. Or you."

He nodded, his face worn-out, his eyes yellowed and heavy.

Alison looked around at her empty garage, out at her car sitting in the gravel, out across the lake, at the way the water looked like oil, so dark and smooth. A piece of glass from her headlight had worked its way into her shoe and now pressed against her foot. She noticed just then something hanging down under the Vette, probably broke loose as she skidded over the road.

"Gordon? What are you doing on Saturday?"

He shrugged. "Not much. And don't try to drag me to the explosion. I hate those things."

"At this point, I don't plan to attend the explosion. Your son is as good at disappearing as you are."

"From you? Then he's a fool."

"Maybe so." She sighed. "I want you to keep the day open, okay? I have a few plans to make."

"Like what?"

"Like I think we need to do something to remember Mr. Rossi. We'll have a wake. A nice one."

"I'm not Catholic, or even very religious. And Rossi—he was a scientist. He swapped all belief for empiricism."

"Then we'll make one he'd like. The empirical wake. The wide-awake wake."

He laughed, almost wheezing, and leaned over against her for a moment. "Okay, then," he said. "You talked me into it."

By the time he left, it was almost three o'clock in the morning. Bill would be up in two hours, readying for work, Sarah with him, cooking eggs. The mornings didn't feel right anymore, Sarah said. Maybe because of Mr. Rossi's box of ashes on the entertainment unit. It made the house not feel like a house anymore, like they were intruders, Alison thought, living in a mausoleum. She pulled the car back into the garage as quietly as she could, then sat listening to the ticks of the engine. No wind tonight, and the lake made no sound.

Sarah had left her mail sitting next to the lamp on the hall table—

several Visa bills, junk mail, and another envelope from Lem and Pammy, stiff with new Polaroids. She shrugged and tore it open, too tired for guilt right now, too drained. She tilted the envelope, and the Polaroid, just one, slid into her hand. This time, it wasn't a ransom photo at all. Instead, Lem and Pammy were wearing costumes Alison recalled from some long-forgotten Halloween party—Lem dressed as Obi-Wan Kenobi, wearing a brown tunic, holding a plastic lightsaber, and Pammy as Princess Leia, her own tunic pleated and white, her long hair wound in buns over her ears. They stood on the porch of Alison's house, *their* house, posing, proud, Lem's stomach grown too big over the years, his tunic raised enough by it to expose his brown sandals, his red-striped gym socks. The trim around the porch had been painted some dark color, and a row of yellow mums lined the sidewalk on both sides. Though she couldn't imagine what the picture *meant,* she didn't much care. And maybe it was simple. Maybe this was only a thank-you from two people who were too shy to come out and say it. They smiled openmouthed in the picture, laughing at themselves, their faces caught in a slight blur, looking dated in the muted colors of the Polaroid, looking silly and otherworldly, looking like something from long ago, from a galaxy far away.

—from the *Haynes Automotive Repair Manual:*
*Chevrolet Corvette, 1968 thru 1982*

Reassembly is the reverse of disassembly.

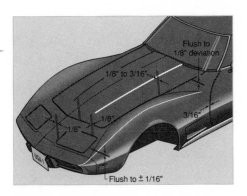

Flush to
1/8" deviation

1/8" to 3/16"

1/8"

3/16"

1/8"

Flush to ± 1/16"

USA 1

# 14

In Wiley Ford, spreading the word about anything was a simple matter of telling Mrs. Skidmore, who was in good standing at several of the local bars and one of the local churches, at the day room of Seven Springs, where she drank coffee all morning, and at the Red Bird, where the third stool next to the glass cake stand was generally understood to be hers. Alison let her know that she wanted everyone, as many as could make it, to gather at Sarah's house tomorrow, that she wanted to do *something,* hold some kind of service to remember Mr. Rossi. Despite Mrs. Skidmore's gruff nod and everyone's general disapproval of Alison at the moment, they all quickly agreed, none of them maintaining a single bad opinion of Mr. Rossi, with the possible exception that he talked too much, a flaw, as Mr. Harmon said, that could not very well be held against the deceased.

By afternoon, she was getting phone calls, people wanting to know if alcohol would be permitted (yes, if they brought their own), or what they could bring (nothing, unless they planned to drink). She told everyone it would be informal, that they might even decide to dance. Alison managed to track down the number of the president of the Tri-State Trivial Gaming Association, and invited her and all her members to attend. She invited Mr. Rossi's nurse from Sacred Heart, and even Mr. Tucker from the funeral home, who said without thinking that he couldn't make it because Saturday was his "best day." Finally, Alison called Frieda Landry at the *Press-Republican* and invited her to come to the lake on Saturday at noon.

"If this is another . . . performance that involves the taking of car parts from the lake," Frieda said, "I believe we've had our fill of that, Ms. Durst."

"Ms. Landry, it is nothing of the sort. It's a wake."

"What's awake?"

Alison rolled her eyes at the wall. "The event. We're holding a wake for Arthur Rossi. You did a column on him once, when he won a trivia contest."

"I *know* Mr. Rossi very well. I also know that he has been cremated already."

"What's your point?"

"Don't misunderstand me—I think it's more than fitting that we memorialize Mr. Rossi. I mean, he was something of a local celebrity. But a wake . . . it's inappropriate, this far along."

"Then it's not a wake. It's a memorial service. Won't you come?"

She grunted, clicked her tongue. "For Mr. Rossi's sake, I suppose I will."

"Good, great. And bring your photographer friend," Alison said.

She spent the rest of that afternoon in her garage, straightening up, putting tools on their hangers, tossing out the oily rags. She fitted the T-top onto the Vette (though the seals were bad), and gave it a going-over with a cloth, just enough to get rid of the dust, then vacuumed out the interior and pushed the broken headlight door closed by hand. She closed the cover on the Haynes manual and left it on the bench, stacked up with all the catalogs and brochures Mr. Beachy had given her, and set her Lil' Wonder All-N-One on top of the stack. If nothing else, she kept a *neat* shop. She smiled again at the photo of Lem and Pammy, which she had tacked up on the wall next to Mr. Rossi's list. They seemed just then like the only things she owned in the world— the photo, the list, and her Corvette, and they felt like plenty.

Bill came home from work and dropped his tool belt on the mud porch, then sat in front of the TV, watching a game show and drinking a glass of milk. He put so much depression into this simple act that the milk might as well have been a fifth of whiskey, the game show a snuff film. Alison worried over him, over Sarah. The two of them seemed to be running out of things to say to each other—Bill worked long hours, and Sarah seemed constantly exhausted and irritable, depressed over Mr. Rossi.

"Bill?" Alison said. He started from his glaze-over and looked up at her. "Did you hear about tomorrow? The wake?"

He looked momentarily confused. "I heard 'memorial service.'"

But yes, everyone seems to be planning to attend." He looked at her a moment longer, then turned back to his milk and the game-show contestants.

She stood in the doorway, watching him. "I need your help." He turned again and looked at her. "Some plans I have to remember Mr. Rossi. But you can't tell anyone. Not even Sarah."

"Not a soul," he said, looking suddenly as if she'd promised to reveal to him the secrets of the UFOs, the ancient gods, and all the magic that resided in the world.


Ernie always kept his office hours at the community college during what he called "suppertime," between five and six o'clock, with the idea that absolutely no one would be by to see him then. And usually it worked. Alison waited until 5:30 to call him, and he answered on the first ring.

"Well, well, how's life in exile?" he asked.

"One excitement after another," she said. "Do you know they actually deliver pizzas right to your *door* these days?"

"I need to get out more." In the background, over and over, was a persistent *thunk, thunk, thunk.*

"Ernie, what are you doing?"

"Talking to you."

"I meant the noise. I don't recognize it. New toy?"

The noise stopped. "Well, I have this basketball hoop that connects to the trash can, and a bunch of little foam basketballs. Not a toy, really. Just a stress reliever."

"By now, I think you have relieved it all, ad infinitum."

"Ooh, Latin. So this is an obscene phone call."

She laughed. "What do you do with your trash, if the can is full of basketballs?"

"I no longer produce any trash. I became perfectly efficient about six months ago. We had a big ceremony and everything."

She smiled. "Ernie, I think I want to teach again. If you give me a little leeway in the syllabus, I want to try a few things."

He was quiet a moment or two. "I always give everyone total leeway. You just never took it. But, Alison"—he sighed—"I finally lost your position, remember? There's a little adage about barn doors and horses that you need to learn."

"I know, I know. Just adjunct is all I'm looking for."

"Spring schedule is set. I could give you a couple sections, but not until next fall."

"That's perfect. But you sound pissed."

"Not pissed, Al. Just wary."

"I'm not going to bail on you, I promise."

"You'll probably have to reapply. I can send the papers. Still at the same place?"

"I'm home," she said.

"Home in Cumberland?"

"Home," she said, "in Wiley Ford."

That night she was up late again, not driving or working on the Corvette this time, but making a few notes, deciding what she would say tomorrow. Near midnight, without any planning or thought, she dialed the number for Max's cell phone. His voice, when he answered, echoed hollow and cavernous, and she knew from the sound exactly where he was.

"I hear they're gonna blow up that hotel tomorrow," she said. "You'll have to find a new ballroom to sleep in." She sat on her bed, her feet curled under her. Outside, voices and laughter sounded, men with lanterns fishing off the docks. They would be there all night.

"Just making sure nobody gets any ideas about any early fireworks shows," he said. She heard him light a cigarette and blow out the smoke. "I'm sorry I didn't get back there when—"

"Or call."

"Or call. My RDX didn't come in until today, and without that, I could blow the whole building and leave the steel frame behind."

"Well, everyone knows how important RDX is."

"Hey, I said I was sorry." She heard his footsteps as he moved around the big wooden floor.

"Speaking of sorry, that article was in the paper yesterday. Your father has been outed, and you got to corroborate. Congratulations." She heard him puff, then blow the smoke out. "How's the old man taking it?" He didn't laugh or hoot, the way she thought he would. Maybe somehow the years of this felt as sad to him as they did to her.

"The old man is taking it disappointingly well, I'm sorry to tell you."

"I'm not a monster, Alison. I just wanted the truth out, I didn't want to gloat."

"You wanted to gloat plenty before it happened. Now that it has, you feel like crap."

His footsteps stopped, and she heard him tapping something. "Don't tell me how I feel, okay?"

She shifted on the bed, her face warming. Two days before, he'd been in this bed, and she had traced his tattoo with her fingertip. "You're right. That's how *I* feel. I got mixed up."

"How can you feel *bad* about tell—"

"Please don't mention 'the truth' again, okay? You keep confusing truth with facts."

He was silent for a few moments. Someone in the woods on the other side of the lake circled it with a flashlight in hand, whipping it out across the water and into the tops of the trees. She imagined for a minute it was Winston Ackerman, like all those old campfire ghost stories about the train watchmen using their lanterns to search for their heads. Only William had kept his head, as far as the story went. Maybe he was looking for his plate of beans or his cat. Maybe he was looking for a way back to his flooded house, or maybe he was looking for some children's children of Colaville, dislodged by the flooding, someone who had heard of him, who would tell his story as though he'd been brave and noble, not stupid and suicidal.

"You won't be here tomorrow, will you?" Max asked, breaking her thoughts.

She shook her head, though of course he couldn't see her. "I don't think so, Max." She didn't mention the memorial service. Outside, the flashlight beam was gone, replaced by more voices and laughter.

Max sighed into the phone. "You know, ballrooms are not much fun without a dance partner."

"I know."

He was quiet a moment. "You know, it's *good* that my father got called on some of his bullshit, finally. I wish you could see that. I just wish you could see it from my side of things."

"Yeah, I wish I could, too," she said.

"So, you really won't be here, even though you said you would."

Alison closed her eyes. It was a mistake, calling him. "Listen," she said. "Be safe tomorrow. Stay downwind. Don't frighten the lieutenant governor. And make sure Tom is safe, too, okay?"

"I haven't seen Tom in about four days, but I'll do my best. . . . Listen, Alison—"

But she didn't want to listen, not anymore. "Just light the fuse, Yosemite Sam," she said, before hanging up, "and run like hell."


Saturday morning, Alison was up before everyone else, sitting on the front porch with a blanket around her, eating a banana for breakfast and watching the lake. The day felt new the way the lake felt new—the same old water, the same old aboveground shuffle, but somehow whatever was emptied had the slow and steady power to refill itself. Some man she'd never seen before paddled a plastic kayak across the lake, leaving a ripple behind, like a water strider. His paddle dripped, the water flashed, and he seemed peaceful enough in his ignorance of the town below, all that hurt and commerce and life and death that had once been the steady rhythm of Colaville, whose big knobby bridge was no longer even visible above the surface. The man finished his paddle, climbed a dock on the opposite side of the lake, and disappeared into one of the houses, carrying his kayak. Alison stood, stretched, left the blanket on the rail and walked to her garage, sat in the driver's seat. With her hands on the wheel, she thought about the first day with the car, and how she imagined driving it off, like John Wayne, into the sunset. The idea made her smile at herself now. The problem with horizons was that they were always on the horizon; you could never get there if you tried. She turned the key, listened to a few bars of Styx (which was getting old, but eight-track tapes weren't exactly abundant anymore), then started the car. The gas tank was nearly empty. She rolled out into the driveway and sat idling.

In a couple of weeks, it would be October, and the days would start to diminish, and the surface of the lake would fill with fallen leaves, slowly sinking. Then the collective paranoia of Halloween, so bad that trick-or-treat was all but a thing of the past, then Thanksgiving, her favorite—just the right size for a holiday—and then the mall orgy of Christmas, visiting Baltimore with Sarah and Bill, Marty's absence almost a presence on such occasions. Years went past in Hallmark cards, a Stonehenge of holidays and deadlines tracking the planets, and none of it mattered. Everything lasted, and nothing did. She might have rebuilt her Corvette down to the last washer and wire, and five seconds after she turned the final bolt, something, somewhere, would start rusting again, undoing itself. Even before she turned that last bolt, even *now*, the present always with one foot in the past, the new always becoming the ruined. Restoration was just a lie, the very best one we have. She turned the key and shut the car down.

The first to arrive, for probably the first time in his life, was Mr. Kesler. He'd traded his jumpsuit for gray slacks, a dark plaid vest, a red necktie, and his porkpie hat. He took off on a walk around the lake while Sarah, still sleepy, helped Alison make lemonade, enough for forty or so, squeezing lemons until their forearms ached and Sarah said the smell was making her sick. Bill had brought home a meat and vegetable tray from Food Lion. The others were late to arrive; she'd put out the word to be there around noon, but most started pulling up, filling the edges of the drive, at almost one o'clock. The van arrived from Seven Springs, Mr. Harmon at the wheel this time, Mrs. Harmon riding shotgun, the two of them in matching

WORLD'S GREATEST GRANDMA and WORLD'S GREATEST GRANDPA sweat-shirts. Tyra Wallace was back on oxygen but smoking anyway. Lila Montgomery was gorgeous in her Levi's and alligator sweater, her cheeks red with the cold. Some of them had brought friends, and some people turned up that Alison didn't know at all, though she recognized a few faces from the Red Bird. They all milled about the front porch, drinking lemonade and coffee, chatting with Bill and Sarah, trading stories about Mr. Rossi that somehow made him more of a character than he'd been—bigger, stranger, smarter.

All of the dancers, Alison noticed, welcomed Mr. Kesler warmly when he returned from his hike, clapping him on the back, shaking his hand. Lila even hugged him; Lila, who said once that you *had* to let bygones be bygones because they would be anyway, no matter what you did. A little while later, Mr. Beachy arrived. He must have closed down the store to be there. He spent a long time looking at the Vette with Alison, popping the hood, peering behind the tires at her work on the brakes, nodding his approval. One of the waitresses from the Red Bird was there, her five-year-old wearing a Spider-Man T-shirt and a Santa hat, pedaling a Big Wheel across the grass. Tanner Mil-tenberger rode down the lake road on his clattering motorcycle, slowed, waved, and drove on. A group of men and boys descended on the Corvette, bragging about the kick-ass cars they'd once owned or the kick-ass cars they planned to own again someday. By the time cars stopped showing up, there were probably thirty or forty people there, on the porch mostly, but spilling into the yard and into the living room, having forgotten why they were there, settling into the rhythm of a party, of old friends, conversing. A few of them took turns passing around and holding Mr. Rossi's box of ashes, though they were awk-ward doing so. Tyra Wallace set it on the kitchen table and announced, as she had numerous times before, that this was her wish, too, to end up as ashes, not to let anybody put her under the ground.

"I'd be afraid down there," she said without a trace of fear in her voice. She pulled away the oxygen mask long enough to light another Virginia Slim, blowing the smoke at Mr. Rossi's box. Alison imagined that one day Tyra would just turn into ash, without benefit of cremation, and would be happy to reside for all eternity in a glass ashtray at St. Patrick's bingo. Mr. Rossi's box made its way around to Lila, who gave it a quick awkward hug. After everyone had had their turn, the box sat ignored on the table in the empty kitchen. They should have gone for the urn, Alison thought. At least it had some shape to it, something to hold in your hands. But even with some shape, an urn just wasn't a very good way to remember someone, no matter how many trout-fishing scenes or *Last Supper*'s were painted on it. The whole idea—a box or urn, either one—just felt tawdry somehow. Keeping a person like they were leftover potato salad from last weekend's picnic. And at least with a burial site, you could go there, pay your visit, and go home. An urn *was* the visitor, a reminder of death living right in your house, a guest who never leaves. Alison stood in the kitchen alone, patting the box on its lid. Then she decided. She took it with her through the side door and into the driveway, opened the door of the Corvette, and put the brass box on the floorboard, wedging it down behind the driver's seat. Then, with hardly a thought, she pulled the shark's tooth from around her neck and curled it neatly atop the box lid.

Two o'clock was nearly here, and soon, Alison realized, Max would be pushing that green button and bringing down the Hotel Morgantown while all the dignitaries and a crowd considerably larger than this one looked on. She felt a little twinge, thinking about the day at the silo, when it blew and tilted and seemed to hold in the air, when she still thought you could hold something in the air. She closed her eyes a moment and wished him to be safe.

Frieda Landry drove up in her big Cadillac, parking not on the street, where everyone else had, but on the grass right in front of the house. She stepped out wearing all pink, from the fluffy feather on her wide hat down to the thickened toenails that peeked out of the ends of her sling-back shoes. She had brought with her the photographer in his safari vest, who had made Tanner Miltenberger into a space alien for one day and put him on the front page of the *Press-Republican*. Finally, everyone who had any designs on coming had arrived, and Alison led them all into the yard, under the pale September sun, under a cloudless sky. Bill had let the grass get too high, and it bent under their feet, almost white underneath.

Alison gathered everyone in the grass near her garage, circled around her, and then she began speaking, without notes this time. She began by telling them about how much Mr. Rossi had loved to dance, and how good he'd been at it, how he'd been something of a Renaissance man, able to speak on almost any topic, how he had shared his knowledge with local children in the elementary schools (she left out the part about the parents who thought his knowledge of whale tongues was obscene), how he'd been that rarest of people, a good man, going about his life with quiet decency.

She wished, right in the middle of speaking, that she were Ernie, that she could seem effortless, and effortlessly engaged. Instead, her words sounded exactly like what they were, a eulogy, one given by a priest who never really knew the person for whom he said the Mass, could never put a face with the name. She faltered a bit, look-ing around at the faces watching her, some bored, some scowling. Lila Montgomery smiled at her. Then Alison reached into the pocket of her jeans and withdrew a piece of paper, unfolded it. She had wanted them to hear some of Mr. Rossi's own words, since hers, as she feared, sounded so feeble. Not the list—that was hers and hers alone. But among Mr. Rossi's few effects—some books, a brass clock he'd been given at retirement, his trophies for trivia contests— had been a typed, yellowed draft of his book, *Funny Facts,* for which he'd never found a publisher. Alison read to them from the last lines of his introduction to the book:

> Whatever knowledge you ~~glean~~ take from <u>Funny</u> <u>Facts</u> will become, I hope, part of your ~~very~~ own understanding of the world, the understanding that whatever ~~you~~ we find along the way is interesting in its own right. A wise man once said, "A clean white pebble is more valuable than a gold nugget, if you've just spent the day looking for a clean white pebble." Well, readers, that wise man was ~~me~~ I, and

I ~~now~~ offer you now the stories of one hundred and
eighty clean white pebbles, each one a treasure.
Carry ~~it~~ them in your pocket, and guard them well.

"So," Alison said, "I hope that each of you will take whatever you
hear about Arthur Rossi today, whatever stories you have to tell
about him, and guard them well."

She looked around; most of the people were looking at their
feet—whether from emotion or embarrassment for her, she couldn't
tell. She was just about to ask if any of them might have a word or
two to say about Mr. Rossi, when Mrs. Skidmore spoke up.

"Okay, then, we'll all set about trading our stories on Mr. Rossi,
and then tomorrow you and your boyfriend and Mrs. Pink Lady over
there can come along and tell us how goddamn stupid we all are."
She stood with her arms crossed, a 7-Eleven coffee cup in her hand.

All around was silence, except for water slapping against the
docks, a dog barking on the other side of the lake. Alison felt her
face growing warm and her hands tensing, and if she'd ever had any
inclination to start a fistfight with an old lady, it was now.

"I don't think this is the time—"

"Why'd you do it?" Mrs. Skidmore persisted. "Answer that."

"I shouldn't have. I—"

"Then why did you?"

Alison closed her eyes. Sarah and Bill, just about her only allies,
had gone up on the porch, Sarah having started to cry almost as
soon as Alison opened her mouth to speak.

"Because that whole mess was a big lie all the way around," Mr.
Davidow said, his apron from the Red Bird still knotted around his
waist. "She just laid out the truth." Grumblings rippled through the
small crowd, little waves of assent or disagreement.

"Old dumb us and our old dumb lie," Mrs. Skidmore said. "I
guess she showed us." Steam from her coffee rose in wisps.

The sun fell behind dark clouds and the wind kicked up, the day
growing colder. Alison held her breath, then let it go. Nothing was
going right.

"And I say you're fussing at the wrong person," Mr. Davidow persisted. "You need to turn your guns on Mr. P. T. Barnum over there." He pointed at Gordon, who looked suddenly as if he were made from porcelain, hardened and white. "The Music Man," Mr. Davidow said.

Somebody, a man Alison recognized from the Red Bird, laughed loudly at this. "Hey," he said, "the high school band can manage maybe seven or six trombones in the big parade." Everyone laughed. Gordon looked as though he were about to be stoned to death. Alison pressed the heel of her hand to her forehead, feeling suddenly like she was standing in front of a surly group of freshmen. The five-year-old in the Spider-Man shirt drove his Big Wheel around and around the crowd, ringing the tiny bell on the handlebars.

"Okay, *listen*," Alison said. "We are here for Mr. Rossi, and—"

"Hey, look!" someone else shouted. "It's Bigfoot!" He waited a beat. "No, hold on a sec, that's just Gordon Kesler in a hat." Again everyone laughed, louder this time.

"Hear, now, Gordon," the first man said, "you got a fancy silver race car sitting right there behind you. Wait around until the lake freezes over, and you can drop it in there, too, a set." By now, the women, polite at first, were laughing as well.

Gordon kept trying to smile, trying to pretend to go along with the joke. He took off his hat and bounced it by the brim in his fingers, then pushed nervously at his glasses, tugged at his earlobes, which were redder even than his face.

"Yeah, go ahead, Gordon. Put the car in the lake. Say it was your uncle's."

"That is *exactly* what I had in mind," Alison shouted. This stopped them. In fact, she'd had it in mind for days, and now here it was, right in front of her. "There's meant to be a car in this lake," she said, all the laughing subsided now, "so, let's put one there."

Gordon looked at her, wide-eyed. Sarah and Bill had moved off the porch and now stood at the edge of the circle, Bill whispering to Sarah. People in the crowd shook their heads and spoke in a tangle of murmurs, none of which made its way to Alison's ears.

"Think about it," she told them. "We roll the car in the lake on the day we remember Mr. Rossi. I bet you'll never forget it. I bet you'll never stop talking about it." If she had expected protests at this point, she didn't get any. It was her car and their lake. Even Sarah looked too shocked to speak, and the thought seemed to hit them all collectively—they could.

"All right then," Alison said, her heart thudding now, "I guess . . . let's do it. Bill? You promised to help, remember?" Bill smiled as he jostled his way through the crowd, moving toward the car. She had imagined Bill and a group of the strongest boys giving the Vette a good headlong shove—Gordon in there, too, his hand pushing—and making it at least up and over the steep bank of the lake. As she thought of this, scanning the crowd for the strongest-looking boys, she heard the door of the Vette open and then quickly slam closed.

She spun around, and Gordon, porkpie hat perched on his head, sat in the driver's seat, his hands on the wheel. He reached across his shoulder and locked the door, then turned the key and started the Corvette, rumbling the ground under their feet.

"Gordon?" Alison said. "What are you *doing*? Get out of there." He blipped the accelerator a couple of times, pretending not to hear her. Fumes and gray exhaust from the car stirred dust from the gravel in rhythmic puffs, the smell settling out over the crowd.

She tapped her knuckles on the window. "Come on, Gordon—get out of the car. Let's put her in the water." From where she stood, she could see Mr. Rossi's box wedged down behind the driver's seat.

He shook his head, squared his jaw, then rolled down his window about an inch, just enough to speak. "No."

"*What?*" She felt her face heat up, sensed the crowd at her back. "Gordon . . . what are you trying—"

"I'm putting it in." He looked at her through the glass, his eyes hard. "Just the way it was supposed to happen."

She shook her head and looked at him. He meant it. "I can't let you do that, and you know it." She hooked her fingertips in the narrow opening. "It's dangerous, Gordon, and the water's cold. Come on out, and help us push. Please." He eased the car forward, jerking the clutch a little bit, and she was forced to step back. He turned the wheel to aim the Corvette toward the water, rolling right to the edge of the bank. The flash of the photographer began going off, one after another. Frieda Landry hauled out her notebook and thin gold pencil. Some in the crowd pushed to the front for a better look. Tyra Wallace lit a cigarette. The scowl slackened in Mrs. Skidmore's face. By now, most there were worried into silence, the teenage boys grinning and agitated, some of the women covering their mouths, some of the men nodding and whispering, as if putting the car in the lake were no different than cleaning the gutters or raking the leaves, just another job to do.

Alison, with Sarah beside her now, moved toward the car, calling his name—"Gordon! *Gordon!*"—as if he were a lost dog they scoured the neighborhood for. Some in the crowd took up the call, asking him to come out, pleading, others standing alongside Bill, still ready to lean in and help push. Gordon shook his head over and over, tight-lipped, not looking at any of them. He shifted into reverse and backed up slowly, scattering Bill and his helpers. He paused only a second before shifting into first, racing the engine, and then popping the clutch—but instead of rocketing the car forward as he'd meant it to, the maneuver nearly made him stall out as the Corvette pitched forward in fits across the grass, tossing him about in the driver's seat. He stopped for a second, bits of clumped mud and grass clinging to the wheels. Alison, all of them, could only watch. He nodded his head, talking to himself, hitting the wheel twice with the heel of his hand, then revved up the engine so the whole car shook, popped the clutch, and fishtailed across the grass. The car ran out of room before it gained much speed, though, sending him into the glassy face of Wiley Ford Lake not like in a movie, not launched into the air with wheels spinning, not arcing out into the deep water, but bucking and lurching, bouncing on squeaky shocks over the steep bank and down into the shallows with a noisy splash, the nose of the Vette nudging the water, engine stalled, the back end angled high into the air, as if the car were only dipping a toe in to test the temperature. The crowd pressed forward as Mr. Kesler sat for a few moments, looking out through the windshield, then shoved with his shoulder against the door twice until it popped open. He stepped out as if he'd arrived at someone's house for dinner, walking out into the waist-deep water, hat crooked on his head, his vest darkening as it soaked through, and then he slammed the door as much as he could and stood there, a little puzzled, while the flash of the camera kept freezing moments in brief whiteness and the crowd held back and Alison stared at him, open mouthed, not sure of what to say, and the engine sent up a hiss of white steam.

And then, all by itself, the Corvette started to roll.

Mr. Kesler moved back, almost losing his footing, and the car made a sound like scraping metal as ripples of water pushed out in front of it, bubbles escaping from underneath, rolling faster now, picking up speed down the steep slope of the bank, but still in slow motion. The water began raining into the open window, raining— only she knew this—on top of Mr. Rossi's hidden bronze box, filling her leather seats with water, filling the floorboards, water now up as high as the T-top, rushing into the space behind the back glass, the front fully submerged, the eight-track and Styx tape filling with water, her brakes, the round lenses of the taillights, the rounded bumper, and then it was gone completely, no more than a glimmer of silver under the water, a slow-moving flash you could almost glimpse, a hidden monster, a mythic fish.

Mr. Kesler smiled and waved his hat, wishing the Corvette a bon voyage. The crowd pressed around the rim of the lake, talking and pointing, many of them clapping now, the photographer snapping photos of Mr. Kesler, of the crowd, of the surface of the lake as the ripples healed over. Frieda Landry gripped her spiral book and her narrow pencil, writing and writing and writing, pink feather bobbing, tongue pushed to the corner of her mouth with the effort of getting it all down. But no matter how much and how fast she wrote, she could never write it all, could never get at everything contained in that moment, for it was too much, too spread out, too full of all those other moments that had already happened or were about to or would in time. She could not see enough, could not write how the Corvette gained momentum as it rolled down the pitched floor of the lake, a kind of slow-motion speed as it receded into murkiness, and how, a minute or two from this moment, it would come to rest five feet away from the stone bridge, its wheels mired in silt.

She could not write how even then the lid and welded seams of the brass box were leaking, how Mr. Rossi's ashes were slowly seeping out of the box, floating, drifting, and dispersing through the water, spreading out over Colaville like a cloud.

She could not write how, only minutes before, about the time that Gordon had closed and locked the door of the Corvette, Max had pushed the green button and the sticks of dynamite buried deep in the bones of the Hotel Morgantown had unfolded themselves in violence and explosion, one and then another and another, and how the building had paused, then buckled, then fallen neatly inside its own foundation.

She could not write about how later that night Alison, in the cold and quiet, would make one more trip to her empty garage and write in, for the last entry on Mr. Rossi's list, "A man in West Virginia had a Viking funeral in a 1976 Corvette."

She could not write about the ghosts of Colaville, shy in their buildings, at home again, coming out slowly to gaze at the silver surface and graceful lines of the Corvette, the prettiest thing they'd ever seen.

She could not write that the shark's tooth felt right at home in the water.

She could not write about the thick column of black dust and soot that rose up as the Hotel Morgantown came down and how, at the center of that roiling black mass, high above, three paper airplanes—white, yellow, and pink—circled around and above all that was broken, like fragile doves, like torn angels.

And she could not write about the fetus growing in Sarah's womb, the source of all Sarah's recent fatigue and the product of Bill's hope—six weeks old as she scribbled, and, according to the list, already forming fingerprints.